"Let me _____
play. A str _____
the fingers _____ *the violin?*

Laurian looked at her fingertips, surprised at his perception, and smiled. "I wouldn't presume to play the violin with Keska Lahti in the world. I play the cello."

His piercing gray eyes seemed to probe into her soul as he studied her. As Laurian looked at him, she began to feel a stirring of desire.

As if he had read her thoughts, Keska smiled. "So, Laurian Bryant plays the cello. I have always considered the cello to have a husky, sexual voice."

She felt herself blush slightly in the dim light and murmured, "Really?"

"Really," he echoed. "The sound of a violin cries out for love," he said gently, "and the cello answers."

After a few moments, Laurian realized she had forgotten to breathe, and still gazing into Keska's molten silver eyes, she drew in a tremulous sigh. The attraction between them was powerful, almost irresistible, and it had been so achingly long since she'd experienced the joy of being held and caressed.

Her pink lips were warm and parted. Keska leaned forward to touch his mouth to hers. The kiss was soft and seeking, a gentle, tender joining that sent a flush flowing down through her entire body . . . .

THE PAPERBACK SHOP
BEST IN USED BOOKS
1824 W. WATERS AVE.
TAMPA, FLORIDA 33604   932-9082

THE PAPERBACK SHOP
8008 W. Armenia
Tampa, Fla. 33604
Ph. 932-9082

WHAT ARE *LOVESWEPT* ROMANCES?

They are stories of true romance and touching emotion. We believe those two very important ingredients are constants in our highly sensual and very believable stories in the *LOVESWEPT* line. Our goal is to give you, the reader, stories of consistently high quality that may sometimes make you laugh, sometimes make you cry, but are always fresh and creative and contain many delightful surprises within their pages.

Most romance fans read an enormous number of books. Those they truly love, they keep. Others may be traded with friends and soon forgotten. We hope that each *LOVESWEPT* romance will be a treasure—a "keeper." We will always try to publish

LOVE STORIES YOU'LL NEVER FORGET
BY AUTHORS YOU'LL ALWAYS REMEMBER

The Editors

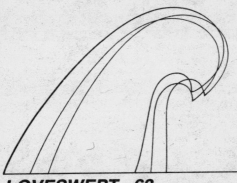

LOVESWEPT • 63

Joan J. Domning
Lahti's Apple

 BANTAM BOOKS
TORONTO • NEW YORK • LONDON • SYDNEY • AUCKLAND

For Bill, my enduring husband.

LAHTI'S APPLE
A Bantam Book / October 1984

*LOVESWEPT and the wave device are trademarks of
Bantam Books, Inc.*

*All rights reserved.
Copyright © 1984 by Joan Domning.
Cover art copyright © 1984 by Steve Assel.
This book may not be reproduced in whole or in part, by
mimeograph or any other means, without permission.
For information address: Bantam Books, Inc.*

ISBN 0-553-21634-1

Published simultaneously in the United States and Canada

*Bantam Books are published by Bantam Books, Inc. Its trademark, consisting of
the words ''Bantam Books'' and the portrayal of a rooster, is Registered in U.S.
Patent and Trademark Office and in other countries. Marca Registrada. Bantam
Books, Inc., 666 Fifth Avenue, New York, New York 10103.*

PRINTED IN THE UNITED STATES OF AMERICA

O   0 9 8 7 6 5 4 3 2 1

One

Laurian Bryant took a deep breath for courage and knocked on the front door of Keska Lahti's house. The three sharp raps jarred on the peaceful country quiet. The only other sounds were those of bees humming busily, birds warbling over their nesting, and the growl of a distant tractor.

As she was waiting Laurian wondered again what might have caused a violinist of Keska Lahti's prestige to retire at the height of his career, giving up fame and fortune for this apple orchard, though she had to admit the surroundings were very beautiful. The large white farmhouse had three gables over the wide veranda, and its surrounding lawn was well tended. The flower beds were bright with yellow daffodils and a rainbow of tulips. She breathed in deeply, smelling the heavenly scented April-blooming apple orchard that stretched between the house and the northern California coastal hills in the west. A rural valley was spread out in front of the house. In the distance lay the city of Santa Rosa.

After a few moments the door opened in answer to her knock and a man in his sixties peered at Laurian with distant eyes over a haughty nose. His voice was far from welcoming when he asked, "May I help you?"

"I would like to speak to Mr. Lahti, if I may," Laurian answered.

"May I ask why, madam?"

His voice was so cool, it seemed likely he might close the door in her face, so she spoke quickly and concisely. "My name is Laurian Bryant. I'm with the Bryant Music Camp, a youth camp for gifted young musicians not far from here on the Russian River. I'd like to speak to Mr. Lahti concerning a benefit concert we conduct each year in August. We thought he might be interested in performing at our concert this year. It's for a good cause."

The eyes of the elderly man made a discreet tour of Laurian's face, cataloguing dark brown eyes, dramatic cheekbones, and a high-bridged nose. Hers was an oval face made almost heart-shaped by a deep widow's peak. A heavy coil of very dark hair was pinned high on her head. The overall effect was cultured rather than beautiful.

A subdued spark of calculated interest that had nothing to do with physical attraction livened the man's cool eyes. "Mr. Lahti never receives unexpected guests," he said.

"I would have called for an appointment," Laurian explained, "but Mr. Lahti has an unlisted number. However, I feel certain he will be interested in our concert. May I speak to him, please?"

"I am George Miller, Mr. Lahti's business manager. I believe I can answer for him," he said. Pausing, he gave a brief, introspective glance at the petite feminine figure under her stylish, pale green dress. Thoughtful speculation crossed his face as he added almost reluctantly, "Keska Lahti does not play the violin for the public any longer. Not for any reason."

"If I may speak to him, Mr. Miller, perhaps I can convince him to make an exception for our gifted young musicians." Laurian had no intention of allowing herself to be shunted off without the chance to tackle Keska Lahti personally.

In the face of her determination amusement flickered in George Miller's eyes. It was something like a challenge when he said, "Mr. Lahti is busy at the moment. He is involved with farm affairs."

The source of his fleeting humor puzzled Laurian. "I'll wait until he's free," she said.

"It will be an hour at least."

"I don't mind. I must speak to Mr. Lahti."

With a slight nod George Miller stepped aside and motioned Laurian into the house. He seated her on an elegant silver and blue brocaded love seat in a sitting room and asked, "May I bring you a refreshment? Coffee or tea? A cocktail, perhaps?"

It was almost four o'clock in the afternoon. Laurian's nervous stomach had rebelled against food at lunchtime, and now it cringed at the thought of a stimulant. "No, thank you. Nothing." She hesitated, then tossed out a conversational feeler. "Mr. Lahti's mastery of the violin is awesome. He must be a fascinating man. I expect you know him well."

"Fascinating, yes," Miller said wryly. "I know him as well as anyone does. We've been associated since he came to the United States from Finland."

"What is he like?"

"One doesn't describe Keska Lahti," he said with a slight smile. "I'm sure you will form your own impressions if he agrees to speak to you. It's likely he will refuse, you must understand."

"I understand. I can only hope."

"I must leave you now, madam," George Miller said, and walked to the door of the sitting room. He glanced at Laurian with that touch of amusement so alien to his superior face, then he disappeared.

Laurian sighed every few minutes in growing apprehension as she waited in the charmingly decorated room. Clasping her hands, she looked around at polished wood occasional tables, at exquisite upholstered furniture, an elegant Persian rug, and a scattering of original oil paintings.

As time dragged by at an agonizingly slow pace, Laurian's wish to be elsewhere grew stronger. It hadn't been her idea to come here to this apple orchard to visit Keska Lahti. Her uncle, Jules Bryant, and the executive board of the music camp had drafted her for the mission by expounding upon the theory that at thirty-one Laurian was the youngest and most attractive woman at Camp Bryant. They had claimed that Keska Lahti was a man after all, and might respond more favorably if she made the request to play at the benefit concert. In the end she had agreed to come because of a real love for the gifted students at Camp Bryant who would benefit from a performance by Keska Lahti, and out of a sense of responsibility to Uncle Jules, who had done so much for her in the past.

Laurian jumped up and began to pace the room. The idea of charming Keska Lahti into doing the concert was ridiculous, she told herself; she wasn't that attractive and she knew nothing of coquetry. She was an expert only at the cello she loved to play and in her knowledge of classical music.

As she anxiously walked around the sitting room she noticed a pair of French doors standing ajar. After she'd curiously peeped through, she drew in a quick breath and couldn't resist pushing the doors farther open to look reverently into a large quiet music studio.

Curtains had been pulled over the windows, giving the room a shadowed, museumlike quality. An enormous baby grand piano took up almost a third of the space. Glassed-in bookcases holding vast inventories of sheet music and books lined the walls.

But Laurian saw nothing but the violin resting on a table, its bow lying beside it. A music stand and a chair were placed near the instrument as if the musician had just stepped out. Keska Lahti must play his violin in this room, Laurian thought. That meant he hadn't given up his music entirely when he'd retired from the public.

Glancing furtively toward the hallway, Laurian listened, her head cocked alertly. The house sounded empty, so she tiptoed into the studio to stand beside the violin.

Even in the dim light its fine, waxed wood gleamed with golden highlights. The elegant scrolled vents framed silent, waiting strings. Her eyes caressed the shape of the instrument with awe.

On the wall above the table Keska Lahti's success was mounted and displayed; medals on satin ribbons, gold and silver plaques, and scrolls. Laurian wondered again what motive had caused such a talented and renowned violin virtuoso to withdraw from the public eye. According to the papers he was only thirty-nine, so half his life would be wasted if he didn't perform again.

Laurian stared curiously at an enlarged, framed photograph of Keska Lahti in white tie and tails. Lordly and distant, he was holding his violin in long, slender hands. He was slim, though well-shaped and broad-shouldered, with fair, slightly wavy hair fanned out over the high forehead of a finely chiseled, aristocratic face. Not an especially handsome man, Laurian decided, but terribly distinguished and supremely self-confident. Her heart contracted at the thought of meeting him.

Knowing she shouldn't be in Keska Lahti's private room, that she should leave quickly, Laurian first had to touch the exquisite violin. Her own career as a cellist had been a disappointment, so perhaps the essence of Keska Lahti's genius would enter her through her fingertips, she thought. Reaching out, she brushed the golden wood with a reverent hand.

Her hand leaped away from the violin almost instantly, and her body jerked in a startled, guilty response when a sharp, disapproving voice said, "May I help you?"

Whirling around, Laurian opened her mouth, ready with an apology.

But the man who stood staring at her was a farm laborer dressed in dusty jeans that rode low on slim hips and fit very snugly around a well-curved pelvis. A wrinkled blue work shirt hung open over a sleekly muscled chest. A New York Yankees baseball cap was jammed down over his forehead, and his eyes glittered in the shadow of the bill as he studied her, waiting for an explanation.

Lifting her chin and speaking as if she had every right to be in the studio, Laurian said, "I'm waiting for Keska Lahti."

At the determined tone of her voice the laborer lifted his brows with a flare of interest and studied every detail of her, starting with the dark hair wound around her head and her full, curving mouth. His inspection made its slow intense way down over her petite, curvaceous body to her slim ankles and high-heeled pumps. Then he shifted his attention back to her face. "I am Keska Lahti." His musical, accented voice held a challenge.

"Keska Lahti, the violinist?" she asked in disbelief, staring at his sweat-stained shirt and the muddy leather gloves on his hands.

"Keska Lahti, the apple farmer."

"There must be some mistake," Laurian said hesitantly. "Is there another Keska Lahti?"

His lower lip was full, the top one narrower and twin-bowed. They parted over even teeth to curve up in a puckish, amused smile. "You think perhaps there could be two men named Keska Lahti?"

"I don't suppose it's likely," she conceded, but could scarcely imagine him as the courtly violinist in formal dress in the picture. This man was bursting with an almost primitive kind of life. He seemed a part of nature and the earth.

Suddenly Laurian remembered where she was—in Keska Lahti's private music studio. It seemed futile to try to explain what she had been doing there beside his valuable violin, so she lifted her chin and walked to the French doors. A vibration of discomforting sensual awareness flowed between them when she brushed past him. Taking a defensive position in the middle of the sitting room, she looked back at him apprehensively.

Closing the French doors firmly, Keska Lahti followed her across the sitting room, stopping just in front of her. "George encouraged me to speak to you," he said, studying her curiously.

Now Laurian could see his eyes, and their intensity seemed to invade her being. They were the color of antique pewter, framed by dark lashes and lit by the sunlight streaming into the room. His brows were dark, too, and sloped from the center down to the ends as a sort of artistic flourish or, if his mood was benevolent, an indication of humor.

His eyes were not only intense, but they were were warm with a masculine awareness that set off reactions all through her body. "You did wish to speak to Keska Lahti?" he prodded with a touch of amusement.

Laurian forced her flustered mind to scrabble back to her mission. "Yes, I did want to talk to you, Mr. Lahti . . . I—I do want to," she stammered. "I've come to—"

"Please sit down," he broke in, motioning to the love seat with one mud-caked, leather-gloved hand. "Perhaps you will feel more comfortable." There was a bright spark of interest in his eyes now. The knowing smile on his lips grew as he watched her nervously pull her skirt over her knees after she had seated herself.

She lifted her chin in a stab at dignity. "My name is Laurian Bryant and I'm connected with the Bryant Music—"

"Laurian," Keska repeated, savoring the sound of her name on his tongue. Stripping off his gloves, he dropped them on the coffee table and sat down beside her. Staring into her face, he murmured, "Laurian . . . Laurian . . . Laurian. A lovely name for so beautiful a woman."

Her lips were still parted from speaking as she stared into his face, at his angular cheekbones, his wide sensual mouth, and at the challenging look in his dark silver eyes. Crossing her legs restlessly, she continued, "The Bryant Music Camp that is located—"

"On the Russian River," he broke in impatiently. "Laurian Bryant, by some unique magic you have impressed my business manager, George Miller."

"Oh?"

Moving closer to her, he slid his arm across the back of the love seat, just above her shoulders. "He suggested I behave myself and refrain from rudeness." Keska Lahti leaned slightly toward her.

Laurian leaned slightly away from him, mesmerized by the play of light in his unique eyes. "Are you often rude?" she asked vaguely.

"Quite often," he answered smoothly, leaning his other elbow on his thigh and his chin on the heel of his hand to look into her face.

"I should be grateful to George then, for asking you to behave," she said with a glance at his neatly curved lips.

"That might be premature. I haven't agreed to comply." His soft, rhythmic accent lent his words a misleading gentleness.

Laurian shifted uncomfortably, wishing the ordeal were over. She'd been a fool to agree to come here to talk to this man, and now she was floundering in water way over her head. Sighing deeply, she said wistfully, "If it would mean you'd behave politely, then I hope George has some influence over you."

"No one influences Keska Lahti," he said in a low voice.

"I don't suppose." She glanced at his warm, interested eyes and away. Then she directed her attention to the message it was her duty to present. "The Bryant Music Camp hosts gifted young music students—"

"You are very serious for so lovely a woman," he cut in, pushing the baseball cap up on his head. A shock of tumbled light brown hair fell on his high tanned forehead.

Disconcerted, Laurian glanced at his wavy hair, then down at his wide shoulders, where a scattering of apple blossom petals were trapped in the creases of his shirt. Just a flick of her eyes on his bare chest was enough to register sleek muscles, curly dark body hair, and smooth tanned skin. He wasn't muscular in the television-hero sense, but there was something acutely disturbing about his slim, supple form.

Taking herself in hand, Laurian valiantly began again, "What I want to ask—"

"Keska Lahti is fascinated by intense, serious women," he said softly, his musical voice the texture of velvet. "You have a tantalizing mystery about you, as of unexplored depths."

Laurian knew he wasn't serious, merely taunting her for reasons of his own, whatever they might be. But his Finnish accent had sent a shiver through her body, and the fact that he spoke of himself in the third person gave the situation a disturbing surrealistic atmosphere.

Wishing herself far away, she looked longingly out the window, which faced the front yard, at her parked car. Then, taking a deep breath, she turned her desperate eyes again to Keska Lahti and said firmly, "Our students are gifted young—"

"Tell me about Laurian Bryant. What mysterious, unexplored depths are there to you?" His eyes searched her face invitingly.

"None!" she exclaimed, her voice rising.

"You seem tense," Keska commented with interest, and rose to his feet. "Perhaps if I serve you a glass of wine, you will feel more at ease."

"No! Really. That isn't necessary, Mr. Lahti," Laurian

protested ineffectively to his back as he walked with a graceful, loose-hipped stride to a cabinet across the room.

When he came back to her, Keska had a cut-glass decanter and two stemmed crystal glasses in his hands. Setting the glasses on the coffee table, he poured something that looked black and sinister out of the decanter and held one glass out to her. "Try this, lovely Laurian."

Taking the glass in defeat, she looked at the purple-black contents suspiciously, then lifted the glass and sipped. When the wine hit her tongue, her dark eyes flew wide open. She fought the shocked reaction of her taste buds. It was only with courageous force of will that she was able to swallow without grimacing. Tears came to her eyes.

Keska Lahti's mouth was twitching when he sat down beside Laurian to touch his own glass to his lips. His free arm stretched out again on the cushion of the love seat behind her back, just short of touching her shoulders. "I made this wine myself from blackberries gathered last fall," he said, lifting the glass to squint at the ominously colored liquid. "It has a fine bouquet, don't you agree?"

For her uncle Jules, who had done so much for her, and for the music camp she loved, Laurian smiled grimly. "It's terribly interesting." Then she dutifully lifted the glass to her lips again while he watched.

The second swallow went down more easily because her tongue and throat were already numb from their first contact with the powerful wine. When the second sip hit bottom, her internal organs heated to a glow, giving her just enough additional courage to begin again. She was desperate to deliver her request and leave this intimidating man. "My uncle sent me to ask you—"

"Laurian, Laurian, lovely Laurian," Keska interrupted, tasting her name as if it had been the wine. "Laurian Bryant." Putting his glass down, he touched the pale green fabric of her skirt where it lay spread out beside his thigh. "You look so fresh and crisp and charming."

Then he brushed at the shirt lying open on his chest. Several apple petals fluttered through the air and landed on his thighs. His brows lifted, and he said apologetically, "But I am dirty and wrinkled and sweaty. Keska Lahti has been working in the orchard all day. I shouldn't be sitting beside you in this condition." His eyes traveled down her body slowly, thoroughly appreciating her freshness, and his hand went back to the fold of green skirt lying between them.

"It doesn't matter. Really," Laurian said, and watched as his fingers petted the soft material only inches from her thigh. She was well aware he was deliberately trying to put her at a disadvantage.

It seemed fairly obvious that Keska Lahti didn't even want to hear about the concert; how could she expect him to agree to play at it? But she had to ask. Taking another desperate sip of wine, she pleaded, "Please, let me say what I've come to say, Mr. Lahti."

"Keska," he said softly. "Please, call me Keska, my lovely Laurian."

She stared at him for a moment, but didn't respond to the request. The glow of the wine had moved rapidly from her empty stomach to spread through her bloodstream. At least she assumed it was the wine that had heated her body. Just in case it wasn't, she pulled her dress out from under his fingers and moved slightly away from him. In case it was the wine she set her glass on the coffee table.

To her horror Keska leaned forward and refilled her glass to the top. When he had finished that task, he settled back. By this time she had lost her grasp on what she had meant to tell him about the camp and the concert, and what she had wanted to ask him to do.

Lifting his distinctive, sloping eyebrows up over his eyes, which were glowing with admiration and amusement, he said, "Yes, you are fresh and lovely, but Keska Lahti has been working all day among the apple trees. It is interesting and rewarding work, but very physical."

He pronounced *apple* with a breathy *ah-h* that made Laurian smile. "I suppose it is."

Her smile encouraged him to go on musingly. "Once I read an item in a newspaper that claimed the odor of male perspiration acts as an aphrodisiac. Do you find that to be so?" His eyes studied her face challengingly.

She stiffened. "Mr. Lahti!"

"Keska."

"Mr. Lahti. That was offensive." She jumped up and faced him with flashing eyes. His scent was predominantly of apple blossoms, grasses, and residual cologne; only faintly of perspiration. She felt a blush rise into her face, a response for the most part to anger and frustration.

"So it *does* stimulate you, then?" he said, and laughed, his grin pushing his cheeks into dimpling creases.

"I don't know why George felt concerned about your rudeness," she said furiously. "Rudeness would have been a hundred times more acceptable than crudity. I think I had better leave." Turning abruptly, she walked toward the door.

Keska jumped up and rushed after her, laying his hand on her forearm to stop her. "But you have come to present a request to Keska Lahti, have you not?"

"You have absolutely no intention of listening to me," she snapped, looking down at the long, tanned fingers on her arm. She could feel their warmth burning her through her sleeve. "Take your hand off my arm. It's pointless for me to stay."

"I have every intention of hearing you out, Laurian Bryant," he said in a sincere voice. "But surely you must realize it is fruitless to speak of business to a man who is hungry and tired."

"*I'm* tired of your silly little games," Laurian said, shaking off his hand and making a move toward the door.

But Keska took her wrist and held her firmly. "No more games, I promise. Please do me the honor of having dinner with me. I will bathe and dress and conduct myself as a perfect gentleman if you will agree to share my evening meal with me."

Shaking her head, Laurian pulled her wrist away from the circle of his fingers. "No, thank you," she said firmly.

"Have you ever been lonely?" Keska asked. When she gave him a sidelong, suspicious look, he continued in his soft Finnish accent. "It is very dreary to eat alone. If you will gift me with your charming company for dinner,

I promise to be quiet and listen to the request you seemed so eager to make of me."

The wine had made its way to her brain with a minor explosion, numbing her resistance, and Laurian considered him doubtfully. The expression on his face was now sincere and disarming, and she frowned over the pros and cons of staying. The cons were self-evident. She had to stretch for the pros.

Though she wasn't convinced it was sincere, his plea of loneliness had caught at her sympathies; Laurian understood isolation. And she couldn't ignore the needs of the talented music students who would benefit from the proceeds earned in a performance by Keska Lahti—if there was an off chance that he might agree to play at the concert after this melodramatic smoke screen he had raised.

The students were important enough for her to take a chance and put herself in jeopardy with this sensual and disturbing man. "If I agree to stay," she said firmly, "I want you to understand that I am *Mrs.* Laurian Bryant. Jules Bryant is my husband's uncle."

Her husband had been gone for four years, but it seemed necessary to use any safeguard available when Keska Lahti stood smiling invitingly at her.

He cocked his head questioningly and murmured, "Mrs. Bryant."

She sighed apprehensively. "I'll have dinner with you if you wish."

"Keska Lahti wishes," he said, his smile stretching into delight.

"You'll listen to what I have to say?"

"I will listen."

"Then I'll stay for *dinner.*" Laurian stressed *dinner* in case he even imagined anything more.

His eyes gleamed. "I'll alert the cook and get dressed. Please be seated and finish your wine. I won't be long."

With an intimate smile Keska Lahti walked gracefully and sensually past her and out the door. She watched him walk down the hall and climb the stairs. Then she went back to the love seat and sat down tensely. Breathing a deep sigh, she lifted the glass and sipped. The dark, potent wine seemed pale and anemic compared to the dynamic man with whom she had agreed to spend the evening.

She frowned, knowing she would have to be on her guard. One temperamental musician, her husband, had been disastrous in her life. To encourage another would be insanity, Laurian told herself, so this encounter with Keska Lahti must necessarily remain impersonal and controlled.

Lifting her glass, Laurian stared at the sparkle of light on the fine crystal and thought, *Uncle Jules, I hope you appreciate what I'm doing for you.*

Then she looked at the closed French doors shutting off the studio, wondering why a man like Keska Lahti had chosen to bury himself in an apple orchard.

Two

It was after six by the time Keska Lahti came back to the sitting room. Time and the wine had done their work, and Laurian felt fluidly relaxed. She smiled languidly at him when he stood before her, her dark eyes glowing.

He had dressed in a cream-colored blousy silk shirt and a pair of beltless tailored black trousers, and looked every inch the polished international artist. The streamlined strength of his body lent an almost animal grace to his movements as he walked across the Persian rug. His light hair waved around his ears and gleamed with sun streaks in the yellow glow of a lamp. When he looked from Laurian's torpid smile to the empty glass on the table, his silvery eyes sparkled with amusement.

"Do you find Keska Lahti more acceptable now?" he asked softly, and lifted her hand. Bowing slightly, he touched the backs of her fingers with his lips. His eyes were linked with hers. When a response to the kiss raced up her arm like an electric shock, Laurian gasped and drew her hand away.

Staring up into the dark gray of his eyes, she repeated tentatively, "Acceptable . . . ?" He looked devastating. The argumentative odor of perspiration had been replaced by a lime scent of after-shave that insinuated itself into her senses. "You look very nice," she offered weakly.

"Would you like more wine?" Keska asked, his smile spreading over his face and sparkling in his eyes.

"Good Lord, no!" she exclaimed. "I should never have had the first glass." To her astonishment a giggle began to climb in her throat, and she choked it down with embarrassment.

Keska's laugh was free as he took both her hands in his and pulled her to her feet. "In that case perhaps we should have our dinner immediately."

"I think we'd better," Laurian agreed, and glanced at him when they walked into the hall. "Your wine is atrocious. Did you know?" If it hadn't been for the wine, she'd never have found the courage to speak the truth.

Keska nodded seriously. "Yes, I know." A smile twitched his lips when he said, "One might hope Keska Lahti will have better luck with apples than wine, might one not?"

His habit of referring to himself by name made her smile. "If you knew your blackberry wine was awful, why did you serve it to me?"

He ushered her into a formal dining room and smiled smugly. "I wondered how far you would go to ingratiate yourself to me to get what you wanted."

"Ingratiate myself!" Laurian exclaimed. "I was trying to be polite. You're impossible, Keska Lahti."

The dining room gleamed with silver and china on snowy linen. The room was warmed by a bouquet of fresh pink tulips and the light of a crystal chandelier.

Keska pulled out a chair and seated Laurian at the table. After he had pushed her chair in, he bent forward and brushed the bare skin of her neck with his lips. His breath curled around her throat as he whispered, "You are right, of course. Keska Lahti is impossible."

A response to the grazing touch of his lips and the warmth of his breath flickered through Laurian's body, and she gasped slightly, then said sharply, "Mr. Lahti, please. . . ."

His hands were on her shoulders, and he murmured in his Finnish accent from just behind her ear, "Mr. Lahti, please—what? Please, no? Or please, yes?"

Laurian made a move to rise, but his hands held her in place. Though she couldn't see him, her body was intimately aware that his was only inches away, just behind her chair. "Mr. Lahti, *no!*" she said angrily.

"Keska."

She sighed. "Keska, no." The sound of his name on her tongue felt exotic and exciting.

To her relief he conceded and took his seat across the round table from her, smiling benevolently. "Actually my intentions were innocent when I kissed your neck. I was curious as to whether all the beautiful hair piled on your head is really yours."

Laurian lifted an exploratory hand to the black hair wrapped around her head and stared at him. He alternated, she thought, between being disturbingly sensual, infuriating, and childishly ridiculous. She couldn't help laughing. "We share instruments occasionally at Camp Bryant, but never hair. It's all mine."

"Beautiful," Keska said, and rang a small silver bell.

In answer a matronly woman with a friendly smile and curious eyes for Laurian served baked salmon, tiny parsley potatoes, and new spring peas in a mushroom sauce. There were relishes and freshly baked bread on the table. The food smelled delicious, and Laurian sampled it hungrily.

When the woman had gone back into the kitchen, Keska said, "It must be stunning when it's free."

She looked at him questioningly. "Free?"

"Your hair. It must be a dark silken mantle when it's loose." His gaze moved over her shoulders and breasts as if picturing her hair covering them.

"Mr. Lahti," she said warningly, putting her fork down deliberately.

"Keska."

Taking an exasperated breath, Laurian repeated, "Keska. Keska, I expected George Miller to dine with us."

"George preferred to take a tray in his room. I believe he imagines he has a scheme to use you to bring about something he feels is necessary."

She stared at him angrily for a moment. "You're determined to put me at a disadvantage, aren't you?"

"Only if you allow it, lovely Laurian," Keska murmured.

At first she scowled angrily, but then she had to laugh. "I've been cooperating very nicely, haven't I?"

"Most gratifyingly," he agreed, and laughed too.

"In that case I'll have to be on my guard," she said, and

picked up her fork again. "Let me tell you about Camp Bryant."

"Oh, no. Not yet. No business while we eat. That would be inviting ulcers. Keska Lahti would like to hear about you, Laurian Bryant."

Glancing up, she smiled wryly. "I think you've already given me an ulcer. And Laurian Bryant isn't very interesting. Keska Lahti is more fascinating. Tell me about you," she said, then blinked. Now he had *her* speaking in the third person.

"Lovely Laurian is interesting—exciting," he said, finishing the food on his plate and laying his linen napkin aside. He hooked one arm over the back of his chair and crossed his legs. "Let me guess which instrument you play. A string. Yes? You have calluses on the fingers of your left hand. The violin?"

Laurian looked at the rough pads on her fingertips, surprised that he had been so perceptive, then she smiled at him. "I wouldn't presume to play the violin with Keska Lahti in the world. I play the cello."

"Do you play well?" he asked, lifting his eyebrows.

"Competently." Laurian paused and pondered him with a little envy for a moment. "I began taking lessons at six, and my parents felt certain I was gifted. But that spark of genius wasn't there, so all I've achieved are proficiency and enjoyment on the cello. In the winter season I play with a symphonic orchestra, and in the summer I teach the string students at Bryant Music Camp."

Keska's face had become serious and introspective while he listened. "Perhaps you are fortunate the questionable gift of genius isn't yours," he said slowly.

She looked at him curiously. "What an odd thing for Keska Lahti to say."

"Perhaps," he answered contemplatively, his expression shadowed. "But at times too much ability can be a burden and a slavemaster, not necessarily a desirable virtue."

A moment of silence elapsed, and Laurian waited for him to go on, to expand upon his statement. She felt an explanation of this feeling might even answer the question of why he had retired from performing. "I suppose I can understand that an exceptional artistic gift can be demanding," she said softly.

"Can you?" Keska said wistfully. His piercing eyes seemed to probe into her soul as he studied her. Then he shrugged slightly, and his expression became teasing again. "So you play the cello, do you? You seem much too dainty and fragile to handle so formidable an instrument."

"I manage," Laurian said, smiling. She shifted in the chair, repositioning all five feet and two inches of her slim, healthy body. "I'm much stronger than I look."

"If that statement was meant to be a warning to Keska Lahti, then I must be very careful," he said, his smile pushing dimples into his cheeks. "Do you wish dessert?" She declined. "Coffee?" He rang the silver bell at her nod and the woman came in from the kitchen immediately with a coffee service on a tray.

Keska took the tray and led Laurian into the sitting room, where he made a small ceremony out of pouring and serving.

Seating herself on the brocaded love seat, she accepted creamed and sweetened coffee, then watched him fix his own cup. He used his hands with a graceful, capable strength. All the muscles under his silky shirt and snug trousers moved with unconscious sensuality, as if he were very sure of himself. It pleased Laurian very much to watch him.

There were faint lines etched across his forehead, hinting at worries and torments. Vertical lines between his brows indicated a temper. Laugh lines around his mouth and at the corners of his eyes balanced the other expressions. Laurian thought that in repose his face had a serious, artistic sensitivity that contrasted with his flippant behavior toward her. She wondered if his teasing might be a shield to protect a vulnerable soul.

Both his face and his body denied the fact that he was almost forty years old. As she studied him she began to feel a stirring of desire. His sexuality was very near the surface at all times, and she couldn't stop herself from responding to it.

As if he had read her thoughts, Keska glanced up at her and smiled. "So," he said as he sat down beside her,

"Laurian Bryant plays the cello. I have always considered the cello to have a husky, sexual voice."

His words might have come from her own thoughts. She felt herself blush slightly in the dim light of a side lamp. "Really," she murmured noncommittally.

"Really," he echoed, shifting his body on the love seat. He crossed one knee over the other and the black material of his trousers pulled tensely around his thigh. "The sound of a violin cries out for love," he murmured with his gentle accent, "and the cello answers."

Laurian's skin stirred with a creeping response to the message in his eyes. Her voice was husky when she said, in an effort to redirect the conversation, "You haven't told me about Keska Lahti."

"Keska Lahti has not heard the rest of your story," he said. "Tell me about your husband."

She stirred irritably and crossed her legs. Then uncrossed them again and nervously smoothed down her skirt when Keska seemed to be following her body movements with too much interest. "I married very young," she said. "At twenty, when I was still in music school. A few years after that I realized I would never become a noted musician or a soloist." Her eyes dimmed with memory. "It was a disappointment, so perhaps that's why the marriage—" She stopped abruptly.

Pursing his lips, Keska waited for her to go on. When she didn't, he finished the sentence for her, his accent softening the painful statement. "That's why the marriage didn't work."

Glancing at him, Laurian fielded his challenging, curious smile, then looked away guiltily and laughed. "I think I've fallen neatly into a trap I set for myself by hiding behind a nonexistent husband."

"When you claimed to be married," he said smugly, "I thought it must be a frustrating relationship, considering your reaction to me." He smiled and put his coffee cup down on the table, then sat back again and touched her cheek with his fingertips. "Your attraction to me has been the most sincere and welcome compliment I have ever received, my lovely Laurian. Don't be embarrassed."

His scent enveloped her, and his gaze touched her face with an almost physical impact. It traced the soft curve of her jaw, fingered the slight cleft in her chin, and melted into her eyes. Oddly she wasn't embarrassed, just vaguely frightened.

When Keska recognized the anxiety warring with the desire in her eyes, he whispered, "I think you are a woman alone who must rediscover the art of trusting and loving a man." His grazing fingertip traced the curve of her cheek.

After a few moments Laurian realized she had forgotten to breathe, and still staring into his molten silver eyes, she drew in a tremulous sigh. Her heart began racing as her body responded to the awareness that his tense, muscular form was only inches away. It could be hers for the asking.

The attraction and pull between them was powerful, almost irresistible. It had been so achingly long since Laurian had experienced the thrill and joy of being held and caressed, but she was afraid. She wanted to run, to escape the confusion building inside her, but she couldn't move.

Her pink lips were warm and parted. Keska leaned forward to touch his mouth to hers, and the kiss was soft and seeking. It was a gentle, tender joining that sent a flush flowing down over her body. His tongue felt hot, burning, when he touched it to the inner surface of her upper lip.

The sound of her cup clattering on the saucer in her trembling hand brought Laurian's numbed mind back to life. She pulled away from the kiss almost sadly.

Rising to her feet, she took a few steps from the love seat and stood with her back to Keska, hugging herself until she felt she had regained some sort of control over her body.

"Tell me what is wrong," Keska said softly.

Breathing heavily, Laurian spoke brokenly in an attempt to explain. "My husband was a— He was a concert pianist. He was a—" She couldn't find the words to describe the disappointment and pain she still felt after all those years.

Keska uncrossed his legs and pulled himself up straight on the love seat. "Your husband was an egotistical, temperamental musician with not enough sensitivity to give his wife a selfless love," he said sharply with poignant emotion in his accented voice. "Is that how it was?"

Laurian turned and glanced at him, startled that he seemed able to read her mind. But Keska wasn't looking at her. He had his eyes on the French doors that closed away his violin and music. "Yes, that's how it was," she said. "I'm sure you can understand how I might be reluctant to stumble into that sort of relationship again."

"Yes, I understand," he said, then after a few seconds he shrugged fluidly and shifted to a more comfortable position on the love seat. "But we have become much too serious, my lovely Laurian. Come sit down beside me and I will tell you about Keska Lahti."

Laurian sat down on a pale blue easy chair a few yards away from him and smiled. "I already know enough about Keska Lahti to realize I'll be safer with space between us."

His eyes gleamed. "I'm Finnish, you know."

"I'd never have guessed—with your accent and your name," she acknowledged. "But what does that have to do with anything?"

"If the Finns are nothing else, they are determined," he murmured. "Once we make up our mind about something, nothing prevents us from triumph." His eyes traveled over her as if he already tasted victory. "And you intrigue me, lovely Laurian."

She glanced wistfully at the door. It seemed quite likely Keska was right, that he might succeed in capturing her in his spell. "I think I'd really better leave now," she said uncertainly, and started to rise.

"Are you a good music teacher, Laurian?" he asked, suddenly changing the subject and throwing her off-balance again.

The ploy was deliberate, and she smothered a laugh of grudging respect for his tactics. "I think I'm a good music teacher," she said.

"Are you kind and responsive to your students?"

"I hope so." It seemed to Laurian that Keska might finally be leading up to the subject she had been waiting so long to present: Bryant Music Camp and the benefit concert.

But he drifted off on another tangent. "I began music lessons very young, at four years of age. My parents had taken me to hear a violinist, and even as so young a boy, I knew the violin was a part of me—my soul.

"A prodigy," he said, dragging out the word with exaggerated sarcasm. "A prodigy. Keska Lahti was a prodigy." He looked at Laurian sharply as if ready to chop down admiration, should she express it.

He relaxed when he saw her neutral expression. "Over the years since that tender age," he went on, "I have had many teachers. Some much better than others. One, I remember in particular, who taught me when I was seven. She would stand behind me with a baton, striking my head to keep time while I struggled with my violin. I didn't need a metronome; I had her baton."

He tapped himself on the head with his coffee spoon, frowning fiercely and intoning, "One and, two and, three and, four and. One and—"

When Laurian laughed, Keska looked up at her, ceasing his hollow-sounding head-tapping. "You think that's funny, do you?" he protested, then laughed and added, "At least she taught me concentration, if nothing else. I could play my pieces on the violin and at the same time concoct methods of killing her—each more horrible than the last."

"I'm not that kind of teacher," Laurian said. "None of us are at Camp Bryant. Will you let me tell you about it now?"

A put-upon expression settled on his face, and he sighed impatiently. "If you feel you must tell me, Keska Lahti will listen."

"Thank goodness," she breathed. "My husband's uncle, Jules Bryant—"

He jerked up straight on the love seat. "You didn't tell me what became of your husband."

"*Keska!*"

"Just answer that one important question, then I'll be quiet and attentive to anything you say."

Laurian hesitated for a moment, then said, "My husband was killed in an airplane crash four years ago."

His face fell. "I've made a joke about a very sad business." He looked genuinely distressed.

"Yes, it was a sad business," she agreed slowly, "but so was the marriage. His death didn't affect me as acutely as it might have if Andrew and I had been happy together."

"I'm very sorry," Keska said.

There seemed nothing to add, so Laurian went back to her subject. "My husband's uncle, Jules Bryant, owns and directs a very respected and well-known music camp that caters to especially talented youngsters between the ages of ten and eighteen. They come from all over the country and they are all gifted musicians."

Pausing, Laurian glanced at Keska's intent face. He looked back at her from under lowered brows and made no comment. "We offer intensive musical instruction," she went on, "both privately and in groups, by teachers of the highest quality. Our students enjoy activities such as river rafting, horseback riding, swimming, hiking, and just rambling around. They are with other children who share their own peculiar interests."

She paused again and added, "Perhaps you remember what it feels like to be a special child in a world geared for average children. At Camp Bryant our children feel secure in an accepting group of peers."

Keska made no comment, though Laurian felt certain she had caught flashes of true interest in his eyes.

"As you might expect," she continued, "we charge quite large fees to pay for teachers, equipment, and a thousand other things. But each year we allocate a certain number of scholarships to be given to highly qualified children whose parents can't afford our fees."

Laurian glanced at Keska and mentally crossed her fingers. "The money for their scholarships is raised at a benefit performance we hold at the end of each season, in August, when our student orchestra plays in concert. At this concert each year, we prevail upon a generous, well-known performer to donate his or her talent to draw a larger audience and thereby a greater profit."

Laurian waited for a moment, giving Keska a chance to volunteer. He didn't, so she asked, "Would you consider performing at our concert this August?"

"I'm sorry," he said without hesitation. "Keska Lahti does not play the violin before audiences any longer."

There wasn't so much as a hint in his tone of voice that he might reconsider.

His answer shocked her into a few moments of silence, and then she started, "But, Keska—"

"No." His full lower lip had settled into an adamant, stubborn line.

Laurian's mouth dropped open as she stared at him blankly, nonplussed. She hadn't expected him to agree readily, but she had expected—what? Interest? Sympathy for the cause? She might have expected the simple courtesy of an explanation. Jumping out of her chair, she exclaimed, "But you led me to believe—"

"I led you to believe nothing, Laurian," Keska said, rising to his feet. "I do not give performances any longer. I am an apple farmer."

"But I spent the evening with you."

"You did indeed." He smiled wistfully and his accent intensified, reflecting a deep emotion, when he added, "I enjoyed your company very much, lovely Laurian. I can only pray you enjoyed mine as well."

She stared at him for a few moments. Then she snorted "Oh!" and marched to the hallway. At the door she turned and said stuffily, "Good night, Keska."

"Good night, Laurian Bryant," he said, and half bowed in the European manner.

Laurian strode down the hallway toward the front door, anger flashing in her dark eyes. She tried to tell herself she had expected nothing *other* than failure in the first place. From the beginning her request for his appearance at the concert had been nothing but a gamble.

What she couldn't forgive him was that he had made such an elaborate production out of putting her off and playing upon her susceptibilities before refusing.

As Laurian's heels clicked furiously on the wooden floor of the hallway, George Miller appeared like a silent wraith from a room down the hall. "May I see you to your car, madam?" he asked in his courtly, distant manner.

"That isn't necessary," Laurian answered tartly. Her feathers were ruffled, and she didn't care to display that sorry state to anyone.

"It would be my pleasure," George insisted, and

opened the door for her. As he followed her out on the veranda he said with satisfaction, "You have made notable progress."

Laurian had started down the steps, but at his statement she whirled around. "Progress? *Progress!*"

George closed the door and took her by the arm, leading her away from the large house and toward her car. "I felt the evening went rather well," he said.

"The evening went well! Keska Lahti subjected me to an evening of taunting, teasing, and ridicule. I even drank his awful wine."

"Oh, my! You didn't touch that vile concoction, did you?"

"I did—like a fool. And after all that, he wouldn't even seriously consider what I had to say about Camp Bryant. He said no. Just no. No explanation. Nothing. Keska Lahti is a—a—" She couldn't think of a name severe enough for him.

"A rogue?" George offered helpfully. "A scoundrel?" The sun had gone down and it was nearly dark. He glanced up at a light that had just come on in one of the three gables over the veranda. "A lonely, confused man?" he added softly.

The last jolted Laurian out of her anger. "Keska Lahti? Confused?"

George didn't elaborate. Instead he suggested, "When you visit the next time, you might plan to arrive at around eight in the morning. Mr. Lahti practices on his violin for a few hours every day."

"Come back!" Laurian snorted and climbed into her car. She slammed the door shut and rolled down the window. "Keska said no with express finality. What would be the point in coming back?"

George put his hand on the door and bent his head to look in at her, smiling slightly. "You've spent three hours with Mr. Lahti, even though he knew what you intended to ask. That, in his case, is as good as a maybe."

Laurian studied him thoughtfully, then gave a restless shiver when her skin and lips remembered his kiss. A gentle breeze was bringing in the scent of apple blossoms from the orchards. Crickets were calling around the yard. The smell reminded her of Keska, and the crickets sounded desolate.

"I'm not sure I have the courage for another encounter with Keska Lahti," she said quickly. "He's overbearing and . . . and spoiled. He thinks he can have everything just the way he wants it, no matter what the other person wants."

"But surely," George said, "you have become familiar with the talented artist's personality while doing the kind of work you do—teaching music and playing cello in the orchestra. You must take into account a gifted musician's temperament."

"There are limits to everything, even temperament," Laurian said, and put her key in the ignition. Then she glanced up. "You don't care much for apple farming, do you, George?"

"It seems a waste, in the case of Mr. Lahti," he answered with a controlled smile. "Good night, madam."

"Good night," she responded, and glanced up at the lighted window in the second-floor gable of the house. Her fists tightened on the steering wheel when she imagined laying herself open to Keska Lahti again.

Shaking her head, Laurian put the car in gear and drove down the driveway. A second visit would be asking too much. She had fulfilled her responsibility to Camp Bryant when she had presented Keska with the opportunity to play the concert.

Keska Lahti could farm and grow apples to his heart's content, cheating the world of his music if that was his choice, Laurian told herself. It was no concern of hers.

The road to the music camp from Keska's apple farm was narrow and winding. When Laurian had almost reached the Russian River, she was driving through a forest of tall, straight redwoods.

Bryant Music Camp was a cluster of two-story chalets on an inner curve of the river, secluded and private. The students wouldn't arrive until May, so all the buildings were dark except the one that doubled as the string students' practice rooms and the teachers' residence. In that building were now settled a skeleton crew of service people and teachers, along with Laurian and Uncle Jules, who had arrived early to get the camp ready for the summer season.

The sky was black overhead and was glittering with huge stars when Laurian parked her car and walked across the dark yard. The subdued night sounds from the pungent forest and the constant splashing roar of the river drifted around her as she walked through the door of the lighted building.

Laurian felt wrung out and exhausted, certainly not eager to talk to anyone when she started up the stairs to the second floor of the large chalet. But Uncle Jules Bryant had been waiting for her and came out of his office on the ground floor as she started to climb the stairs toward her room.

Jules was a dumpy man of seventy-three. He had almost youthful energy, a halo of wild white hair, a beaming smile on his cherubic pink face, and hands that were pushed into the stretched pockets of a vintage sweater. "Ah, my dear, you're back finally," he said. "So how did it go? What did Mr. Lahti say?"

Laurian stopped in the middle of the stairs and looked back. "He said no."

Jules started up the stairs after her, his forehead wrinkled with disappointment. "You were with Keska Lahti all this time and he still said no? How can that be?"

"Keska Lahti likes to do things with a flourish," Laurian said, and ran up the rest of the stairs.

With Jules on her heels she walked into a room that was warm with soft pastel colors against cherry-wood paneling. Her Camp Bryant room had a comfortable bed, a scattering of cozy furniture, and wall hangings of her own choice; it had become her home away from home in the last years.

"Tell me all that happened," Jules said, and sat on the edge of a chintz-covered easy chair.

Laurian slipped her shoes off and threw herself into another easy chair. "I feel as if I've had an encounter with a tornado," she said, and related the course of that evening's events, carefully minimizing Keska's seductiveness and her reaction to him. "He scares me," she finished.

"You've been frightened ever since Andrew," Jules said, obviously reading between her lines.

She looked into his kindly, beloved face and said softly, "Uncle Jules, don't start telling me there's more to life than music and work, or that I should enjoy myself more, or that I might learn to love another man. It's not your fault that Andrew and I didn't have a happy marriage. You were only his uncle, not his keeper. I appreciate your concern, but please don't try to push me into anything."

"When do I ever push you, my dear?" He looked insulted, but his eyes were sparkling.

"When *don't* you?"

Jules laughed and then gazed at her thoughtfully. Finally he said, "So this George Miller person thinks it would be productive for you to go back to Keska Lahti, does he?"

"I'm not going," Laurian said flatly. "I can't hold my own in his kind of game playing."

"Not even if there's a chance that he would agree to play the concert? Think of the money. . . . I imagine we could charge a hundred dollars a head for that performance and still fill the house."

Laurian shook her head slowly from side to side.

Jules pressed one finger against his lips, then said tentatively, "It sounds as if Mr. Lahti found himself attracted to you. He's not an unappealing man, is he? What harm is there in a little flirtation, eh?"

The harm was that she had already foolishly come too close to surrendering to Keska's blatant seduction attempt. Laurian had no wish to become enmeshed with another egotistical musician. "Just because Keska Lahti is an attractive man with a fascinating talent doesn't mean that I'm going to rush after him like any other love-starved groupie," she said irritably. "The way he acted, I imagine he expects that kind of behavior."

Uncle Jules said nothing. He smiled knowingly.

"I wonder if he's ever been married?" she pondered curiously.

"I believe there was something in the papers a year or

so ago," Uncle Jules murmured in a detached voice. "An item mentioning a divorce shortly before Lahti withdrew from the public eye."

"Really?" Laurian frowned thoughtfully. "I wonder if—" She broke off and gave Jules a suspicious look, realizing she had almost allowed herself to be manipulated again. "I'm not going back to that apple farm. Ever."

He smiled and sighed.

Laurian frowned at him. "We can get along perfectly well without Keska Lahti. There are other important musicians who will play at the concert for us."

Jules smiled and nodded, but his face had suddenly begun to look sagging and tired. His blue eyes rested upon her with the warm affection of years of closeness.

After a few moments of silence his gentle acceptance began to wear on Laurian. "The benefit money isn't everything," she said defensively.

"Of course, it isn't, my dear," Jules said softly, and rose to his feet. Before he went out of her door, he looked back and said, "Do you know we still have no student flautist for the summer? The orchestra simply won't sound right without a flute. It's such a shame we've already filled our gratus quota of students, because I think I remember a young girl from New Jersey who is an outstanding flautist and who would like very much to join us." He sighed deeply. "But she can't afford us and we can't manage another plane fare, can we?"

"Uncle Jules," Laurian protested faintly. "What are you trying to do to me?"

Three

At 8:07 the next morning Laurian drove into Keska Lahti's yard and parked her car. Her head was full of dark thoughts about Uncle Jules, George Miller, and everyone else who had made her feel guilty about not talking Keska Lahti into playing at the concert. She would never have come back to this farmhouse of her own volition.

She felt especially annoyed at Keska. If he had explained in a final and civilized manner the reasons for his refusal, it would have been the end of this farce, and she wouldn't have felt obligated to return for another try. But with his secrecy he had left alive a frustrating spark of hope. Laurian felt it her duty to fan this hope in case the spark meant a concert performance was possible. She sincerely doubted the likelihood, however.

The truly disturbing fact of it all was that Laurian felt an underlying, breathtaking thrill of anticipation over seeing Keska again. And she knew that would never do. She had no desire for a relationship to develop between her and that temperamental man. She was not a masochistic woman.

To defray the handicap of her attraction to Keska, she had dressed very casually in a pair of navy-blue pants and a loose white cossack blouse with embroidery and a tie belt. Vanity had forced her to wear at least a minimum of makeup; she had put on highlighting around her eyes, a hint of pink lipstick, and just a touch of perfume. Her dark hair was braided into a thick, heavy club that hung almost to her waist. A smile crossed her face when she thought she could use the braid as a weapon, should the need arise.

Humor aside, the point was that her costume didn't look seductive in any way, so she apprehensively turned off the motor, opened the door, and stepped out of her car.

George Miller was strolling from flower bed to flower bed in the front yard, already impeccably dressed in a three-piece suit. "Good morning, madam," he said as if he had been expecting her. "A fine morning, don't you agree?"

Laurian stood motionless beside her car, her answering greeting struck silent on her tongue. The sound of string music emanating from the house had taken her breath away.

Her entire life had been devoted to classical music, but never had Laurian heard a violin brought to such exquisitely full life. The music wrapped itself around her and captured her mind in an ephemeral, silken web. It shook her emotions to listen to the sound. And Keska Lahti was only playing scales.

The treble of the birds and the whisper of the breeze, the smell of the flowers and damp grass, faded into nothingness as she listened with parted lips and speeding heart to the lilting, full-bodied sound of the violin. Her knees weakened when the scales ceased and the sound shifted into the complex melody that she recognized as Bloch's "Nigun."

The violin began low and throaty, sending out a sad mournful message that pulled at her. Then it rose to a high thin cry, and the notes rolled up a pinnacle of grief . . . or wanting. The sound seemed to call out, then answer its own impassioned query with loneliness.

George had walked across the yard to stand beside Laurian, but she didn't notice him until he said softly, "You may join Mr. Lahti in the music room if you like."

For a second she stared at him blankly until she could will her mind away from the spell of the music. "I wouldn't want to disturb him," she whispered.

"I'm sure you wouldn't distract him; an audience brings out the best in him. A gift such as his is meaningless unless it is shared. He knows this."

Laurian wanted desperately to go into the house to watch Keska Lahti entice that incredible sound from his violin. But she hesitated and listened, enthralled, for a few moments. Then she said regretfully, "He might think I've come back to harass him about playing the concert. I'm not sure I'd be welcome." The music pulled at her like a siren, and she had to tense her muscles to resist going to it.

George allowed a slight smile to cross his lips. "Have no fear. Mr. Lahti would not hesitate to tell you frankly if he didn't want you with him. Then you could leave, and no harm would have been done. I suspect he will welcome you."

Only seconds of vacillation passed before Laurian walked up the steps of the veranda and opened the front door as silently as she could. Once inside the house, the pure soaring sound of the violin curled itself around her like a lover's arms, urging her forward, touching every nerve in her body.

Breath-catching emotion filled her chest to bursting as she walked quietly toward the French doors that stood open on the other side of the sitting room. Stopping just short of entering the music studio, Laurian gazed with rapt eyes through the door at the man and his violin.

Keska sat in his chair, half facing the door, though unaware of her. He wore heavy laced boots and was dressed in clean, faded jeans and a blue shirt with the top three buttons open. The baseball cap and his muddy leather gloves had been thrown on the table beside a pile of sheet music.

Slender, elegant fingers moved smoothly on the neck of the violin and drew the bow over the strings. Neither the hands holding the violin nor the expression on Keska's patrician face could have belonged to a simple farmer.

His chin and cheek were cuddled in a lover's embrace over the violin resting on his shoulder. The emotion on his mobile features changed fluidly from phrase to phrase, sometimes from note to note, of the haunting music produced by his talented hands.

The strong shape of his chin seemed vulnerable in his

preoccupation. His lips were slightly parted and curved in an expression similar to sensual passion. The light brown hair waving on his forehead and around his neck seemed as alive and vital as his music.

His gray eyes looked inward, reading his emotion into the sounds of the violin. Though there was passion in Keska's face for the music he created, there was also a heavy frown of loneliness and discontent pulling his brows down over his eyes.

Afraid to move a muscle lest she shatter the spell, Laurian listened and forgot she'd had dire anxieties about this dynamic man. She became a willing prisoner to the binding, ethereal timbre of Keska Lahti and his violin.

Suddenly he sensed Laurian's presence and his face came to life as he looked at her. His discontented frown washed away immediately. Without interrupting the complicated musical piece he was seducing out of the violin, he touched her enraptured face with his warm gaze. His slow, embracing investigation gave Laurian a sensation of being stroked lightly on her lips, shoulders, and rise of breasts.

The intangible touch of Keska's music and his eyes was more powerful than the effect of his wine, and Laurian's bones seemed to turn into liquid. Her heart leaped in her chest as if it wanted to fly to him. She looked wistfully at the slim, vital length of his body, at the curve of his thighs and the strength of his shoulders, at the skill and artistry of his hands.

As soon as Laurian recognized the invitation in the curve of Keska's mouth and in the depths of his eyes, her body answered by demanding to be close to him, to touch him, to hold and be held, to be a part of the man and his music. Her brain had barely enough rationale left to put a brake on her rebellious bodily desires.

Then his eyes linked with hers and he mouthed "No" without missing a beat in his playing.

For an instant Laurian thought unreasonably that Keska had rejected her body's intense desire, and she winced with hurt. Then her mind snapped on, and she realized he had only reaffirmed his refusal to play at the benefit concert.

Her relief brought beads of perspiration popping out on her upper lip as she fought to control her sensual reaction to him. The safest course would be to leave the room immediately, she told herself, but she couldn't bring herself to break away from the spell of his music.

Sighing, Laurian shrugged slightly and answered his "No" by lifting her hands, palms up, in exaggerated resignation. When the sound of the violin moved seductively over the sensitive flesh of her hands, she dropped them instantly.

At her gesture of acceptance Keska smiled and nodded, inclining his head toward a chair a few yards away from him in the music room.

When Laurian walked into the studio, the music issuing from the strings under the bow he held so lightly in his fingertips made an unbelievably smooth transition from Bloch to a wailing, agonized, impassioned gypsy love song.

The sound and the emotion sent almost unbearable tremors running through Laurian's body, and she dropped weakly into the chair, lifting her eyes to meet Keska's gaze. The flaming, ardent passion of the gypsy music was mirrored in his face, though she also caught an underlying teasing amusement.

The fact that he found humor in the situation gave Laurian the strength to give a firm though silent answer to the seduction in the music. "No, Mr. Lahti," she mouthed. Her hand closed around the thick dark braid of hair that had fallen forward to rest on her breast. It might have been her weapon, but the gesture was symbolic. Despite her better sense she had become tightly enmeshed in the spell of the man and his love song.

At her mute rejection the music made another mercurial switch to a somber funeral dirge, but Keska smiled at her with no apparent insult. And then his eyes turned inward with concentration. He went back to Bloch's "Nigun," picking up amazingly at the precise place in the music where Laurian had interrupted him.

Without his disturbing attention she allowed herself to relax and lose herself to his playing, to the magic of Keska Lahti's violin. The pieces he played for practice were intricate and obscure, meant to stretch his abilities. They might have been dull and technical exercises under another hand, but Keska brought them to full, exciting life.

Laurian's respect for his genius built to worship. Her only thought when he put down his violin and bow after two hours was that it was criminal for Keska Lahti to hide his magnificent gift in an apple orchard.

With practice over, Keska stretched, reaching for the ceiling with his fists, contracting the muscles in his body to bring it back to fascinating life. Then he relaxed and picked up the Yankees baseball cap, brushing his hair back before setting the cap on his head. He looked at her from under the bill and asked in his intriguing accent, "So, lovely Laurian. What do you think?"

She realized instantly that he expected praise as his due; it was time for applause and bravos. But she decided to take another route in dealing with Keska Lahti. He obviously enjoyed playing games, so she'd have to learn the rules—or make up her own. Smiling slightly, she shrugged and said, "That wasn't bad—for an apple farmer."

For a few seconds his face turned chilly with surprise, but then his eyes gleamed under the cap. A slow smile spread across his lips. "Can it be that lovely Laurian has ceased to ingratiate herself?" he murmured approvingly. Pleasure shone in his eyes. "Our association should become interesting."

Belatedly she paused to wonder how wise it had been to tease an egocentric and temperamental man, but it was too late to back out now. "I think I'd prefer a simple truce," she said wryly. "Why did you stop performing for the public, Keska? It's a sad loss for us."

He studied her introspectively for a moment, and then he got up, stuffing his leather gloves in his back pocket. The fingers stuck up in a cluster on his streamlined hip and waggled when he walked toward the door. He held out his hand to her. "Come see my apple trees, Laurian."

Standing, she put her hand in his, steeling herself against a reaction to the warmth and pressure of his talented fingers. "Aren't you going to answer my question?" she asked as they walked through the sitting room to the hallway.

"Keska Lahti will answer," he said, "but you couldn't understand if I explained here in the house." He led her through the kitchen and into a sunny, fenced backyard.

A large, rectangular bright-blue swimming pool lay before them, flanked by deck chairs and tables. "Keska Lahti lives well for an apple farmer," Laurian commented dryly.

He laughed. "It isn't necessary to revert to the primitive to come close to the land."

Beyond the pool was a small tight windowless shed with a feather of smoke rising from a chimney in the rear. He pointed to it and announced, "My sauna. I keep it heated and ready for use at all times. I wouldn't be a proper Finn if I didn't." His eyes hit her face. "Would you like to try it out?"

A picture of Keska sitting naked in the steam flitted through Laurian's mind, embarrassing her. Shaking her head quickly, she smiled and said, "I thought we were going to look at your apples."

"Some other time, then," he conceded, and led her through a gate in the fence. They walked into a field that was knee-deep with pasture grass and wild mustard weeds blooming like a sea of gold.

Beyond the field was the orchard of mature, gnarled apple trees. They were lacy with beginning leaves and pale pink apple blossoms. The trees were planted in symmetrical rows with freshly harrowed earth between them. The smell of newly turned soil rose up to wed with the perfume of the flowers. The scent reached out and took Laurian into another world, a strange and different world that was far removed from reality.

Keska held her hand, threading his way between the tree trunks until the house was out of sight. Near the center of the orchard stood a green tractor with a pronged cultivator attached behind. It was silent and waiting, and Laurian realized Keska must have left it there when he had met her in the house yesterday afternoon.

It seemed incomprehensible that he would use his magical hands for so mundane a task as driving a tractor and cultivating an orchard. "This is what you do?" she questioned dubiously, staring at the machine.

Keska nodded and took the leather gloves out of the back pocket of his jeans to lay them on the tractor seat. "This is what Keska Lahti does. If I didn't, the weeds would grow and leech the nutrients out of the soil. I mustn't allow my apple trees to starve, must I?"

"But *why*?" Laurian demanded. "Why waste yourself?"

"Waste myself?" he repeated impatiently. "Can't you see the beauty here?"

"Of course, I can, but—"

"No buts. Come and see my favorite place." Taking her hand again, Keska tugged her along through the trees until they stood beside a tiny stream that trickled through the middle of the orchard. It was only about four feet wide, but it splashed and gurgled merrily around the rocks of its bed. The sound was a perfect tenor accompaniment to the high-pitched warbling of the birds nesting in the branches. He leaned his shoulder against a tree trunk and looked keenly at Laurian, waiting for her reaction.

She nodded her head and smiled. "It *is* beautiful here. So peaceful. It's a secret little world, isn't it? We're alone in it."

A smile of approval spread over Keska's face, creasing his cheeks as he nodded. Then he turned serious and said, "In all my life, before I came to this apple farm, I've never known anything but music and the violin. I'm almost forty years old and I've had no other experiences. When—"

He broke off and studied Laurian for a moment, as if evaluating her. Perhaps he felt he couldn't trust her completely, because he didn't finish the thought. Instead, he said, "I have been a property belonging to other people and to the world all my life. Keska Lahti is a very valuable asset—praised, lauded, bought, and used."

Laurian looked into his serious gray eyes and felt sympathy. "I realize your life must have been very structured and that you've had little freedom," she said slowly. "But it isn't easy to separate the man from the talent. It's all a part of you."

"Perhaps," he said, and paused for a few moments,

then went on. "A little over a year ago something happened to make me realize that I must find out who Keska Lahti really is." He studied her, searching for understanding. "Even if no one else can, I must come to know the man behind the violin. I need to find out if he has any value as a human being."

"It's obvious there's a man behind the music," Laurian said sincerely. Hadn't she been fighting against responding to that very human male ever since she had met Keska?

"I'm not sure it's obvious," he said skeptically.

"Do you think you'll find what you're looking for here?" she asked, and walked under the tree to stand beside him. The branches hung over them like a canopy. When a breeze swept through, a shower of pink petals drifted down on them. "Are your answers here in the apple orchard?" she asked again.

Taking a deep breath, Keska reached up and gently bent a branch down to look at a cluster of delicate pink flowers. "My apples are a beginning. At least here in the orchard I am close to the earth from which all things spring." He glanced at her and smiled. "Perhaps Keska Lahti will spring from the earth, too, a complete man."

Suddenly a honeybee swooped down from the sky to light on a blossom on the branch Keska held. Laurian stepped back quickly, startled and half afraid. She was ready to run if the insect so much as hinted at a hostile motion.

Keska laughed and reached out with his free hand to pull her closer. "The bee won't hurt you unless you touch him," he said softly. "He's interested in other things."

"I hope so," Laurian said, hanging back.

Holding the branch steady, careful not to disturb the bee, Keska put his arm around Laurian's waist, drawing her close against his side.

"Watch the honeybee," he murmured. "See how he kisses the flower, how he caresses her and loves her?"

Laurian relaxed, and her body softened against him. Her thigh was pressed against his and her breast against his chest. She sighed as she dreamily watched the bee nuzzle the bloom.

Keska's voice became deep and intimate, his accent musical, when he said, "What the bee is doing is very close to lovemaking, don't you agree? See how he enters the flower, drinking her sweetness." His arm tightened around Laurian, and she nestled her cheek into the curve of his shoulder.

Warmth spread over her, and a heavy flush of desire burst from the center of her body as she watched the bee embrace the flower, sinking his head into her pink core.

Keska's lips touched her cheek, moving on her skin, and his arm pulled her even tighter against his hard, muscular body. His whisper was a sensual caress when he asked, "Do you think the flower enjoys the act of love?"

His breath flowed over the skin of her face, bringing every cell to life. She gazed enviously at the joined bee and flower, then turned her head to look up into Keska's molten silver eyes. She read the message of desire written in their depths. "I think the flower must be very, very happy," she whispered.

Keska's lips came down to cover hers, moving and tasting, seeking and claiming Laurian as his own.

She put her arms around his shoulders, touching the warmth at the back of his neck and threading her fingers through his thick wavy hair. Opening her lips, she invited his kiss and tasted the honey of his mouth. She met his tongue and pressed her eager body against his hard lines. In the embrace they melded into one and shared the beginning of their passion.

Keska released the branch gently and carefully, leaving undisturbed the link between bee and blossom. Then he encircled her with both arms, shifting her to rest against the full length of his body. His arousal was no secret.

His hands moved with the sensitivity of a gifted artist over her shoulders and down the sweeping curve of her back. He touched her neck and wrapped his hand with her thick braid of hair. His lips moved on hers, hard and demanding, until the sensation had spread through every fiber of her body, bringing her to radiant, humming life.

When Keska pulled back and looked down into her

face, Laurian felt breathless and molten, acutely aware of wanting him, of being at home in his arms. The full curve of his lower lip was soft with desire, and his smile was impish when he whispered, "I think the bee enjoyed making love just as much as the flower."

Her breath came in sharp little gasps, and she smiled at him, her eyes as black as a moonless night.

"You are so beautiful . . . so very beautiful, so special, my lovely Laurian," he said softly, his gentle accent stroking her. He touched the buttons on her blouse with tentative fingers and raised his brows.

The choice to make love had been left to her, and sadly there was only one answer she could give. "I can't—not yet. I can't be intimate without commitment and love," Laurian whispered reluctantly. "I don't know Keska Lahti well enough."

Mustering sheer willpower, she tried to draw away, but Keska held her against him with one hand on the small of her back and the other firmly wound in her braid. The club she had laughingly thought to use as a weapon had become a booby trap. But she couldn't rouse herself to mind and rested her cheek on his shoulder.

"The lovemaking between the bee and the flower was a very natural and beautiful thing." His hand moved lightly down to rest on the curve of her hip, his thumb moving in inviting circles. "It can be so for us too."

Laurian sighed deeply and lifted her head to look up at the branch and the cluster of apple blossoms. "But the bee is gone now, isn't he? He took what he wanted, and there sits a poor lonely flower, with nothing but memories," she said, and pulled away from Keska, holding her braid as she slid it out of his hand.

He kissed her forehead, the curve of her cheek, and her chin before he allowed her to step back. "It is the bee who has lost the most," he whispered, his face shadowed. "If you didn't want to be close, then why did you come back to Keska Lahti?"

Though Laurian knew it was wise to be cautious, she felt painfully confused, and the words stumbled over each other when she said, "I came this morning to hear you play your violin."

Angry creases slashed down between his dark brows, and his face looked stiff and hurt. "You see?" he said in a low, heavily accented voice. "Now you know why I retired from performing on the violin. When you do this to me—that is why Keska Lahti has become an apple farmer. Because even when I kiss you, you see me as nothing more than an extension of the instrument I play and of the music I produce."

He turned abruptly and walked away through the apple trees, his back straight and insulted.

Laurian stared after him, frozen in confusion. "Keska . . ." she whispered.

Then she came to life and ran through the trees after him, calling, "Keska, I don't see you as an extension of your violin. I didn't see you like that at all."

When he reached the tractor, he pulled on his leather gloves and said, "But you didn't come back because you were fascinated with me as a man." He glanced at her, climbed up on the tractor seat, and held up his gloved hands. "All you see are these hands that might be put to use to play the violin at your concert. I knew if I kissed you, I would find out the truth."

"Keska, were you testing me?" she cried in disbelief. *"How could you!"*

The tractor engine roared to life, drowning out any answer he might have offered. Laurian watched the big machine move away, ripping up ripe brown earth. Anger rose inside her like a minor volcanic eruption. Keska Lahti had led her into passion and she had scampered right after him. She'd fallen into the snare even though she'd known better from the moment she had seen him.

But the aspect of the situation that made Laurian most explosively furious was that Keska was right. She had come back this morning under ~~duress~~ and only because she wanted a chance to talk him into playing his violin for the concert. Everything else that had happened had been unplanned and even unwanted. Laurian had had no intention whatever of responding to the man.

Fury and frustration teemed in her emotions until action was imperative. Diving down like a bird of prey, Laurian grabbed up a clump of dry dirt and set her feet.

She pitched the clump viciously at Keska's infuriating back. It hit the green fender over the back wheel of the tractor and exploded into fragments.

When the clod hit, Keska turned with a surprised look. Then he gave a charming smile and waggled the gloved fingers of one hand at her. Even though he had turned away as the tractor rolled down the line of trees, it was obvious he was laughing.

Eyes flashing, every nerve bristling, Laurian marched through the orchard, dodging trees. Berating herself for stupidity, she walked through the field, heading toward her car.

George Miller saw her coming and stepped down off the veranda to intercept her.

"Don't say anything, George," Laurian ordered, her nostrils flaring warningly. "I never want to hear another word about Keska Lahti again, ever."

"I understand, madam," he agreed sympathetically, and followed her at a discreet distance as she walked furiously toward the driveway.

"An obstinate man is our Mr. Lahti," he offered offhandedly as she climbed into her car.

"Contemptible," she snorted.

"Trapped."

"Trapped?" she repeated, pausing with her hand on the ignition to glance at him suspiciously.

George smoothed back a strand of hair that had fallen out of place. "Mr. Lahti made a decision to retire from his life as a performing violinist on the crest of a shattering emotion. Now he finds himself in an entangled situation of his own devising. His pride prevents him from returning to the life of music he loves." He smiled in his stiff manner. "He's a rather stubborn man, even for a Finn."

"What shattering emotion?" she asked.

"It wouldn't be my place to speak of such things," he said.

Laurian started the car after an annoyed pause, put it in gear, and then leaned out the window to look at George. "Keska is going to have to find his own way out of his trap, I'm afraid. I've got problems of my own."

As she drove down the driveway the sound of Keska

Lahti's haunting music leaped to life in her memory. When her lips remembered the touch of his mouth, the two memories collided to crescendo into an explosion that left her shaken and trembling. She refused even to consider the possibility that she was falling in love with him, but the sobering suspicion was in the back of her mind.

After she got back to Camp Bryant, Laurian paced around Uncle Jules's office. "I can't believe I did such a thing," she exclaimed. "I threw a clump of dirt at Keska Lahti. That infuriating man has reduced me to acting like an irrational child. It's humiliating."

Jules was sitting behind a large desk strewn with paperwork, listening to Laurian tell a stringently censored version of what had happened. "So he quit performing to find himself," he mused after she had finished.

"I hope he isn't appalled by what he discovers," Laurian said, her dark eyes flashing.

A knowing smile curved Jules's lips. "Perhaps Mr. Lahti is not the only one who will discover something about himself."

Laurian turned to look at him with narrowed eyes. "I didn't like what I found out about myself this morning. I've always prided myself on my composure, but Keska ripped my poise to shreds, and then he laughed at me." Her face was flushed, her eyes were glittering, and her pacing fairly vibrated the room.

"How odd," Jules mused. "I don't believe I've seen you act this alive in years."

"I'm not alive, I'm furious."

"Whatever." He laughed softly. "Perhaps Keska Lahti is not the only volatile artistic personality among us."

"I am *not* temperamental," Laurian cried. When she realized her voice had risen shrilly, she cleared her throat and sat down, folding her hands sedately in her lap. "I'm not temperamental," she said quietly. "It's just that Keska Lahti brings out the worst in me."

Uncle Jules shuffled some papers from one side of his desk to the other, then said, "I wonder what we can do to convince Mr. Lahti to abdicate his retirement—while helping him preserve his integrity, of course."

"I doubt he has any integrity," Laurian muttered darkly.

"Do you suppose he might take an interest in instructing our string students?" he ventured. "Or at least in conducting a workshop or two this summer?"

"You'd subject our innocent students to Keska Lahti?" Laurian objected. "He'd demolish them."

"Perhaps," Jules said, running his fingers through his white hair. "But you might suggest it to him."

"I!" she exclaimed, jumping up to pace again. "I never intend to see Keska Lahti again. I can't seem to control myself around him."

"Ah, so," he murmured. "Such is life. But my heart weeps for the beautiful music lost to the world if Keska Lahti doesn't make a comeback. You understand?"

"Yes, I understand," Laurian said. The memory of the sound of his violin still sent shivers of pleasure over her skin. "What I *can't* understand is how such an irritating, intimidating man can produce such heavenly music. I refuse to go back, but I hate thinking of never hearing Keska play again."

The thought of never seeing Keska again, violin or no violin, contracted her heart into a painful lump in the middle of her chest.

An overly innocent smile sent a flurry of wrinkles over Jules's cherubic face. "Isn't it a shame you can't hide in his music room like a little mouse in a corner? Then you could enjoy his playing without having to deal with him."

Several moments of silence stretched as Laurian bit her lip. Her gaze grew contemplative. "I wonder . . ." she said vaguely, and thought about a little mouse skulking behind Keska's back.

Four

Several days passed before Laurian capitulated to her need to hear Keska play. Then with great caution and secrecy, she spent the next three mornings indulging in a pure musical thrill through his unknowing cooperation. Each morning at around eight she parked her car at the mouth of his driveway and crept silently up to the house to sit on the lawn outside the open window of the music room.

Listening to the breathtaking music of his violin without watching Keska seemed incomplete and frustrating, but Laurian had no wish to brave another personal encounter with him. She always seemed to come out second best. As the days passed she relaxed and thoroughly enjoyed the clandestine experience of basking in the sounds of his morning practice, letting his musical essence flow around her and carry her away.

George Miller knew she came every day, and he didn't object. In fact, he seemed amused by her conspiracy, becoming almost an ally when he provided her with a lawn chair for comfort.

But by now April had turned into May, and Laurian's fourth morning visit would be her last opportunity to listen to Keska play; it would be her last illicit concert. In less than a week Camp Bryant would open its doors for the summer season. Preparing the music camp for an onslaught of young musicians would take all her time. The cooks, teachers, and house mothers, the lifeguards and recreational directors, would begin arriving today and from now on every moment would be filled.

As she walked up the driveway her steps were silent in

rubber-soled tennis shoes. Looking slim and crisply morning-fresh in white pants and a silky blue blouse, Laurian glanced at the house and smiled. It served Keska right to entertain her despite himself after the way he had manipulated her. She didn't feel the slightest guilt as she seated herself on the lawn chair positioned at the side of the house near the open window of the music room.

He had already begun to play, and the complicated textures of Vivaldi floated around Laurian, enchanting her sensibilities. After a few moments she frowned slightly; his playing lacked something today, though she couldn't put her finger on what it was. Perhaps it was just an off day for him.

Then Laurian's mind began drifting; she started wondering what it might be like to accompany Keska's violin with her cello. Even the fantasy of such an experience sent a shiver of anxiety running through her.

Though she had been trained to be a soloist, somewhere along the line her self-confidence and her faith in her ability had disappeared. Playing as a member of an orchestra was one thing, but the very thought of facing an audience in solo paralyzed her. The knowledge that she hadn't developed to her full potential was one of her greatest disappointments in her career.

Accepting the fact that she could never play with Keska, Laurian relaxed and gave herself up to the sensuous pleasure of drifting with the beauty of his music. Her eyes wandered dreamily to the trees in the orchard. The blossoms had lost their petals, but the leaves had filled out the branches with a mellow, fresh silvery green color that made a perfect backdrop for the music flowing out to them.

Wild, earthy smells arose from the soil and plants around the house to join the sweet strains of the violin. Laurian breathed deeply, taking in the fragrance of grass, wild flowers, the tangy scent of lime—

Lime! Stiffening in the lawn chair, tightening her fingers apprehensively around the arms, Laurian turned her head slowly and looked into Keska's delighted eyes. He was sitting on his heels a few feet behind her, his elbows on his knees. Grinning smugly, he said, "Good morning, my lovely Laurian."

Glancing toward the window, she cocked her head and listened to the string music for a moment; no wonder it had a lifeless quality. She looked back at him and said sheepishly, "That's a record?"

"Obviously," he said, nodding sagely.

"How did you know I was here?"

With a graceful movement Keska twisted himself around to sit on the grass beside her lawn chair. A snug turtleneck knit shirt showed off his well-muscled chest and broad shoulders. The gold color reflected the sun streaks in his hair and darkened the tan of his face and the gray of his eyes. He pulled his knees up and clasped his hands around his legs.

When he had made himself comfortable, he looked at her with sparkling eyes. His voice was warm and caressing when he said, "I shall always know when you are near. Your presence throbs through the air, carrying the message that lovely Laurian is close by." His smile was charming and inviting.

Laurian smiled a twisted grin; every time the man opened his mouth, the most ridiculous statements came out. But ridiculous or not, her pulse made bounding little leaps through her veins as she looked into his eyes. Her expression softened at the seductive invitation in his words. Then she frowned slightly and said, "George is a traitor. He said he wouldn't tell you I have been coming."

"George is a good and faithful friend to Keska Lahti," he said, and laughed with delight. "He didn't betray your secret outright; he only dropped hints. Why didn't you simply come into the music room?" He waved at the chair and the window. "This wasn't necessary."

"You more or less vetoed my visits the last time I was here."

Laurian refused to feel embarrassed at being caught lurking around his house, though she was annoyed with herself. Her subconscious must have known from the first that it was inevitable that she be found out, that she end up sitting here beside him.

Shrugging elaborately and lifting her hands, she

added, "I'm sorry, but I still enjoy listening to you play your violin, even though you made it clear my interest in your ability insults you. I can't help my perverted tastes in music. So what choice did I have but to hide?"

Keska looked into her face piercingly for a few seconds, perhaps trying to read her thoughts and motives. Then he settled back on the lawn, stretching out full length, with his hands clasped under his head, to gaze up at the fluffy clouds drifting across the wide blue sky. "You could have bought a record to listen to my music more comfortably," he said. "Obviously you can't tell the difference between a record and the real thing, or I wouldn't have been able to surprise you this morning."

"I could have bought a record," she agreed, dismissing the fact that she already owned every record or tape he had made over the years.

He glanced at her. "Then why *did* you come back here?"

"Why, indeed?" she responded, a question more for herself that Keska. She let her eyes run down his slim form, over the flare of his shoulders, the curve of his chest, and around the slim hips under his trimly fitted brown trousers. He had his feet crossed, and the position of his legs emphasized his masculinity. Her desire for sexual fulfillment had lain dormant for quite some time, but since she met Keska, everything seemed to have gone out of control.

"*Why* did you come back to Keska Lahti, Laurian?" he asked again, breaking into her thoughts.

A relationship had to be based on much more than strong biological urges, so the truth wouldn't do. "My uncle Jules wondered if you would agree to instruct our string students," she said. "If you don't feel you can do the benefit concert, perhaps you wouldn't mind giving a few hours of your time to teaching the students. Your experience and expertise would be invaluable to them."

"And that's why you came? To ask me that?" he said skeptically.

"Yes, I'm asking you because with your knowledge of music you have a great deal to offer our students," she said stubbornly. Rather than look at Keska, Laurian studied her slim fingers, clasping them in her lap. But even studying her hands wasn't safe, because she began to imagine what it would be like to touch him with them. She had a nasty suspicion she wasn't fooling Keska for a moment and glanced up to add weakly, "Uncle Jules insists that you would be a great asset to Camp Bryant."

"Why didn't Uncle Jules come to me in person to present this request?" he asked softly, sitting up again and leaning closer to her. He lifted a hand to touch her arm with one finger, barely grazing her blue silk sleeve.

She laughed nervously to cover the reaction he had kindled. "Uncle Jules is no fool. He's wise enough to send a patsy to do his dirty work."

Letting his burnished silver eyes roam down over her breasts, Keska murmured, "Uncle Jules would have been in no danger from Keska Lahti."

"Does that statement mean that I am?"

His eyes caressed her face. "That depends upon what constitutes danger in your mind. Does the passion of Keska Lahti frighten you?"

"Your particular brand of humor intimidates me," Laurian said, and stood up.

Keska reached out and took her hand, looking up at her from his seat on the grass. "I wasn't making a joke. You are a very unique woman, and my feelings have been running very deeply ever since the first moment I saw you. I believe I love you, my beautiful Laurian." His brows lifted, and he looked surprised, as if the statement had been spontaneous and unexpected.

Laurian stared down at him, into his eyes. Her heart began pounding in her chest, and her mouth was propped open mutely. Then she remembered how serious he had sounded the last time. He had seduced her with his talk of apian lovemaking, and then he had figuratively rubbed her nose in her explosive reaction to him.

Pulling her hand away, she said in a voice that sounded oddly husky, "I'm sure Keska Lahti has many passions. Isn't that the way of an artist?"

His forehead was still wrinkled and puzzled. "It's true I've had passions of many kinds before, but never like this one."

Laurian knew she'd be a fool to take another chance, so she backed away, ready to bolt for her car. "Would you agree to give a little of your time to instructing our students?" she asked desperately. "You could choose your own hours and conduct the seminars in any way you like."

Keska rose to his feet with a fluid, graceful motion and looked at her with a rejected, hurt expression. "Keska Lahti knows nothing about teaching children. I would be useless in your school."

He was so close that she might have touched the curve of his chest if she reached out, or she could have laid her fingertips on his lips.

Slipping her hands safely into the pockets of her pants, she retreated toward the driveway, saying over her shoulder, "I thought you wanted to learn about life. If you do, children are an effective beginner's course— better than apples. You could learn a great deal from them."

His face brightened as he followed her, as if something had become clear to him. "You want Keska Lahti to come to your camp to be with you in your home territory. Is that it, lovely Laurian?"

"No!" she exclaimed. "I mean, yes— I'd be pleased if you would help instruct my students."

For a moment Keska tilted his head and studied her discomfiture, and then he smiled and held out his hand. "Surely you don't have to leave yet. Come see my apple trees. Conception has taken place."

"*What?*"

Throwing back his head, he gave a clear, pleased laugh. "The honeybee who so obligingly violated the flower has impregnated his victim. Come and see my fetal apple."

His whimsy was impossible to resist, so Laurian put her hand in his and walked beside him into the field. When she glanced at him, she saw a triumphant, amused smile on his face and flares of excitement gilding his eyes. "You're completely insane, did you know that, Keska?" she said, and laughed.

"That may be true," he agreed, nodding solemnly.

"And as for your bee making love and impregnating

the flower—I happen to know he wasn't even a male. The bees that pollinate flowers are females. The male bees do nothing but laze around the hive."

"Foolish male bees," Keska murmured, and took her hand, threading his fingers between hers. "You may be scientifically correct about the bees, but I prefer my version of the story."

"So do I," Laurian admitted softly.

The sound of violin music faded into the distance as they walked into the orchard. Laurian's heart raced as they wound their way into the privacy of the gnarled trunks, walking under the canopy of silver-green leaves. A flock of migrating songbirds, pausing on their way north, sang excitedly in the trees. The beat of her heart matched their fervor as she reacted to the nearness of this exotic man.

Keska found the same tree they had kissed beneath, the one beside the small babbling brook. He pulled down the same branch on which the bee had caressed the flower. Laurian recognized it and was charmed to realize their interlude had been important enough for Keska to remember, even though it had ended badly.

"You see?" he said proudly, touching the end of a twig. "Keska Lahti's apple. Our apple."

A marble-size nub had grown where the flower had been. The stamens were dry and brown on its end, sticking out like the whiskers on the nose of a seal.

She inspected the apple dutifully under his doting eyes and laughed. "You act like a new father. If these are your babies, how are you ever going to sell them when they're ripe?"

Keska grinned and let the branch snap back up into place. "I'm not a father, I'm a guardian. When the apples come of age, I will push them out into the world as one must do with one's charges."

Taking her hand, he led her down the row of trees toward the end of the orchard. His expression became serious and he asked, "Did you have children in your marriage, Laurian?"

"No," she answered after a brief pause, and glanced at him, then away. "My husband was like a child, and he was all I could handle."

"Did you wish for a baby?" Keska asked softly. "Do you have an instinct for motherhood?"

Her sigh was deep. "Yes, I would have liked a baby. I enjoy children very much."

Keska didn't respond to her answer, and Laurian couldn't resist her curiosity about his private life. "Do you have children?" she asked.

"Not now," he said in a low voice, the creases deepening across his forehead. "Once I did—a beautiful baby girl. She was my treasure."

When he walked on silently without explaining, Laurian asked gently, "What happened?"

Lifting his head, Keska looked at her with eyes as heavy and gray as a brooding ocean. "Her name was Melanie. When she was a little over two months old, she died quite suddenly. Crib death, they called it." His chest lifted and fell in a deep sigh.

"I'm so sorry." Laurian pressed his hand in sympathy. "How awful. It must have been terrible for you."

His brows came down over his eyes and he grimaced. "It was terrible for my wife. She was alone when it happened. I was away on a tour, giving myself to my public. Because of my performing commitments, I was never home." His fingers were tight and tense around hers. "Out of the nine weeks that my baby girl lived, I had spent only ten days with her. You see how I cheated myself?"

As he spoke they walked out of the far end of the orchard into the warmth of the brilliant sunlight. Keska shook himself slightly as if to cast off the painful memories. "But it is too delightful a day to think of sad things. The past is the past, and nothing can change what has happened." He pulled Laurian forward. "Climb the hill with me, my lovely Laurian. Then we can look down over Keska Lahti's apple farm."

Tact and sympathy forbade the questions she wanted to ask: Had the death of his baby caused him to retire? What had happened to his marriage that it ended in divorce? She climbed the steep hill beside him in frustrated silence.

The hillside had not been cleared. It was dotted with

boulders, rotting logs, and scrub oak trees. Clumps of blackberry brush were heavy with beginning fruit.

When they reached the crest of the hill, they sat down side by side on a flat, grassy patch to look out over a perfectly serene pastoral view. Keska's big white house sat elegantly in the midst of an ocean of green fruit trees. It was brightened by the intense colors of the flower beds and the blue of the swimming pool. The valley stretched for miles beyond the house and the orchard, disappearing into a hazy horizon.

Laurian sighed, breathing in fresh, smog-free air. "Are you content here with your apple orchard, Keska?" she asked, looking at him. "Do you miss the excitement and fulfillment of performing in front of audiences?"

A shadow darkened his face for a second, but it was quickly covered. "Can one ever be completely content?" he hedged, shrugging. "I am content at this moment to be here with you, my sweet Laurian."

His eyes softened as he looked at her. Reaching out, he cupped her cheek with one palm. With the other hand he traced the curving line of her jaw and the shape of her lips. When he turned toward her, his knee bent over and rested on her thigh. The touch sent a flame of anticipation jetting through her veins.

Laurian's lips parted breathlessly as she surrendered to the magic of his sensitive hands and to the exquisite pleasure they awoke in her. When she closed her eyes, she felt his fingertips graze their fiery way up over the bridge of her nose to touch her eyelids and outline the deep peak of dark hair on her forehead. "You are so beautiful, Laurian," he whispered.

When she opened her eyes, she saw an expression on Keska's face that punctuated his statement as truth. She didn't stop him when he touched the coil of hair on her head. He pulled out the hairpins holding it in place and the heavy, thick hair tumbled down her back. His lips were parted and his expression intense when he spread and smoothed the dark cascade over her shoulders and forward over her breasts.

"So marvelous, my love," he whispered, pressing a thick, silky tress to his cheek. A gentle, inviting smile curved his lips. His gray eyes were flecked with the warmth of gold. "I was content on my apple farm until you came to me, Laurian," he said, and then he lifted her hair in both hands and buried his face in its perfume.

Laurian hesitantly put her hand on his head, and his crisp wavy hair caressed her palm. "I was content, too, Keska. I don't know what's happening to me." Her breath caught in her throat, and she seemed to have no control at all over the reactions of her body.

Lifting his head, he smiled at her. "You know, lovely Laurian. You know what's happening to you . . . to us." Desire intensified his accent, and he pulled her close. "Something so beautiful . . . so special."

With a low cry deep in her throat she put her arms around him, pressing her face into the curve of his sun-warmed shoulder. Her hands moved impatiently over the taut muscles of his back and arms.

Lifting her face with a hand under her chin, Keska touched her lips in a tender kiss. Then the kiss grew in intensity. He urgently explored the depths of her mouth, spreading a sensation of joining, imprinting her sensitive membranes and her tongue with his taste and his heat. A skyrocket of desire shot through Laurian's body, and she arched against him.

Without breaking off their kiss, Keska slowly lay back in the pungent wild grass, pulling Laurian down with him in the circle of his strong arms. Their bodies were touching from face to feet as they lay on the crest of the hill. He pressed his thigh between her legs, his tense muscles caressing the most sensitive part of her body.

If Laurian had once had a will or a resolution to resist him, it disappeared now as her hands roved feverishly over his lean supple body. Her quest and her hands were urgent on his body. His hands were as feverish as hers as they both became familiar with the shape and gift of desire.

When Keska lifted his head, he rested his weight with an elbow on either side of her shoulders and smiled down into her face. "I think you have wanted me almost as much as I have dreamed of you, my sweet Laurian," he murmured. "Is that so?"

Her lips felt swollen and ripe from his kiss, and she

was acutely aware of his thigh between her legs. Her smile was playful when she said softly, "I'll admit I've thought about you now and again." Every minute . . .

One of his fingers stroked a quivering line up her neck and over her cheek, then fingered the mass of silky black hair spread out on the grass around her head. "Why did you come into Keska Lahti's house, into my life to destroy my tranquillity?" he asked softly.

Reaching up with a trembling hand, she touched the faint roughness of his jaw and the smooth tanned skin of his cheek. With both hands she pulled his head down and kissed the aristocratic arch of his nose and the indentation where his jaw met his neck.

Then she looked into his eyes and laughed. "You're the one who shattered the tranquillity, Keska Lahti. My intentions couldn't have been more innocent when I came to your house. You insisted upon complicating everything with your atrocious wine and your silly little games."

"But I couldn't resist you, Laurian. Surely that must have been clear." He laughed and dropped his head to touch his lips to the curve of her neck and to the pulse at the base of her throat. He kissed the satiny skin just above the top button of her blouse.

Replacing his lips with trembling fingers, Keska undid the top button and then the others, until the swell of her lace-covered breasts was free to him.

The touch of his moist, hot lips on this intimate skin sent messages of unbearable urgency flowing down to a lower, even more sensitive part of Laurian's body. She gasped at the strength of her need.

When he lifted his head, Keska's hand moved to cover the curve of her breast. His fingers circled lightly over the rigid nipple pressed into the flimsy lace. The touch seemed to burn through her body and she clutched his shoulders tightly.

Breathing heavily, Keska rolled over, turning on his back. He pulled Laurian into his arms, on top of his body. Burying his face in the dark hair that cascaded down over him, he whispered, "If you came into my house and my life to charm me, my sweet, sweet Laurian, you have done much too thorough a job of it."

Laurian brushed her hair aside, looking down into his eyes. Every cell of her body, every nerve, was aware of the hard lines of him under her. But something about his words tweaked a suspicious chord in her mind. "What do you mean?" she whispered.

"I want you so badly, Laurian, my angel," he whispered, his hand moving over the curves of her buttocks, pressing her down against his offering. "Make love with me, and Keska Lahti will do anything you want, give you anything. . . . I'll give you my love . . . my life," he whispered, punctuating his words with fevered kisses. "I'll play my violin for you forever, my sweet. I'll even play your concert for you . . . I'll teach your students for you. . . . Anything you ask." He smothered her face, her neck, and then her lips with his soft, urgent kisses.

Because the pleasure of his mouth on hers was so joyous and welcome, and because her body demanded his touch with a will all its own, his words didn't register in her mind at first. When they did, she stiffened and lifted her head.

For an instant it seemed her heart stopped, then it started up again in a huge, humiliated surge. "Do you think . . . ?" she started, and rolled her body away from his.

"Laurian, stay," Keska murmured pleadingly, holding her by the hands. "Come back to me."

She pulled her hands away and sat up to button her blouse with fingers that were shaking with a mixture of passion and disbelief. "You can't imagine that I'd—"

"What is it, my love?" he asked softly, touching her sleeve with his fingertips.

Rising to her feet, Laurian slapped angrily at the grass, and twigs caught on her white pants. Then she looked down at Keska with eyes that were flashing black anger. "You can't possibly think I'd barter my body for your musical services! How *could* you suggest such a thing?"

Pulling himself up to a sitting position, Keska reached out for her hand. "Laurian," he said softly, "you misunderstood."

Dodging his hand, she gathered her hair together and twisted it to fall behind her shoulder. "I didn't misunderstand. You said you'd give me anything, even the concert, if I'd make love with you. Well, I don't sell my body for anyone or anything! There is no musician worth that—not even Keska Lahti!"

"Please listen to me," Keska said, rising to his feet.

"Every time I listen to you, I get into more trouble," Laurian said furiously. Marching to the trail they had climbed, she started down the hill.

Keska followed her, and his voice had also become angry when he said, "You aren't being fair to me. Besides, I think you have no place to act so self-righteous, Laurian Bryant. Can you deny you were sent to me because of a notion that so attractive a woman might seduce Keska Lahti into agreeing to perform? This isn't the first time that trick has been tried on me."

"O-o-ooh!" she exploded. It was demeaning to know he was right. That was exactly why she had been sent to him. And it was all her fault, because she had been dumb enough to go along with Uncle Jules and the camp board.

At the bottom of the hill, just before she stalked into the orchard, Keska took her arm and stopped her. "Please don't be angry, my Laurian. Talk to me. Let me attempt to make amends."

"Don't touch me!" she said, jerking her arm away. "Go spray your apples or something, but leave me alone."

He walked beside her silently with his head bent, thinking, through several rows of trees.

Laurian suddenly stopped and faced him. "I would have made love because I'd begun to care for you, Keska," she said in a voice thick with hurt. "Why do you have to ruin everything by being so glib and flip? Not everyone is bent on plundering Keska Lahti for anything they can get."

"You do care for me?" he exclaimed, his face a map of surprise.

"I don't know *what* I feel," Laurian cried, and felt her throat choking up. When tears rose in her eyes, she turned abruptly and marched out of the orchard into the field.

Keska walked with long strides beside her. "Come into the house. We must talk."

"No, there isn't anything to talk about," she said, and turned down the driveway toward her car.

"When will you come back, my Laurian?" he asked, standing forlornly at the edge of the field, watching her.

Laurian felt so confused, she couldn't answer without sobbing, so she simply shook her head and walked to her car.

"I'll wait impatiently for you, Laurian," he called after her. "You will come back."

"I'm not going to come back to this farm, ever. It isn't safe for my peace of mind," she said. "I must be a slow learner or I wouldn't have been here today. But now I've gotten the message, Keska Lahti. I can't expect any respect from you, so I won't come back." Before he could answer, she climbed into her car.

After she had started the motor, Laurian looked back at Keska. He stood halfway up the driveway at the edge of the field looking after her. The sun made gleaming gold out of his light hair. The shape—and feel—of his body would always be branded upon her consciousness.

As Laurian looked at him she realized both her body and her mind were reaching out for him. Very reluctantly she had to admit that she had begun to fall in love with Keska Lahti. He had caused her nothing but confusion, embarrassment, and frustration from the first moment she had seen him, but still, a special magic had flared between them.

Even though she had known better from the beginning, she had allowed herself to fall in love with another egocentric, temperamental musical genius.

This admission was so shocking that after Laurian had put the car in gear, she flooded it by desperately jamming her foot on the accelerator.

"Heaven help me," she murmured as she restarted the motor and turned out onto the road. "Because no one else is going to be able to."

Five

The next two weeks were so busy, Laurian had little time to think about Keska Lahti. When the music students began to arrive, they consumed all her energies.

The very bright, individualistic youngsters brought with them the expected contingent of adolescent emotions. They ranged from the fairly well balanced to the rebelliously high-spirited to the painfully shy. She had to deal with potential homesickness, personality conflicts between roommates, and strong creative personalities. Laurian loved working with these young people who were on the brink of adulthood. In general she had a close, warm rapport with her students. Even so, it took the entire first two weeks to sort them out and settle them into a routine at Camp Bryant.

With few free moments even to think about Keska, Laurian was not able to tamper with the temptation to go back to his farm to test her confused feelings by seeing him again. Given spare time, she might have done just that.

Of course, it piqued her vanity just a little to realize that he could have come to see her. Obviously he didn't care as much for her as he had indicated. But she imagined Keska's pride would never allow him to pursue her once he'd been refused. More reason not to put herself in jeopardy by going back, she told herself.

Unfortunately never in her experience had Laurian been so physically affected by a man. Big, brawny muscle builders had never appealed to her, but the streamlined masculinity of Keska's body tormented her. She couldn't erase her memories of his kisses and the touch of his hands. They caused her long hours of frustrated restlessness at night.

Nor could she ignore the fascination he held for her. The unhappiness Keska had known in the past and his present soul searching drew at her sympathies. She wished there were some way she could safely comfort him without risking herself.

On the first morning of the third week since she had left him, Laurian sat bristling with annoyance as she listened to her most talented student violinist play.

Roger Oliver was a fourteen-year-old boy with a mop of curly brown hair, balky blue eyes, a petulant and unhappy mouth, and a mind of his own. He had the hands of an angel on his violin, but the personality of a werewolf. Her own hands were clenched into fists to restrain herself from ripping up the sheet music from which he was playing.

A talent such as Roger's was born to only one out of thousands, perhaps millions. He could skyrocket to fame and success as he matured if only he would allow himself to be taught and molded. Unfortunately his parents worshiped the earth under his feet. They had instilled in Roger the notion that he was above such ordinary mortals as Laurian Bryant. He refused to listen to her instructions.

She scowled at him as he butchered the selection by Schubert he was playing. Everything that he did was talented and harmonic, but it simply wasn't what Schubert had intended to happen in his music when he wrote it. Roger played as if he had a grudge against the violin and malice against the world. But at least the boy wasn't talking to Laurian. His verbal sarcasm was even more brutal than his interpretation of the music.

Roger reminded Laurian just slightly of Keska, though Keska was more like a vampire who seductively sucked the life out of his victims rather than a snarling werewolf like Roger.

It was a welcome interruption when one of the other teachers walked quietly into the practice room and whispered to Laurian, "You have a visitor in Jules's office."

Laurian glanced at Roger, who ignored her disdainfully, then walked out of the room irritably. Jules had gone out to take care of business, so the office directly across the hall was unoccupied for the day. She walked through the door, cringing when Roger's individualistic handling of his violin followed her inescapably.

But Roger's music, the camp, even the world, were struck from her consciousness when Laurian saw her visitor. Keska Lahti stood smiling at her, his gray eyes warm and delighted.

He wore a silky blue-figured shirt with a pale blue scarf knotted around his throat and a pair of gray slacks. Apparently he had come in the role of a musical artist rather than an apple farmer. She wondered skittishly why he had come to Camp Bryant at all—no matter in what capacity.

"Keska," she said, hoping he wouldn't guess the excitement bubbling through her system, or see the tumbling of her leaping pulses. "Hello."

"Hello, Laurian," he said in a soft questioning voice, apparently unsure of his welcome.

"This is a surprise," she said in an equally curious voice.

"Yes, it is to Keska Lahti also."

"Oh . . . ?" she responded weakly. That ended that inane phase of the conversation.

In the silence that followed, his eyes made a tour of her body. This gave Laurian the opportunity to wish she had dressed a little less casually that morning. If she had known Keska was coming, she certainly wouldn't have chosen white shorts and a pink T-shirt with quarter notes scattered all over her breasts—even though the skimpy outfit was almost a uniform at the camp for both teachers and students.

Her hair was tied back with a pink satin ribbon and the thick, shining black tail lay forward over her left breast. She tossed it back over her shoulder when she realized it was jumping with each jarring beat of her heart. "Why are you here, Keska?" she asked finally.

He lifted both hands in a helpless gesture and said sadly, "I've missed you so very much, my lovely Laurian."

His brow contracted in a slight, annoyed frown, and he glanced at the open door as Roger drifted into a particularly bizarre flight of music. Then he looked at

Laurian again and asked, "Why didn't you come back to me?"

"You missed me?" she said in surprise.

"I did, and now I've come to apologize to you. My behavior and the unfortunate choice of words I used the last time we were together were inexcusable and uncalled for. Will you please forgive me?" His expression was intense and sincere, pleading.

Laurian's heart leaped against her rib cage in alarm. When Keska set out to be engaging, he became irresistible. "I'm amazed," she said cautiously. "Isn't an apology out of character for Keska Lahti?"

He lifted his shoulders disparagingly and pushed his hands into his pants pockets. "I am ashamed to admit that it is, lovely Laurian. But you are making a new and different man out of Keska Lahti. I can't bear for you to be angry with me. I can't sleep at night, and my apples hold no interest for me. All I can think is that my lovely Laurian despises me." His gray eyes were inconsolable. "You must forgive me."

Laurian stared at him suspiciously, completely bewildered. "I'm not very proud of how I acted that day either," she said. He was overdoing his apology by an appreciable degree, but she couldn't stop herself from feeling pleased and happy.

Roger played a particularly jarring phrase and a momentary grimace passed over Keska's face. But then he smiled pleadingly at Laurian. "George won't speak to me because I chased you away. He's so angry he has gone to visit his sister in Arizona. He loves you too."

The mention of love flushed her skin, and she crossed her arms in front of her body. Digging her fingers into the flesh of her upper arms, she reminded herself that if she responded to him, there was a strong chance she'd end up tattered emotionally. She said nervously, "I suppose I can forgive you, if you wish."

"Keska Lahti wishes," he said happily, breaking into a brilliant smile. Taking a step toward her, he reached out with his arms.

Backing away, she put up her arms to ward him off. "No!" she exclaimed. "Please don't, Keska. I'll forgive you. I'm not harboring any hard feelings toward you."

"But . . ." He raised his sloping brows.

"But everything has happened too quickly between us." She gestured toward his arms. "This sort of thing has to stop." Sitting down on a straight chair on the far side of Jules's office, she tensed her body against her own wishes and desires, clasping her hands around her bare knees.

Keska took the chair beside her and leaned forward, his lime scent drifting around her. "But why, Laurian?" he asked with concern. "You said you had begun to care for me. Has that feeling died?"

She glanced up into his eyes. They were tragic with intense feeling. Overly tragic, it seemed, and she suspected he was trying to coerce her. Taking a deep breath, she asked, "What do you want from me, Keska?"

"I want to be close to you. You have captivated me and I wish only to love you," he said softly. "Nothing more."

His words pierced through the armor of her ambivalent suspicion and intensified her own wishes. The pleading in his eyes tugged at her. The curve of his shoulders and chest kindled desire. She looked at his hands and remembered how they had felt touching her breasts.

Just then Roger hit a sour note and his music broke off abruptly. Laurian glanced toward the open door of the office and thought, Roger the werewolf; Keska the vampire.

She looked back at Keska. "If I tell you a little bit about my marriage to Andrew Bryant, then maybe you'll understand why I'm reluctant to trust myself to you."

"I would like to understand," he said softly, and leaned forward attentively on his chair.

Roger started playing again and Laurian grimaced before taking a deep breath. "Andrew was a brilliant pianist," she began. "We met when we were at Juilliard together as students. We were married just out of school. At first I loved him very much, and I think Andrew loved me, too, in his own way—within his limitations." She paused for a moment, remembering how very young and full of dreams she had been.

Keska hooked an elbow over the back of his chair. "And then?" he encouraged.

"And then the novelty of being in love wore off for Andrew. I played the cello quite well, and he saw me as some sort of threat to him. He wanted to be the best and only star in the family."

"He felt insecurity?" Keska murmured. His lip twisted in response to a discordant squeal of the violin in the room across the hall.

"Oh, I don't think so," Laurian said. "Not Andrew. He was full to bursting with self-confidence." She frowned over her memories. "So much so that he couldn't understand when I didn't quite live up to his idea of perfection. When I soloed, he criticized everything about me, from the way I held my cello to my interpretation of the music I played. He even found fault with my stage presence."

"In his insecurity he felt the need to corrode your self-confidence too," Keska said softly, his eyes on her face. "You must be a very excellent cellist to have been so threatening to him."

"Maybe he *was* insecure," she said after a pause, then shrugged. "At any rate he certainly was successful at undermining my confidence. After a few years of Andrew, I didn't have the courage to attempt a solo performance any longer. He was a genius at manipulating me and playing upon my sympathies. Though I can't blame him completely, because I was immature and I let it happen. Toward the end we didn't even have love in our relationship. My function was simply to feed Andrew's ego."

"I'm sorry," Keska said, "because you are a sweet person and you deserved much, much more, Laurian." He frowned for a moment, then asked, "And he was killed?"

"Yes, in a plane crash on the way to one of his concerts. I'm ashamed to say the accident almost gave me a sense of freedom. I suffered from months of guilt over that feeling."

"But with your freedom you still didn't redirect yourself toward your own musical ambitions?"

For a few moments Laurian listened to Roger's immature musical creativity. His entire life was waiting and she almost envied him.

Giving a short laugh, she said, "By that time it was too

late to plunge into a very competitive field again. And I didn't seem to have the courage to face an audience with my cello, even after Andrew was out of my life."

Keska took one of her hands and held it between both of his. "But you survived your unhappiness. You seem a very mature and strong woman now."

Laurian smiled and looked down at the tan of his fingers around the fair skin of her hand. "I hope so," she said. "If I'm mature now, it's because of Andrew's uncle, Jules Bryant. When he realized what had happened between Andrew and me, he forced me to take an interest in this camp and to audition for the symphony orchestra. I owe my life to him . . . literally."

"I'm glad you had him," Keska said. "My admiration for Uncle Jules has mushroomed. The man must have remarkably good sense."

"He's a sweetheart." Laurian looked steadily into Keska's eyes. "I've told you this story because it explains why I can't trust myself to another gifted musician. It explains why I can't let a relationship develop between us, Keska. I'm no match for you."

His brows lifted and his eyes widened. "Do you imagine *I* would diminish you to build my own ego?" His fingers tightened on hers. "I have nothing to prove, Laurian. I am Keska Lahti."

Laurian thought about that for a moment, then she smiled. "No, I don't suppose there's much competitive threat on your level, is there? Even so, everything that's happened between us since we met has happened much too quickly for comfort. I need to have you slow down."

"You wish to be my friend before becoming my lover, is that it?" Keska asked, and lifted her hand to his lips, his eyes warm.

Laurian pulled her hand away. It was probable that she was accepting both options when she said, "I don't mind if we work on being friends."

"Thank God!" Keska exclaimed, and reached out to take her long heavy tail of black hair in his hand. "I was afraid you would have nothing whatever to do with me after I had insulted you so." He pressed the fragrant hair to his lips.

Laurian jerked it away from him. "Friends, Keska . . . *Friends.*"

There was a challenge in his laugh, but he let the issue drop. "Now, will you please tell me who is playing the violin?" he asked. "He is annihilating poor Franz Schubert. Do you allow your students that sort of interpretation in this school of yours?"

Laurian grimaced. "What you hear, Keska, is Roger Oliver, our prize prodigy. He's fourteen and incorrigible. I wouldn't allow his individuality, except that he refuses to listen to me."

"Fourteen!" His eyebrows rose as he listened, then an expression of grudging interest crossed his face. "The boy seems very talented. Despite his handling of the material, he has an amazing touch on the violin."

For a few minutes Keska sat listening. A frown deepened on his face and he rubbed one finger speculatively back and forth over his jaw. Finally he glanced at Laurian and asked, "Could I look at this young rebel?"

"Be my guest," she said, and led him across the hall to the practice room where Roger was tormenting his instrument.

Keska stood just inside the door, his head tilted to one side. His gaze was fixed on the gangling adolescent boy. After a few moments he walked slowly across the room to sit down in a chair close to the young violinist. His body was tense with fascination.

As soon as Roger realized Keska was there, he lowered his violin and scowled. "I didn't invite an audience," he said rudely in a voice made changeable by puberty.

Keska pursed his lips slightly at Roger's tone and his eyes narrowed. "Nor *should* you invite an audience," he said carefully. "You are far from ready." Annoyance made his Finnish accent more pronounced.

Laurian leaned against the wall in the back of the room, biting her lip to control a smile as she watched the two temperamental violinists square off belligerently.

Roger lifted his chin. "Who asked for your opinion?"

"No one asked me," Keska answered in a deceptively soft voice. His nostrils had taken on a pinched look. "I have chosen to offer my advice. You have been playing Schubert as if his music were written by Beethoven.

Schubert is humble and delicate, not powerful and cataclysmic."

Face reddening angrily, Roger glared at Keska. "Where do you get off telling me how to play my violin? Who do you think you are?"

Keska's pinched nostrils turned white at the edges. He rose to his feet with exaggerated dignity and said imperiously, "*I* am Keska Lahti."

"So what?" Roger sneered insolently. "Buzz off, turkey."

Laurian pushed away from the wall and quickly walked forward. This confrontation was certain to require a moderator—or a referee, she thought. "Roger!" she exclaimed. "Keska?"

Neither one of them paid any attention to her. Keska's face turned a dull red, then paled with anger. His body stiffened and pulled up to his full five feet ten inches. His chest expanded to press against his shirt and the muscles of his arms strained his sleeves.

Laurian could almost feel him vibrating with indignation. His jaw knotted as if he were biting off words he would liked to have said. She put her hand on his arm. "Keska, maybe—"

"I'll handle this, Laurian," he grated out, shaking off her placating touch. His voice was icy and stringently controlled when he asked, "Do you have parents, Roger?"

"Of course, I have parents. The stork didn't bring me." Roger sneered. Turning his back, he tucked the violin under his chin and said, "I'd appreciate a little privacy. I have to practice." Positioning the violin, he pulled the bow across the strings.

Two strides took Keska to the boy's side. He grasped Roger's hand and lifted his bow off the strings. Snatching both the bow and the violin, he placed them on the table, ignoring the boy's outraged objection.

Taking Roger's arm in one strong inflexible hand, he propelled him across the hall and into Jules's office despite Roger's protests. Laurian trailed anxiously behind.

Plunking the boy down in a chair, Keska picked up the

telephone and demanded in a thickly accented voice, "Tell me the number where I might reach your father."

Some of the bravado faded out of Roger. He glanced at Laurian, looking worried, then at Keska. "You'll be sorry if you call my father. He'll tell you where to get off."

"The *number*," Keska snapped.

"Keska," Laurian said nervously. "Maybe you shouldn't—"

Keska irritably waved her into silence and glowered at Roger expectantly. Roger reluctantly recited his father's number, then bit his lip as it was dialed.

Laurian heard only one side of the telephone conversation that followed.

"Mr. Oliver," Keska said when the ring was answered. "I am calling from the Bryant Music Camp concerning your son Roger. . . .

"No, he is well. There has been no accident. . . .

"Because of the boy's *attitude*. That is why I am calling. He is rude, uncooperative, and he resists instruction. I don't see how he can *possibly* benefit from his summer at a music camp unless he applies himself—

"Who am I? *I*, Mr. Oliver, am Keska Lahti.

"Thank you, you are very kind to say that. But my concern now is for your son. I am *donating* my time to the instruction of the string students at Camp Bryant this summer. And I expect your cooperation in convincing Roger that it will be in his best interest to *listen* when I *speak* to him."

After a few seconds of nodding, Keska held the instrument out to Roger.

Roger's one-sided conversation consisted of several "But, Dads," then a series of sulky, intermittent "Yes, sirs."

After he had replaced the receiver, he turned to Keska and said sullenly, "I'm sorry I talked to you like I did, Mr. Lahti. I didn't realize who you were."

"You have no right to speak to anyone as you did, no matter who they are," Keska said sternly. Then he cocked a forefinger at the boy and smiled.

Laurian followed, bemused, as Keska led Roger across the hall to the music practice room.

"Now," Keska said, motioning the boy to a chair, "the first thing we must discuss is artistic temperament."

When Roger had seated himself, Keska straddled another chair and propped his arms on the back. "You have a bent for the creative temperament, without a doubt. But you must learn to use it with discretion and responsibility—for effect only. If you feel the urge to exercise your temperament upon Keska Lahti again, do not forget that I have had twenty-five years more experience than you. I have perfected my eccentricities to a fine art. If you feel compelled to challenge me, Roger, you will in all probability come out second best every time."

Laurian stared at Keska in surprise. The fact that he didn't take his own vagaries seriously shifted his bizarre behavior into a totally different light.

When the boy stared rebelliously at him and declined to answer, Keska suggested mildly, "Perhaps you would be so kind as to play your selection from Schubert for me again."

Relieved the lecture was over, Roger picked up his violin and applied his bow while Keska listened contemplatively.

Laurian slipped out into the hallway and nabbed a passing teacher. "Quick!" she said. "Round up every string student you can get your hands on. Tell them to come to this practice room immediately. Keska Lahti is going to give a lesson."

Before Roger had finished his piece, most of the young string students—more than twenty-five—had filed silently into the practice room to take seats on chairs or on the floor.

When Roger lowered his violin, Keska got up and took the instrument from him. "That was very nice," he said. "You do have talent, no doubt about that. You handle yourself well, Roger, and perhaps you may be gifted. But you are difficult to evaluate because of your poor habits. Now I will show you how Schubert meant the music to be played."

Keska lifted the violin to his chin and positioned the bow. Then he noticed the group of students breathlessly watching him. His eyes shifted to Laurian and his brows pulled down in silent, questioning accusation.

She smiled sweetly. "You said you would be donating your time to teaching the string students at Camp Bryant this summer. I heard you. It seemed a shame if the rest of our strings couldn't take advantage of this session along with Roger."

Keska's eyes bored into hers for several seconds. Then an oddly pleased smile crept across his face. He looked into each eager young face, then at Roger and said, "Keska Lahti will demonstrate how Schubert should sound on the violin."

As the clear, sweet, controlled strains of Keska's distinctive violin playing filled the room, Laurian watched the rebellious resentment fade from Roger's face. Grudging respect began to take the place of petulance. After he had listened for a few minutes, the boy leaned forward with fascination and excitement to watch every nuance and movement of Keska's hands.

For two and one half hours Keska charmed the students. He teased them by giving his instructions in Finnish, then pretending surprise when they didn't understand. He flirted outrageously with the girls. He led the group in an exuberant rendition of "Raindrops Keep Falling on My Head" before he directed them in more serious music. Subtly, under the cover of his foolishness, he guided and taught them. Finally he pleaded exhaustion and dismissed a class that was still reluctant to leave.

"You do this every day?" he asked Laurian after the young musicians had gone. Flopping down on a chair, he stretched out his legs and rubbed his head. "How do you stand it? No wonder you are so tiny and delicate. The energy of these students must wear you away."

She laughed and sat on a chair beside him. "I don't put quite as much effort into it as you do, Keska. They loved you."

"They were polite," he said with false humility.

"And you enjoyed it too. Admit it."

"I only acted as if I did out of consideration for those tender young spirits," he said, reaching out to take her hand. "I had to be considerate after you tricked me into doing the class."

Laurian squeezed his hand. "I didn't trick you. Your

mouth did. You were so angry at Roger that you backed yourself into a corner."

"Angry! Keska Lahti does not become angry—ever. I wasn't."

"Then why was your nose all pinched and white?" Laurian asked, laughing.

Keska touched his offending aristocratic nose with one finger and grinned. "I concede defeat. I may have been slightly annoyed." His eyes glowed an invitation. "Come look at my apples, Laurian. They have doubled in size since the last time you saw them."

Laurian's face became serious, and she looked away from him. She was very aware of the warmth and pressure of his hand on hers. If she went with him to his secluded farm, she would be making a conscious commitment. It was folly to think they could spend time together as platonic friends.

When she didn't answer immediately, Keska murmured puckishly, "Unless you don't wish to be seen with a 'turkey'?"

Laurian glanced at him in surprise, and then she laughed. "Roger is all charm, isn't he?"

Keska smiled slightly. "I can understand what he is feeling—the frustration. I went through something similar when I was his age. Possessing a passion for the classical grandeur of the violin, but at the same time wishing to be a hot rock star so the girls would scream and faint at my feet. An adolescent virtuoso isn't eagerly received among his peers. Roger has more than the usual young problems, and it makes him sour. He needs sympathy, though he makes it very difficult for anyone to give it to him."

Laurian looked at him for a few moments. "I'm touched that you can recognize both the humor and the pathos of Roger."

"Then come see my apples," Keska said.

Keska and Andrew were two very, very different men, she conceded. It was unfair to have compared them, but she wasn't ready to take a chance yet. Pulling her hand away from his, she said, "Perhaps I'll look at your apples another day."

Rising to his feet, Keska leaned forward to brush her

lips with a kiss, then sighed deeply. "You see why I feel sympathy for Roger? My violin and my talent still discourage the women I wish to be with." He touched her cheek lightly with his fingertips. "The one woman I wish to be with."

Giving a theatrical shrug, he walked to the door and paused to look back at her, his eyes inviting her to change her mind and come with him.

Her mouth tingled from the touch of his lips. It was all she could do to stop herself from rushing away with him. His slim muscular form, his caressing gray eyes, and his seductive hands were a vision that sent flares of desire bounding through her body. "I've got to think first, Keska. I've got to be sure it's the right decision before I come with you."

"I'll wait, my lovely Laurian," he said softly.

"You're welcome to come back to camp to give another class, Keska. Come whenever you wish. We'll work around you." Her voice sounded husky and turbulent. "I'd look forward to having you here."

He pursed his lips. "We'll see," he said, then smiled and disappeared through the door.

Laurian sat limply in her chair, limbs trembling as she tried to calm her restless desires.

Uncle Jules walked into the practice room not too long after Keska had left. When he saw Laurian's flushed cheeks and brilliant eyes, a smile wreathed his face and he sat down beside her. "An interesting man, your Keska Lahti," he said. "Very charming to speak to. When I came home, I found the camp enthralled by his presence."

"*My* Keska Lahti . . ." she repeated dreamily.

Jules's eyes twinkled. "So he has met our students? You have presented our case quite convincingly?"

"I suppose," she agreed, her eyes blank and focused upon an inward picture of Keska.

"I think our summer might prove exciting, don't you agree?" he said, and sighed with contentment.

"Possibly, you old romantic." Laurian laughed as she stood up.

"And is it also possible that Keska will do the concert in August?" Jules asked.

"I wouldn't think of asking him again," Laurian said firmly. "Whatever he's working through has to be done without anyone harassing him. You'd better try to find someone else to play at the concert."

Jules smiled benignly at Laurian. "I have a few possibilities in mind who would play for us. But I think we will wait and see what happens. Eh?"

"I wouldn't count on Keska," Laurian said, and walked to the door of the practice room.

Jules's brow wrinkled thoughtfully for a moment, and then he said, "One wonders why Keska Lahti chose to buy an apple orchard so near our humble music camp. He could have located himself anywhere in Oregon or Washington, or in many other more productive areas of California if he wanted only to grow apples."

Laurian stopped short with her hand on the doorknob. Several different thoughts shot through her mind. That Keska's retirement had been well thought out. That he was much more interested in the music camp than he had let on. Her final reluctant suspicion was that he might have used her to make it appear he had been forced into giving his time to the camp. Then she decided her suspicions were unfair.

"I'm beginning to wish I were a secretary or a computer expert . . . or tone-deaf," she said unhappily. "Then I could be sure that whatever happened between Keska and me wasn't just a professional thing. Then I wouldn't suspect he was using me, and he would have no cause to suspect I was after his violin. Everything would be so much easier."

Uncle Jules rose to his feet and crossed the room to pat Laurian on the shoulder. "The young are so impatient. Relax, my dear. Allow everything to take its natural course."

Hugging him briefly, Laurian smiled and said, "There is no natural course with Keska Lahti."

Six

Laurian lay restlessly awake for most of the night after Keska Lahti's visit to her classroom. As the events of the day scampered around in her mind, she spent a great deal of time trying to understand her shocking attraction to him. Then, since her obsession for Keska couldn't be easily understood, she spent several more frustrating hours trying to balance her captivation with him against her apprehensions about him. What it boiled down to in the end was that since she had met Keska, the life she had for almost four years considered orderly and contented had suddenly begun to appear dull and unfulfilled.

The night progressed endlessly, one dark hour passing after another with no distraction other than the fresh sounds of running river water and of rustling trees outside her open window. Occasionally she heard the call of a bird that also seemed troubled with insomnia.

Eventually Laurian convinced herself she had made too much of Keska's dramatic and unexpected visit to her. He spoke of love, but it had taken him weeks after their last encounter to act upon the emotion he claimed to feel, so she rather doubted his love ran too deeply. He probably had other more obscure motives for his attentions.

Turning over one more time, she untwisted the nightgown tangled around her legs and straightened the sheets. Then she firmly turned her mind off, telling herself she had been making a tempest in a teapot and a mountain out of a molehill.

With that her brain raced off on a quest for other clichés that fit the situation, until she ordered herself sternly to stop, be done with it. "Listen to me," she whispered irritably to her restless, feverish body. "There's more to life than the little physical indulgences you've got in mind. Keska isn't lying awake tossing and turning in his bed over you, so just forget it."

Her choice of words had been a mistake, because now she became obsessed with images of Keska lying in bed, his sleek, tanned, muscular body naked on top of rumpled sheets, his arms held out to her. When Laurian finally did sleep, her rest was broken by embarrassing, graphically sensual dreams.

She felt exhausted when she awoke suddenly, much too early the next morning. In her half-asleep blur she couldn't figure out what might have aroused her at such an ungodly hour and she burrowed her head sleepily back into the pillow.

When the sound of violin music penetrated her consciousness, she sat up instantly, cocking an ear. Had she overslept? Were her students downstairs in the practice room, waiting for her?

Flustered, she squinted at her watch and flopped back on the bed. It was only a little after seven. What student had the nerve to make that kind of noise so early on a summer-vacation morning? Roger, probably.

Then Laurian listened more closely. The music wasn't noise. And Roger wouldn't be playing a Paganini caprice. Her pulses leaped to attention as she strained to listen. When she jumped out of bed, all the agonies and uncertainties she had endured in the night evaporated in a blaze of thrilled anticipation. Keska was here. He had come to her.

Dashing water on her face, brushing her teeth, dabbing lipstick—her hands shook with excitement as Laurian prepared herself. After she had brushed her long black hair, she pulled it straight back from her widow's peak and fastened it into a tail with a wide gold clasp. A bare-shouldered white sundress with red piping and narrow straps seemed just right to wear this day. It fit her flatteringly and flared around her knees.

None of the wise advice or clichés she had spouted to herself in the night seemed relevant when Keska Lahti was so near. The distant strains of his violin were like siren calls, irresistible.

Pushing her feet into white sandals, Laurian ran downstairs. She paused just a second or two outside the door of the practice room, trying to wipe an idiotic grin off her face and to gather her wits—unsuccessfully in both cases. Then she walked through the door and closed it softly behind her.

Keska was unaware of her as he sat in a chair near an open window in the front of the large room. An empty violin case lay near his feet. He was intent upon creating the music that enticingly swirled around Laurian as she stood motionless, breathlessly watching him.

A white tennis shirt set off his tan and his muscles. His longish light hair gleamed with gilded sun streaks. His face was alive with the vibrant emotion of his music. It was the face of a mature man, Laurian thought as she studied him, the face of a man who wasn't afraid to admit his emotions as many men were.

The sadness of the losses Keska had suffered was printed in a tracing of lines across his forehead. Anger had been expressed and frustrations had been faced to leave faint grooves between his sloping brows. But laughter had softened all the emotions etched on his features.

Laurian saw an underlying tenderness that balanced the emotions, and the well-developed ego that was natural to a man of his talent and ability. The tenderness initiated the wave of love that surged through her. A gentle smile crept across her lips.

As if the wave had reached out and engulfed him, Keska sensed her presence. He glanced up and lowered his violin to smile at her. "Good morning, my lovely Laurian," he said.

"Good morning, Keska," she answered. Walking across the room, she sat down sideways in a chair near him, propping her arm on the back. "I'm surprised you could find time to show up here when you have so much to do on your apple farm," she teased. "Do you realize what time it is?"

"So Keska Lahti woke you up, lazy Laurian," he said, his Finnish accent a caress. "I played fortissimo, but I couldn't be sure how soundly you were sleeping in the room above my head." He pointed at the ceiling with his bow. "There are many things I must learn about you."

There were many interesting things about Keska that Laurian wanted to learn too. How he looked when he slept was high on the list. She warmed at the thought and asked, "How did you know where my room was?"

"I told you once that I always know when you are near, my Laurian," he said, his pewter-gray gaze embracing her. "My senses seek you out."

Little tremors ran over her skin and she laughed softly. "I think it's more likely you have a whole network of spies and information sources."

"That too," he admitted, and grinned, his cheeks pushing into dimpled creases. "Everyone at Camp Bryant has been quite friendly and helpful. Especially Uncle Jules."

"I'm sure they have been. Keska Lahti seems to awe everyone into cooperation," Laurian murmured wryly. "But what are you doing here so early in the morning?"

Keska cuddled the violin under his chin, tilting his head to hug it with his cheek. As he began to play a mellow simple little melody, he said, "I noticed the acoustics were very good in this room, much better than in my music room. I thought it might be interesting to try them out."

"Did you?" Laurian said, her dark eyes gleaming skeptically.

His gaze came to rest on her, wandering over her form as he played the soft and sentimental ballad. His lips twitched, curving into a smile. "I'm sure you know that practice becomes boring after a while. The same thing in the same place, day after day after day. One needs change."

"Does one?" She leaned her cheek on the back of her hand, her eyes linked with his.

"One does, and I was right," he murmured. "It is much more fascinating to practice in your building." A sad, romantic folk song issued from the strings of his violin and he sighed. "I'm here this early because I couldn't sleep well last night for one reason or another."

"Really?" Laurian said, her eyes laughing. "How odd. I wonder why?"

"I wonder," Keska said, and gave her a caressing look. "Have you ever heard the fable of the ant and the grasshopper?"

"Probably not the way you're going to tell it." She crossed one leg over the other, swinging her sandaled foot.

Keska switched to the playful fingering of a children's tune and frowned very seriously as he told his story. "There once was an ambitious ant who did nothing but play at farming and fiddle around on the violin. He fell in love with a beautiful, very intense grasshopper who thought she knew much better than the ant what life was all about. To his dismay the desirable grasshopper did nothing but repulse the ambitious ant." Keska fell silent and gave his attention to the dancing music he played.

After a few seconds Laurian laughed. "That doesn't make sense. What is the moral to the fable? If there is one."

"The moral is that if the ambitious, amorous ant fiddles around with a reluctant, very lovely grasshopper long enough, he may discover the secret of life. And if she is agreeable, he will find happiness and contentment in the end. That is the moral," Keska said solemnly, his eyes sparkling. "I hope."

"That's a pathetic fable," Laurian said, shaking her head.

"I know. But as you see, I'm here—fiddling around." Keska's violin gave a laughing little trill.

Then he lowered it, leaning the rounded end of the body on his thigh. "Would you please accompany me on your cello, Laurian?" he invited, his eyes intense and questioning.

The request was so sudden and unexpected, she could almost feel anxiety drain the blood out of her face. Each one of her muscles tensed until her whole body was stiff. She shook her head and said in a choked voice, "I'd rather listen to you play."

"It would be fun for us to become one in our music," Keska said softly, studying her keenly.

"Yes— No, really I can't," Laurian said, her breathing picking up until she was almost hyperventilating. "I'd rather not."

"Don't be afraid of Keska Lahti. You are my equal." The meaning behind his words was rich with promise.

"I'll think about it," she said miserably, wanting to accept, but terrified and thoroughly intimidated.

"Yes, you must think about it, my lovely Laurian, because sooner or later you *will* play with me." His voice was low and confident; his eyes had taken on a metallic gray of challenge as he looked at her. "Soon, Laurian."

He lifted his violin to his chin and went back to playing the difficult and convoluted measures of the Paganini caprice.

The sound of his caressing violin sent chills and shivers through Laurian's body. Or perhaps the tremors had arisen from his last statement; she wasn't entirely certain whether Keska had been referring to a duet on the violin and cello, or physical lovemaking. But excitement flooded her no matter which he had been predicting.

Laurian melted into the pleasure of listening to his music. Relaxing languidly in her chair with her elbow cocked over the back, she rested her cheek on the back of her hand and watched him, mesmerized.

Though Keska had withdrawn from her into his music, his eyes rested dreamily on her face. The free, soaring, seductive sound of his violin reached out and held her, pulled her, invaded her body.

The expressions that moved fluidly over his features made Laurian one with him, opened to her his emotions as the notes flowed exquisitely between them. His high notes balanced her on a tightrope of sheer pristine purity. The aggressive masculinity of the moaning low notes sent shivers through the soft parts of her body.

Keska shared with Laurian his joy of creating beauty, his restless wish to refine and improve. Together they exulted in the triumph of a perfect phrase and frowned in annoyance when a sound didn't meet perfection.

Laurian had been allowed into the most secret and inner soul of Keska Lahti, and she felt a part of him. He offered himself and she received him joyfully, with tremulous excitement.

The music began to fade from her consciousness as she concentrated on his expressive face. His sloping dark eyebrows changed shape as they moved from passion to annoyance to happiness. His lips were slightly parted, faintly pink, and very alive, full and sensual.

Laurian didn't hear the singing of the violin as she looked into Keska's eyes and recognized his dynamic inner force. Those eyes, his lips, all of him, was as intense as it would be when the time came for him to make love to her.

She gazed at the chin and cheek pressed against the violin and wished they were caressing her body. Her attention shifted to the slim fingers moving confidently on the bow and strings, caressing the violin to ecstasy. Sighing wistfully, she lovingly traced the muscles in his upper arms. Their tight, rounded shape moved under the short knit sleeves of his shirt. Shoulders made wide and strong from physical labor curved in around the feminine form of the violin. His collar lay open at his tanned neck and the unbuttoned slash of his shirt framed a teasing V of smooth chest skin and a hint of male body hair.

Her lips parted with her frustrated need to see more of his body, to become intimate with all of the sleek frame hidden under shirt and belt.

Suddenly Laurian realized Keska had stopped playing. She had no idea how long the silence had stretched with his bow held motionless over the strings. Her eyes lifted to his face.

Keska smiled tenderly, his lips soft with a passion that matched that in her face, his eyes dark with invitation. "I am pleased my lovely Laurian is beginning to notice the man behind the violin," he said in a husky caressing voice. "You see, the ant has persevered in his fiddling and now he will find happiness with his most beautiful grasshopper."

Laurian smiled at his whimsy. When her desire was so welcomed and prized, she could feel no embarrassment at being caught showing it. "I've always been very, very aware of the man, Keska," she whispered.

Putting his violin and bow down on the table, he rose to his feet and took Laurian's hands, pulling her up so he could put his arms around her.

Just as his lips were centimeters away from hers, the door of the practice room burst open explosively in the kinetic, breathless silence. They both jumped, startled that there might be an intruder in this, their private universe.

Laurian glanced toward the door and breathed, "Roger." She gave a tremulous little disappointed smile that matched Keska's.

The boy stopped short just inside the door and stared at them. His brow wrinkled with embarrassment under his tumbled brown curls, and his face glowed red. He didn't seem to know how to handle the mortifying situation he had blundered into.

"Oh . . . I guess you're busy," he said, "I didn't mean to break into anything . . . but I heard you playing," he said to Keska, his words delivered in spasmodic bursts. "I knew it was you. It couldn't have been anyone else. I wanted to ask you something."

Roger glanced at Keska's arms around Laurian and cleared his throat. He wiped his palms on the sides of his wrinkled khaki shorts. "I guess I can come back later . . . since you're busy."

Keska grinned as Laurian pulled back out of his arms. His voice was tight with laughter when he spoke to Roger. "It isn't necessary to leave. Stay. Whatever Keska Lahti was busy doing can be done much more efficiently later." He glanced at Laurian, a secretive, questing glance. "In privacy on my apple farm? When your time is free?"

Her eyes were fixed on Keska's tempting lips. "Why don't you hang around camp until I'm done with my teaching?" she said in a whispery voice. "I'll go to your apple farm with you after the student orchestra has finished practicing this afternoon."

Keska's lips curved into a smile. "The day will stretch into a million years, my lovely Laurian."

He sighed and turned to Roger. "What question did you want to ask Keska Lahti?"

Roger had been watching the romantic interlude

keenly, possibly storing information for later use. But he had heard only snatches of the conversation, and he looked thoroughly bemused. His Adam's apple bounced when he swallowed.

Then he looked at his violin and remembered what he had meant to ask. "I don't know why I can't play my music any way that seems right to me. Why isn't my own interpretation more creative? Why do I have to follow the directions on the sheet music?"

Laurian walked to the back of the room, preparing to leave Roger to an expert. But she stopped and turned disapprovingly when she heard Keska's answer. "You can play the music any way that suits you, Roger."

Before she could protest, Keska went on. "You can play any which way you like, but everyone will think you lack sensitivity for your craft. They'll think you don't know what you are doing and that you don't understand music. Besides, the composers who wrote their themes had a vision that they put down on paper. Those gifted artists have been long dead and they are unable to protect their works. It wouldn't be fair to steal and distort their dream, do you think?"

Roger flopped down in a chair with a dark, rebellious look.

Keska took another chair and settled himself into a position of feline relaxation. He lifted his brows. "If you have emotions that demand to be released, you should compose your own music."

Roger's face brightened. "I have," he said almost shyly, and he perched on the edge of his chair with his violin and bow held in his fists.

"I thought as much," Keska said. "Would you play one of your compositions for me?"

"You might think it's amateurish," the boy said hesitantly.

"I don't believe I will. I have respect for you."

When Roger lifted his instrument and began to play, Keska pulled himself up in his chair and leaned forward intensely, his head cocked and his face transfixed.

There was a unique anguished quality to the boy's music that lifted the hair on Laurian's arms and filled her throat. She watched Roger with something akin to reverence for a moment. The combination of the rich, tumultuous emotion of Roger's music and Keska's gentle encouragement of the boy filled her eyes with tears.

After a few minutes she crept out of the room and closed the door silently.

The day passed on peaks and valleys of excitement and impatience. Keska spent the hours with Laurian, lending his musical expertise to her classes. And she spent the hours wishing the time would fly by instead of creeping as it did. Every time she thought of his secluded farm, her face blushed a blooming pink with anticipation.

Early in the afternoon the entire student body met in the auditorium as an assembly. It was a dissonant and high-spirited fledgling orchestra.

Before the practice began, the youngsters tuned their instruments with much more exuberance than seemed necessary. The timpanist beat out a clashing rock rhythm. The trombonists "accidentally" nudged the heads in front of them with the slides on their horns. Roger sat sulking among the violinists, pouting because another student, an older girl, had been chosen first violinist. Confusion reigned.

Keska sat beside Laurian midway back in the empty auditorium, grinning. They watched Uncle Jules repeatedly rap his baton on the podium, trying to capture the attention of his boisterous group. When the old man had finally commanded their attention, the students began to squint seriously at their sheet music. They played remarkably well for so early in the season, though it was instantly apparent that about half the musicians were individualists, wandering off into flights of pitch and tempo.

"When is this concert to be held?" Keska asked Laurian sotto voce, every one of his laugh wrinkles deepening.

"In August," she replied.

"Is it *possible* they can be ready?"

"We've got two and a half months to work with them. You'll be surprised."

"I'm afraid I will have to be."

But even before the two-hour session was over, the young musicians had settled down under Jules's influence, and a tenuous harmony began to bud. Keska watched and listened with complete absorption, smiling when the music went well and wincing at each discordance.

When Jules dismissed the class, the group of striving musicians turned into a shrieking stampede of hungry, liberated teenagers. They cleared the auditorium with startling dispatch.

Jules joined Keska and Laurian, wiping his flushed perspiring face with a large white handkerchief. "Each year these young ruffians seem to come stocked with more energy," he said, and laughed. "I'm becoming far too old for this sort of thing." He cocked a speculative eye at Keska. "Do you conduct, Keska?"

"I have led an orchestra or two on occasion," Keska admitted. "But I would be panicked if you suggested I might face *this* group."

Jules laughed and ran his fingers through his fluffy white hair, raising it around his head. "Caution, as they say, is the better part of valor," he agreed sagely.

"I noticed you don't have a flautist," Keska said. "The orchestra hardly seems complete without a flute."

Jules gave his face one last swipe with his handkerchief and tucked it away. "Odd that you should mention that," he said innocently. "Laurian and I had a discussion about that very fact nct too long ago."

Refusing to acknowledge any of the silencing looks Laurian threw at him, Jules continued. "As a matter of fact there is a girl, a flautist, in New Jersey who applied for a grant to come to our camp." He sighed. "Unfortunately the limited money we earned at the concert last fall didn't stretch far enough to pay her plane fare. We must wait until this fall for more funds." Gazing mournfully at the ceiling, he added, "We are so hoping the income from our concert this August will be much larger and bring in much greater revenues, so that we can give assistance when it is needed for deserving children."

Laurian sensed Keska's body tensing rigidly in the seat next to her. Crossing his arms over his chest, he stared straight ahead, his lower lip protruding.

The silence in the big empty auditorium seemed deafening, and Laurian shuffled her feet in irritation at Uncle Jules. It wouldn't surprise her in the slightest if Keska's interest in her would evaporate after such a poorly timed reminder of the concert.

"Such is life," Jules murmured when no response from Keska was forthcoming. "Such is life."

Laurian glared at him out of the corners of her eyes. He was gazing at the unoccupied stage, apparently in a state of abstract depression. It was an act she had seen before when he wanted something.

Keska wasn't fooled either. Taking a deep breath, he asked, "Do you accept private donations?"

"Of course," Jules said, glancing at him in annoyance when he realized Keska had no intention of being manipulated. "But you mustn't think I was suggesting you have a financial responsibility."

"I know exactly what you were suggesting," Keska murmured, his voice tinged with amused respect as he studied Jules's venerable face. "It would give me pleasure to donate the plane fare to bring the young flautist to Camp Bryant. Then my conscience would be clear."

A mischievous smile brought Jules's face to life. "Ah so . . . I tried, didn't I?"

Keska was clearly restraining a laugh. "So you did," he said, then turned to Laurian with a grin. "Are you free to admire Keska Lahti's apples now?"

She nodded and put her hand in his as they walked to the exit of the auditorium. When they reached the door, Keska paused to look back toward the stage thoughtfully. "Is this where you hold the concert?" he asked casually.

"Oh, no," Laurian answered. "This room is much too small. We use the Luther Burbank Center for the Arts, in Santa Rosa. It's large enough, and so much more sophisticated and beautiful."

"Mmm-hmm," he acknowledged as if he were familiar with the center.

"Why did you ask?"

"Simple curiosity," he answered tersely, and started to turn back toward the door.

Before he went out, though, he smiled and raised a

hand to Jules, who sat dwarfed in the middle of the empty auditorium, watching them leave. Jules saluted them both with impish and knowing good humor.

It occurred to Laurian as she and Keska walked out of the auditorium and across the camp that Keska was much more tempted by the opportunity to play the benefit concert than he would ever admit.

Seven

When they had driven to the farm, Keska parked his car in front of the garage beside the big white house. He got out and came around to open the passenger's door for Laurian.

"The house looks deserted," she said nervously as she put her hand in his. "The farm is so quiet and peaceful."

A smile curved his lips, a knowing expectant smile, as Keska answered softly, "It *is* deserted. George is still in Arizona and I have given the housekeeper the day off. We are alone here. Just you and I."

When Laurian was on her feet, Keska put his arms lightly around her waist and brushed her mouth with a grazing kiss. Though her lips responded to his touch, she felt herself go stiff with an embarrassing uneasiness. A shyness settled around her when she thought of the ultimate intimacy that would come.

It would take courage to bare her body, strip away her shields, and open herself completely to this man. Suddenly it seemed she hardly knew him. He was a stranger.

Keska seemed instantly aware of her ambivalent reticence. "Don't be afraid, Laurian," he said softly. There was no demand in the gentleness of his embrace, only affection and happiness. "I love you very much," he said, looking down into her face. His lips brushed against hers again, a teasing invitation.

Smiling tremulously, she drew away from the kiss. "I think you must have been very sure of me when you came to the camp this morning."

"No, Keska Lahti wasn't sure at all, only hopeful," he said, answering her smile. "That is a large part of your charm, that you are not easily compliant or predictable. You make any reward most precious."

"Where are we going?" Laurian asked as he led her away from the house.

His smile was white against his tan. "Before we do anything else, we must visit our special apple."

"Visit an apple!" she exclaimed. "Now?"

Keska led Laurian into the field where the spring grass had turned into purple-blooming hay. "I want you to take pleasure from me, Laurian," he said seriously. "So we will move slowly until you feel comfortable. When two people have waited long, as have we, they can savor the moments jealously and relish the anticipation."

A pause hung between them before she glanced at him. "Thank you, Keska," she said softly. "You're very special to understand how I feel."

He pressed her hand and they ambled slowly toward the orchard. "The little honeybee with his ardent lovemaking has given us a gift of fertile value," he said.

The memory of the bee with his head buried in the core of the flower sent erotic sparks dancing through Laurian's body. When she looked into Keska's face, she saw the sparks reflected in his eyes, along with amusement. "You seem to have some sort of fixation on insects—with your honeybees and ants and grasshoppers."

He grinned and nodded. "Yes, it seems so, doesn't it? But you can't deny they are fascinating creatures. So small and fragile—like you, my most lovely Laurian. Yet without them the world would be a barren, lifeless place, as my world would be if you rejected me. Because of ants and bees and grasshoppers the earth is green and lush with life." His arm tightened around her waist as he looked down into her face. "They are tiny beings who live by biological instinct."

The lacy, fragrant apple trees of the orchard closed intimately around them. He stopped to brush Laurian's cheek with his lips. "And Keska Lahti is very interested in instinct and biological urges at this moment," he whispered.

Laurian sighed deeply and pressed her face against the warm pulsing skin of his neck. Her own biological urges were reviving. They had begun leaping through her veins in a staccato dance rhythm, flushing and prickling her skin.

For some reason her embarrassment had disappeared with the touch of his hands and lips. The reticence had been erased by his clean lime scent and by the sensation of his quick breath against her hair. "You're sure you want to see your apple now?" she asked tentatively.

In answer Keska's warm mouth covered hers, moving and searching, sampling and tasting her. Laurian melted with a growing need for him. His hand clenched in the fall of thick hair hanging down her back and he pressed her close to his body. When he lifted his head, his eyes were filled with melting love.

"Our apple was conceived on the first day we kissed," he murmured in a husky voice, his accent thickened by emotion. "So the apple is a symbol of our love, Laurian. Of course, we must visit the apple. We must watch our love grow to maturity and perfection."

"What a sweet thought," she whispered, looking up at him through a mist of tears. "I love you, Keska," she said, her voice choked with a vast, deep sentiment. "Oh, my darling, I love you so."

A breeze whispered through the trees, swaying the fruit-sprinkled boughs. Laurian couldn't be sure whether the motion came from the world around her or from the explosive thrill of love and excitement bursting inside her.

Crushing her in his arms, Keska showered kisses on her cheeks, around her face, and over her mouth. Then he lifted his head and smiled down at her. "We must visit our apple to pay homage to the kind and generous Fate who brought us together," he whispered.

The brook had less water flowing around the rocks now that spring had progressed into summer. Keska and Laurian stood beneath their special gnarled apple tree and looked down at the hypnotic motion of the water, conscious only of the touch of their bodies, one against the other. The clean, crisp scent of the soil and the sun-heated apple trees enveloped them.

Keska reached up and pulled the branch down. The perfectly shaped green apple had grown to the size of a large walnut. It hung on an inch-long brown stem, alone

on its twig. The other fruit had been pruned away to give
it a place of honor. The strong, healthy miniature apple
was growing vigorously on its tree of life. "Your apple is
beautiful," Laurian sighed.

"Our apple," he insisted.

"Our apple is so very beautiful," she said softly, speaking of the love it represented.

Keska stood behind her, his free arm around her
waist as he held the branch. The full length of his body
was pressed against her back. Heavy surges of hunger
pulsed through her veins as she felt the shape, the beat,
and the breath of his slim strong form. "So very beautiful," he whispered against her ear.

She reached up and touched the small green fruit very
gently with her fingertip. "Nothing will ever happen to
our apple, will it?" she asked. "It'll continue to grow
strong and healthy, won't it?"

When Keska's arm tightened around her, pressing her
against his body, she turned her head and looked
questioningly into his face. "Won't it?" she whispered.

"How can one predict what will happen in the future?"
he murmured. "We must snatch the beauty and tenderness of these minutes we have been given . . . the hours
and the days."

"Not forever?" she asked, a shiver of apprehension
running through her. Love had just begun to bloom,
and she couldn't bear the possibility that it might end.

Keska felt her shiver. "We have become too serious,
lovely Laurian," he said. He released the branch carefully and watched it spring back into place. The apple
bobbed, then settled on its stem. "This is a day for celebration, not questions and predictions."

He turned her toward him and raised his brows. "I
believe you have become tense again." Taking her hand,
he led her in the direction of the farmhouse. "Keska
Lahti can see in your face that you are anxious, my lovely
Laurian. You must try my sauna, then your tensions
will melt away." His eyes sparkled when he added, "Or
perhaps you would like a glass of my blackberry wine."

"Good Lord, no! Spare me your wine, please," she
exclaimed, and flushed over the notion of spending time
naked with Keska in the sauna. "If my only choice is

between your wine and your sauna, then by all means let it be the sauna."

"That would have been my choice, too, my Laurian," he said, his accent enhanced by whatever images he was seeing behind his suggestive eyes.

Then he laughed. "But you mustn't criticize Keska Lahti's wine. If you hadn't drunk it so cooperatively that first afternoon, then you might have had the sense to slap my face and leave in horror, mortally offended by such a fellow as Keska Lahti." They had left the orchard and were walking across the field toward the house. "Admit it," he challenged. "You were shocked by me when we first met, and only the wine made you stay."

"I won't admit it," she protested. "I wasn't."

"I don't believe you."

"All right, you were awful. I hated you."

"No, you didn't hate Keska Lahti. You were afraid of me."

"Terrified. What made you act the way you did to a total stranger?"

Keska laughed and led Laurian through the gate, into the backyard. "I couldn't help it. You were so naive and serious, but the instant you saw me, all your hormones leaped to attention and reached out to me. In the face of such a marvelous compliment, what could I do but tease you and see what could happen next?"

Laurian smothered a laugh and forced a frown. "Keska Lahti, I think you are, without a doubt, the most egotistical and insufferable man I have ever met."

"I know," he agreed cheerfully, and stopped to face her, his mouth only inches away from hers. A teasing smile twitched the corners of his lips.

Laurian put her finger against his inviting mouth and laughed. "Unfortunately for me, you're also the most irresistible man I've ever known."

Her smile faded as their eyes held, trading and sharing desires. "The sauna . . . ?" Keska murmured, drawing out the word slowly. He stepped back and allowed his eyes to trace the shape of her breasts, the flare of her hips, and the slim lines of her legs.

Laurian felt nude before him. But there was no shyness now, no reserve, no inhibitions to hold her back from Keska. His slow, loving seduction had done its work. Her skin crept with dimpling, raging reactions to his visual touch.

When Keska read her eagerness in her eyes, a smile curved his lips. Taking her hand, he led her into the small, windowless building beyond the swimming pool.

After he had shut the door, they stood facing each other in the intimate privacy of a tiny anteroom that was lit only by a small yellow bulb. There were wooden benches lining the walls and a cupboard holding towels and robes. The walls were tightly paneled in unfinished, sanded wood. Hot dry air escaped from the secret inner chamber on the other side of a solid door.

Breathless and motionless, Laurian gazed at the man before her. In the dimness his face looked exotic and sensual. His eyes were dark, glittering with his need for her. The vibrating silence between them spoke more clearly of their passion than any words might have.

Her heart raced when Keska lifted his hands to slowly pull his white knit shirt up over his chest and off over his head. His wavy hair was tousled when he dropped the shirt on a bench and stood quietly, watching her. There was no sexual pressure, only a simple sensual offering of himself to Laurian. His gift was the freedom and time to know him.

Lips parted, she stepped forward and touched the curve of the tanned muscles on his chest. When she lay her palm over the rough, crisp, curling brown hair scattered from male nipple to male nipple, the sensation tickled the nerves in her seeking hand.

Glancing into his face, Laurian saw that her touch gave him pleasure. Smiling, she let her hands wander up around his broad shoulders, up his neck until she touched his full lower lip. She traced his angular cheek and the sloping curve of his eyebrow. Then she smoothed the mussed wave of his light brown hair.

Both her mind and her body found him desirable and perfect. His perfection lit a scorching flame inside her body that paled the intensity of the heat coming from the sauna.

Keska's eyes turned sultry in answer to Laurian's fever. His hands was trembling when he touched her bare shoulders to trace the narrow red straps of her sundress. The delicate touch sprayed a fierce quiver over her skin, and she closed her eyes when he found and undid the zipper at the back of her dress.

Very slowly Keska eased the confining material down over Laurian's body. His hands lingered on her nude breasts, shaping and cupping them as the dress slipped down around her waist. Bending his head, he kissed the valley he had uncovered. She touched her lips to his sweet-smelling, gold-streaked hair.

The sundress fell in a white circle around her feet, and she slipped out of her sandals to curl her bare toes into the warm floor boards. Keska looked at her with eyes that worshiped a beauty she had never realized she possessed.

With seductive hands that had been trained from the earliest childhood to evoke magnificence, he brought her body to singing life. His fingers curved around her waist, her hips, smoothed up and down the lines of her thighs.

Touching the creamy lace panties that hid the throbbing, eager core of her, he said softly, "You are perfection, my lovely Laurian."

Then, taking a large thick yellow towel out of the cupboard, he wrapped her and held her close against his bare chest. Reaching behind her head, he unfastened the gold clasp that held her hair. He lifted the heavy dark silken veil forward to flow down over the knotted towel covering her breasts.

Laurian clung to him, her fingers digging into the smooth skin on his back. "Keska . . . I love you," she whispered urgently. "I've never known anyone like you. I'm— I need—" Breaking off, she pressed her face into the warm curve of his smooth shoulder.

His voice trembled when he said softly, "Sauna is not a sexual experience, my love. It is a spiritual preparation for the bliss to come. It is almost a religious experience, and you are the goddess I worship."

Lifting her head, Laurian brushed her toweled breasts against his chest and smiled up at him. "I'm no goddess, my love. I'm nothing but an earthy woman, and I want you."

His lips were soft and relaxed as he brushed them back and forth, so excruciatingly slowly, over hers. His fingers shook as he touched the rolled knot of towel at the rise of her breast. "Our first lovemaking must be transcendent, my sweet Laurian," he whispered with an exciting huskiness against her ear.

"It is, Keska," she gasped. "It is already. I need you and want you, my darling."

Pulling back, he kicked off his shoes, slipped off his trousers and briefs together, and threw them aside with an utter lack of self-consciousness. He smiled impishly at her. "I am yours, Laurian."

"I'm glad you are. I'm so happy." Breathing raggedly, she gazed at his long, sleek, completely masculine, eager form. The hard angles of his finely honed body thrilled her.

Each muscle fit into its exact place. Even his bones curved seductively. His waist was slim and his hips flat. His spine arched fluidly, and his legs were long and lightly fuzzed. His buttocks were high and well rounded.

The ferocity of the hair at his pelvis and the force of his masculinity softened her body to moist readiness. His catlike, graceful bearing seemed a preview of his sexual finesse. "You are magnificent, Keska Lahti," she whispered, her eyes glowing.

"I, too, am just an earthy man, with needs and desires, as you can plainly see. All my needs are for you, sweet Laurian," he said, and laughed softly as he wrapped a towel around his hips. He opened the door of the sauna, bending his head to touch Laurian's tumbled hair with his lips as she passed.

Breathtakingly dry, exhilarating heat met and merged with the fire in her body. The tiny, wood-paneled room was unfurnished except for a double tier of wide plank benches and a large pail of water. Wavering heat rose from the rough surfaces of big rocks in a heated metal bed in the rear of the room. Laurian imagined heat must be rising in waves from her aroused body with equal intensity.

When Keska threw several dippers of water over the rocks, steam boiled up into the room, curling around and embracing their bodies. The white cloud pulled them together, pressed them against each other, though they weren't touching.

Spreading a towel over the lower bench, Keska held Laurian's arms and urged her down onto her back. He tucked another rolled towel under her head for a pillow and sat down beside her, facing her, his lean hip pressed against the curve of her thigh. His eyes had gone misty with yearning. He touched her hair gently, smoothing and petting it, spreading it out around her head and shoulders. Lifting the silken mass, he pressed his face into its perfume.

Fingers of white steam caressed their bodies. Laurian melted languidly into the heat and passion she felt. Lifting her arms, she held Keska, loved him. Curbing her impatience to possess him, she learned the lesson he taught—to extract the essence and thrill of each moment before going on to the next.

Moving her hands over his steam-slicked shoulders and his strong arms until she threaded her fingers into the hair on his chest, Laurian began to be familiar with the vibrant male body that would become a part of hers.

Her heart was racing and her body demanded release. "My darling," she whispered, "you must be a magician, a sorcerer. I've never felt like this before . . . I've never been alive before."

Smiling down into her face, a message of the coming union in his eyes, Keska said, "I am no magician. You are the one who has put me under a spell—because I swore I would never love again." His lips came down to cover hers, and he touched his tongue to the sensitive inner surface of her mouth.

When the kiss ended, Keska lifted his head and leaned sideways to throw another dipper of water on the heated rocks. The sizzling explosion raged through Laurian's ears. It matched the tempestuous boiling in her own molten, rushing blood.

Keska shuddered as he curved his fingers around the slope of her shoulders. His touch burned like flame as he traced the edge of her towel, mounting both swelling breasts, exploring the valley between. He undid the knot that held the towel and spread the two sides apart, uncovering her wanting body.

Very slowly, like the most agonizing caress, he hooked his thumbs in the elastic of her panties and peeled the lace down over her hips, down over her legs, and off her feet. His eyes probed and adored her femininity.

He explored every hollow and space of her body with his lips and tongue. Laurian moaned frantically when sensations rippled out over her skin from his touch.

"So beautiful, my Laurian. . . ." Keska whispered in a voice made musical by his sensual accent. "My sweet. . . . Oh, God, I want you, my entrancing Laurian. Are you ready, my love?"

Her hands curled convulsively around the bulge of his upper arms. "Oh, yes, Keska," she moaned, lost and drowning in her need. "Please, yes . . . now."

Keska pulled her up. Her towel fell away and he lifted her easily into his arms. As he carried her out of the sauna, the crisp, fresh summer air hit their heated bodies, blasting them into life.

Urgently seeking, joining tongues, he invaded her mouth with a foreshadowing of the mating that would come as he carried her to a small, velvety patch of lawn beyond the pool. It was a hidden secret niche in a corner between the house and the fence. The apple orchard huddled around the yard, shielding them with privacy; the dark evening sky lit with the first two glittering stars was their roof.

Allowing Laurian to slide down his body in a slow erotic motion, Keska set her on her feet. She watched breathlessly as he dropped his towel, which hadn't been able to hide his thrusting need for her. Then he held Laurian's hands and lowered her to the soft, fragrant grass. She lay on her back and held out her arms to him.

Keska dropped down to press his body against hers. His chest brought her breasts to life. He thrust his thigh demandingly between her legs. His mouth took her lips insistently. Murmuring breathlessly, disjointed, excited words, he lapsed into Finnish in his intense need, but Laurian knew what he wanted, what he needed. As she spoke her own desire the sensual scent of the roses growing beside the house reached out to blanket them.

His hands moved over Laurian with shaking insistence, seeking out and discovering what would be his.

She explored him with little cries of passion. When he lifted his body and entered her, she took him desperately and gave herself with complete freedom and joy.

The melody of love they played in duet was a rhythm as old as humankind, as new as their love. It ended with a crescendo that shook them both into oblivion. Their cries of release were heard only by sleepy, nesting birds and by crickets busy with their own noisy courtships.

After a few minutes Keska lifted himself away and held Laurian in his arms. Kissing her gently, almost in awe, he whispered softly against her cheek. His words were made more romantic because she couldn't understand them.

"I love you, my darling," she answered fervently, kissing his moist neck. Then she lifted her head and whispered, "I don't understand Finnish."

He looked up at her with deep, tender eyes. "You know what I am saying, my lovely, marvelous Laurian."

"Maybe," she added, touching the bowed curve of his upper lip. "But I want to understand every word so I can remember them forever, so I can write them down in my mind, in my book of incredible events. Tell me all over again in English." Her thick, long hair slipped forward in a flood to fall over his face and neck. She twisted it back over her shoulder.

Keska pulled it forward again and smoothed it across his chest. "I have only been saying one thing—that I love you more than I knew it was possible for me to love. I said that you are beautiful, so very exciting and passionate."

Laurian took his hand and kissed the palm, then each of his talented fingertips. "Oh, Keska, I love you too," she cried, and nestled her head into the curve between his neck and his shoulder. "I feel so full of love and contentment that I can hardly bear it. I can't understand how anything so wonderful as you could have happened to me."

His arm tightened around her and he sighed happily. After a few moments he asked, "How many items do you have in your book of incredible events?"

Lifting her head, Laurian laughed softly. "This is the

first and only event in the book. My life began when I met Keska Lahti."

Slipping his hand behind her neck, he pulled her down to meet his lips, then said, "Keska Lahti doesn't need a book, because lovely Laurian is branded across my heart. I shall never forget this day, this moment with you."

Night darkened as they lay side by side on the pungent grass with the scent of rose blooms drifting around them. When more stars began blinking on in the navy-blue evening sky, they got up to splash and play in the warm water of the swimming pool.

Laurian stayed with Keska on his apple farm that night. She slept beside him in his huge four-poster bed, warm and safe in his arms. She was content with life and supremely happy.

Once in the middle of the night she awoke to stare into the darkness with a feeling of confusion. For a few seconds she couldn't remember where she was. When awareness dawned, a flood of tenderness washed over her and she reached out to touch Keska.

But he wasn't in the bed with her, not beside her. She was alone with nothing but a residual scent of him lingering, a muskiness tinged with lime. A spurt of anxiety lifted her straight up in bed. Gathering up her loose hair, she listened intently.

The house was silent, and Laurian reached out to fumble for the switch of the bedside lamp. Jumping out of bed, she put on one of Keska's robes and walked out into the upstairs hallway.

As if by instinct she knew where she would find him. Creeping down the stairs in her bare feet, she walked through the hallway to the sitting room, past the brocaded love seat to the open French doors of Keska's music room.

A small lamp spread its yellow glow, reflecting on the piano and glinting metallically on Keska's medals and precious plaques. It shone gold on Keska's light hair and shadowed his introspective face.

A short brown robe was belted around his body. He was sitting, his legs stretched out in front of him, bare feet crossed, holding his bow in one hand, twisting it back and forth between his fingers. His face was thoughtful as he frowned intently at the exquisite violin lying on the table beside him.

For a few moments Laurian stood motionless, watching him, hesitant about breaking into his mood. Then she walked across the studio and dropped to her knees beside him, putting her arms around his waist. "What are you thinking about, my darling?" she asked softly.

Keska smiled and lay the bow aside so he could run his fingers through her flowing mass of hair, caressing her tenderly. "Could you be happy married to an apple farmer, lovely Laurian?" he asked wistfully.

"I don't recall any apple farmers asking me to marry them," she murmured, her eyes glowing like black diamonds in the soft light.

His grin pushed his cheeks into creases. "One is now . . . but can you be happy in this kind of quiet life?"

Laurian's first impulse was to shout "Yes, yes." Then she hesitated and wrinkled her brow. *Could* she be happy on a farm? Her life had always been linked to the sophisticated world of classical music. So had his.

After a few seconds she looked at Keska searchingly. "I think a more appropriate question is whether Keska Lahti can be happy managing an apple farm."

"I love you, so that means I must find happiness with my apples," he said, his eyes sliding sideways to rest on his violin again.

"I don't understand," Laurian said softly, tightening her arms around him.

Pressing a palm on either side of her face, Keska bent forward and kissed her lingeringly on the lips. When he raised his head, he said, "Tell me how I can choose between my heart and my soul, my sweet lovely Laurian."

She looked into his gray eyes for several seconds. "I can't, Keska. A man must have them both, mustn't he?"

Shrugging away his earthshaking questions, he gave a wry, twisted smile. "I think we have become too serious again, my sweet."

His hands gave an exquisite demonstration of his

remarkable genius as he explored the mysteries of her body, bringing it to singing life. After a few minutes he said in a velvety, husky voice, "Can you think of a possible way to lighten your mood?"

Laurian could. "This is a music room, isn't it?" she said. "As long as we're here, we ought to make beautiful music together, shouldn't we?"

Keska grimaced and groaned over her blatant play on words. And the temper of the atmosphere almost instantly lifted into laughing, giggling excitement.

Eight

The next several days passed for Laurian as if on a pinnacle of continuous rapture. Most of each day was spent
with Keska at the camp, and the evenings on his farm
were exciting and sensual. Since they were absorbed in
coming to know each other in the most intimate ways,
questions about the future were put on hold.

It pleased Laurian very much that Keska seemed
drawn to the music camp. He came early in the morning
to practice on his violin. Then he stayed for hours helping tutor her string students. The smoothing, maturing
progress of the orchestra fascinated him.

Under his influence the eager young string musicians
were developing into the most adept Camp Bryant had
ever hosted. Keska made their classes exciting and
interesting with his uninhibited delight in music and
his wry humor. He always offered a sincere empathy
for the unique problems of the musically gifted
children.

Keska made the classes so fascinating the students
were always reluctant to be dismissed. "Play for us,"
they would beg in an effort to hold him. Generally he
complied simply because he had an extrovert's appetite
for sharing his music and for entertaining an audience.

Laurian never tired of watching him and listening to
him play, but she often wondered just why he had abandoned public performances when he derived such
extreme pleasure from giving them.

Then one morning the young students went into a
particularly imploring act, insisting, "Play for us—just
one piece . . ." In their enthusiasm for music they had

already held Keska and Laurian long after the class period should have been over. "Please . . . please . . . please," echoed through the room, drowning out Keska's halfhearted refusal.

"What are you trying to do to Keska Lahti?" he moaned. "You are going to wear me out—make me an old man before my time." His gleaming eyes denied any aging.

"Come on," they cried. "We played for you. It's not fair if you won't play for us."

"All right, all right." He laughed, waving down the clamor. "I'll agree to play on one condition." He hesitated for a moment, then pointed a finger at Laurian. "I'll play my violin only if your talented teacher will accompany me with her cello."

"*No,* Keska!" she whispered harshly, her body stiffening. Apprehensive perspiration instantly popped out on her forehead.

It terrified her to think of presenting herself on the cello without the security of an orchestra surrounding her, not even when the audience was only a group of students. Especially not with Keska. She couldn't bear for him to find fault with her abilities.

Laurian knew the insecurities and anxieties crashing down around her were probably unrealistic, but they were real and frightening nonetheless.

"Why won't you entertain us?" Keska asked softly after a few moments. "With your background you are undoubtedly an accomplished and capable musician. All of these young people have heard you play at one time or another, so they know your abilities."

"But . . ." Laurian started, almost cringing in her panic. True, she occasionally demonstrated a musical point for the students on her cello, but that was entirely different from pitting her talent against Keska Lahti's in front of an audience. Her chest tightened until she almost couldn't breathe.

Smiling tightly, she shook her head firmly. "They want to hear you, Keska. You play for them."

The class went into an uproar, insisting on a duet. Everyone in camp knew there was more than a professional relationship between Laurian and Keska. It captured young imaginations to think of these lovers joined in music too.

Keska stood off to the side, watching Laurian keenly, now that he had forced the issue of her playing. He shifted his position to stand with the students and lifted his hands pleadingly and persuasively.

Laurian knew that if she continued to refuse, she'd be setting an enormously bad example for impressionable students who were all headed for performing careers. She nodded rigidly, then walked reluctantly across the room on trembling legs to bring out her cello and bow. The class quieted instantly and watched with great interest.

Keska smiled encouragingly, his brows pinched with concern. "What would you like to play?" he asked.

Her heart was thumping as she walked to the music cabinet, and her breathing speeded as she paged through the sheet music. She felt as if everything she had ever learned about music had been erased from her brain as she stared at the violin-cello duets.

Finally she picked up a couple of folders and glanced at Keska. "Kodaly? *Allegro Serioso*?"

It seemed an appropriate choice, Laurian thought, because this circumstance was acutely "serioso." And besides, it was familiar to her. She had played it years ago with a violinist in school, and she knew the notes by heart. Her stomach twisted into a knot as she watched Keska nod. He would have nodded agreement to anything she chose; what did he have to lose?

"Keska Lahti will struggle through," he murmured as he took the violin music from Laurian. Then he hovered close while she spread the cello music on a stand and took her position on a chair.

Shaking out her full blue skirt, she glanced apprehensively at him as she plucked at her peasant blouse and nervously smoothed the dark hair coiled high on her head. Then there wasn't any other choice but to settle the bulky, highly polished cello between her wide-spread knees. Its weight seemed to drag her down when she supported the long neck on her shoulder.

Leaning close, Keska fussily straightened the pages of her music, his eyes resting teasingly on the span of her legs. Leaning even closer, he whispered softly, "It is difficult to resist a cellist, my lovely Laurian. You take your instrument between your knees as if you were clasping the body of your lover." His teeth gleamed white against his tan when he grinned. "As you might hold the fortunate body of Keska Lahti. Perhaps I am jealous of your cello."

"*Shhhh!*" she hissed, glancing at the young class. They were watching avidly, but they couldn't possibly have heard his suggestive, whispered words. "Go sit down, Keska," she whispered back. "We're *playing* this morning, not fiddling around." Her anxieties had lightened a few degrees in response to his nonsense.

Keska laughed softly, then placed a chair a few yards away, facing Laurian. He made an enormous production out of laying out his sheet music.

Finally he picked up his violin and bow, sat down, and shifted around until he had found the optimally comfortable position. In a silky bohemian shirt and snugly fitted trousers, his slim body seemed to curve into the chair bonelessly. His knees fell away from the center, spreading wide. He tucked his feet back under the chair. Even his hair settled into relaxed waves around his ears and over his forehead.

Laurian watched him, bemused, and wished she could feel that comfortable and relaxed. Every nerve in her body was pulled as taut as a piano string. Her knuckles were white from a death-grip on her bow.

Keska lifted his violin and cuddled it under his chin, his eyes sinking into a gray, dreamy mood. His right arm lifted. His bow rested on the strings and he raised his eyebrows. "Ready?" he asked softly. It was an oddly sensual invitation.

Anxiety instantly doubled. Laurian felt glacial ice settle in her chest. But she placed her bow on the cello and nervously fingered the strings on the neck. Her mind blank, she fixed her eyes on the opening notes of the piece. Then, by sheer strength of will, she licked her lips and forced herself to nod readiness.

The cello began alone with a deep, soulful pleading sound. Keska's violin joined with a pure, soaring answer. Laurian paused at the command of the music, then knit her cello into the fabric of his playing, frowning with concentration.

Instantly she knew she was playing woodenly, merely delivering the correct notes and matching Keska's pace. Her face froze in mortification. But she had no choice other than to forge her way through this humiliating experience and never, never let it happen again. Proceeding desperately, she played note by agonizing note, phrase by miserable phrase.

Suddenly Laurian's attention jolted to life. Faltering, she missed several notes, then scrabbled to synchronize her cello to Keska's violin. Her head jerked up. As her eyes left the sheet music her memory took over automatically to produce the notes on the cello.

She stared at Keska in questioning disbelief. He had abruptly changed the tempo! His attention was on the music, but his innocent and guileless expression told her he had done it deliberately. He was intentionally making this ordeal more difficult for her!

It was almost impossible to believe a man as gifted as Keska Lahti could be so *cruel*, Laurian thought, deeply hurt. All his pretty words about trust had been meaningless. Why on earth would he have done such a thing to her?

Then he did it again; he slipped into a tempo just a few degrees slower. Since it wasn't such a surprise this time, Laurian lost only two notes before she had readjusted to his meter. Anger raged. She'd show him he couldn't intimidate her!

Though she glared at Keska, he blithely kept his eyes fastened to his sheet music. Fury overrode anxiety completely, and her dark eyes flashed with hostile emotion as she redirected her attention to the *Serioso*.

Suddenly the poignant duet they were playing seemed a fraud after what Keska had done to her. It was ridiculous when Laurian heard the violin call seductively. Defiantly she answered in the husky voice of the cello, echoing his pleading tone. First one led, then the other. At times they scampered after each other in a joyful game. They chased each other playfully over the peaks and valleys of music. But Laurian knew if she ever caught Keska, he'd come away bleeding.

The emotions of Laurian's subconscious began to handle the music. That left her conscious mind completely free to concern itself with the hurt she felt that Keska had deliberately put her at a disadvantage and had tried to make a fool of her. She stared at him furiously.

Luckily, by watching him, she noticed a slight quirk of his eyebrows the next time he altered his pace. Laurian picked up the tempo immediately and triumphantly followed his modification.

When she did, Keska glanced up from his music and smiled at her, his expression pleased and satisfied, one of encouragement. He mimed a kiss by pursing his lips.

That's when Laurian noticed her cello music was soaring confidently and that her muscle tension had evaporated. Keska hadn't intended to make her fail. He had set out to shock her out of her unreasonable fear of playing with him. Her anger died instantly when she realized that he must have been very sure of her talent and he had been confident she could handle his challenge.

Warmth spread through her relaxed body as she gazed at Keska and sank into the sensuous pleasure of giving herself over to the emotional music.

Kodaly's *Serioso* was a generous composition, giving equal rights to both violin and cello. First one dominated, then gave way to the other. They soared and sank; echoing, calling, answering, and teasing.

At times Keska's violin swooped down to harmonize with the throaty depths of the cello, matching its sexuality. Then it would rise to trilling peaks of excitement. Laurian followed to his peaks and supported him, sustaining his fever. At other moments the cello would ascend and the violin would pause to listen to the siren song, then answer in plucking, urgent, pizzicato joy.

The fevered pitch in the music built until the two instruments rose to a towering pinnacle as one, then dived deep into ecstasy. The violin gave a galloping response and soared back up to a fine, exultant, trebling climax. The cello followed, proclaiming its own fulfilled passion. Then the violin swept up the scale to an ecstatic note so high, it was almost out of hearing range. The cello ended with a low consummated moan.

When the sound died away, Laurian's body was flushed and swollen with a sensual joy. She met the gaze of Keska's hot, hooded eyes and they sat motionless for a few moments, bows silent on strings, sharing a gratified emotion that was similar to the one they felt after making love. They were fully one.

The class burst into applause and cheers, shattering the mood. Keska put aside his violin and stood up, waving them to silence.

He looked at the young musicians sternly for a few moments, then said, "You listen to everything your lovely teacher tells you. Laurian Bryant is a very, very talented musician." He gave a brief, fierce look at Roger for emphasis. "Now, shoo. Get out of here. Go have fun."

After the class had stampeded out of the practice room, he stood in front of Laurian. "I meant it," he said sincerely. "You are a truly gifted musician who lives her music. You know that, don't you?"

Her gaze lifted to Keska's face. She studied his expression for a second before she answered uncertainly, "No, I guess I didn't really know. I lost my faith somewhere along the way."

Laurian hadn't moved since the piece had ended. Her cello was propped between her legs and her bow drooped from a hand that was supported against a knee. Shaken and bemused, she tried to understand the thing that had happened between them—to her.

Dropping down to sit on his heels, Keska put his arms around the pulled-in waist of the cello, leaning his elbows on Laurian's knees. "Your confidence wasn't lost, my sweet," he said with a smile. "It was there all the time, just waiting to burst out in amazingly superior music."

"It only made an appearance because you forced me to trust myself." She laughed and tapped him on the sun-streaked hair with her bow. "You're lucky I didn't hit you over the head with my cello when you changed tempo on me."

"I had faith," he said smugly. "That's why I could afford to take a chance." His expression turned serious. "The past is the past, my lovely Laurian. You must let previous unhappiness go and live your life freely."

"Yes," Laurian said, nodding. "It's time I do that. It's easier to do when you trust me the way you do." Then she looked into his eyes. "Can you take your own advice and come to terms with your worries too? Can you face your past?"

Keska gave a sheepish grimace. "The past isn't my problem, the future is. I must carefully arrange my life for the maximum benefit to all concerned."

Then a smile pushed up his cheeks. With his arms around the cello and a hand on each of her wide-spread legs, his fingers closed around her thighs. "I'll tell you what. Keska Lahti will bring you home to the farm, and I'll allow you to perfect your seductive grasp on the cello." His hands moved up her thighs to the joining of her legs. "It might be helpful for you to use my body as a model."

Laurian laughed softly, warm with a surge of desire that sprang up from the motion of his artistic hands. "So you think I need to improve my style, do you?" Neither one of them was talking about the cello or music.

Bringing his sloping brows down in concentration, Keska pursed his lips to give the matter several seconds of serious thought. Then he said in a soft, velvety voice, "In the last few days I have felt nothing but the greatest admiration and gratitude for your style."

Lifting her hand to his lips, he nibbled the sensitive skin of the palm. "But even one so expert as my Laurian must keep in practice and explore exciting new concepts. Don't you agree?"

"Oh, I agree wholeheartedly," she murmured breathlessly as he kissed the tender skin at the curve of her wrist.

"Then come and see my apples," Keska whispered. "George will be back tomorrow, so this is our last day of freedom in the Garden of Eden."

Laurian shivered slightly when his wandering lips nibbled their way up her arm and kissed the inside bend of her elbow. Curving her hand around the back of his neck, she played with the crisp wave of his hair and laughed softly. "I don't know how you can say such ridiculous things and have them sound so charming."

He laughed, too, and stood, taking the cello away from her. "Don't you know by now? Keska Lahti is gifted." As he leaned the cello in the corner he looked back with snapping eyes. "Actually, Laurian, you bring out an embarrassing foolishness in me. So you must take the blame for the poppycock I spout. Do you want me to control my tongue and try to be more conservative?"

"No. Absolutely not," she said, and walked out of the building with her hand warm and eager in his. "I've never known a Garden of Eden until I met you, and I couldn't bear to lose it now."

Two days later George Miller came to visit Laurian at Camp Bryant. Within the bounds of his dignified self-possession he seemed delighted to see her. "You're looking very well, madam," he murmured.

"And you, George," Laurian said. "Your visit is a surprise. I'm so pleased you've come to see our camp—unless you have something else on your mind." She looked at him questioningly.

"Oh, no," he answered. "I simply felt I needed a little outing. It tends to become rather quiet on Mr. Lahti's farm."

"I imagine," she murmured, and couldn't help smiling. It had been far from quiet on the farm while George had been gone.

"I assume you and Mr. Lahti have resolved your differences?" he inquired.

"More or less." A smile hovered around her lips.

"I thought as much. Mr. Lahti's disposition seems to have altered during my holiday," he said approvingly. "Perhaps you would show me around this camp of yours, madam."

"I will, George, if you could bring yourself to call me Laurian instead of madam."

He glanced at her with a subdued twinkle in his eyes. "When I can call you Mrs. Lahti, I will relinquish the madam."

"Why, George, you sound like a marriage broker, or a cupid."

"I, madam?" he protested. "Really!"

George seemed keenly interested as Laurian showed him through the school. Then she began a tour of the grounds. The path they turned their steps to was bordered by towering redwoods and followed the curve of the wide, muddy-blue river. The cloying scent of wet vegetation and the summer forest hung around them in clouds.

"How did you happen to become connected with Keska, George?" Laurian asked after they had walked a ways. "Your personalities seem to originate from the opposite sides of a wide gulf."

George smiled nostalgically. "When Mr. Lahti first came to this country, I was connected with an agency that dealt with the advancement of young musicians. He came to us from Finland very young, very enthusiastic, and with great dreams. At twenty-two he had conquered all the peaks in Scandinavia, so he meant to turn his sights toward the world of music in the United States."

"And the rest is history," Laurian said, smiling over a young Keska.

"He was an instant success in the classical music world. It was a very thrilling and euphoric happening for him, and he dove into the sea of acclaim with energy and passion. His enthusiasm tended to get in the way of his wisdom and he overextended himself, accepting every engagement offered."

"He's a fantastic performer," Laurian said proudly, wondering once again why he had quit.

"That he is. But our personal connection came about because he was lonely and homesick at first," George went on. "I took him under my wing, so to speak, and we developed a friendship."

Laurian smiled at him. George wasn't half as stuffy as he liked to project, she realized. "I'm glad you did."

"Then when I suffered a heart attack a few years ago, leaving me unfit to handle my duties at the agency, Mr. Lahti convinced me he needed me to take care of his affairs. He doesn't, in fact, but our relationship has become a rather fulfilling one. Certainly for me, and I flatter myself it is for him also. He is like the son I never had. I am fortunate."

Laurian touched his arm. "Keska is fortunate also. He tries awfully hard to hide it, but he's a very kind, nice man, isn't he?"

"Indeed, madam."

"Do you know his family? Does he have parents, brothers or sisters?"

George smiled slightly. "Mr. Lahti is an only child, but his parents are quite interesting people. His mother was at one time a rather fine ballerina and his father plays a French horn in an orchestra. Mr. Lahti and his family are quite affectionate, but they all seem quite—uh—volatile. I've heard them erupt into some rather shocking disputes. Though, oddly enough, everything smoothes out in a matter of hours, sometimes even minutes."

Laurian laughed. "I'm not surprised that they're volatile if Keska's personality runs in the genes."

"They care deeply for each other."

"I'm glad," she said, and lapsed into silence. After a few minutes, she asked hesitantly, "Did you know Keska's wife?"

George gave her a quick, sharp glance, then looked straight ahead, down the path. "Yes, I knew her quite well."

"What was she like?" She paused, then tacked on, "Was she pretty?"

"Helvi is a quiet, gentle Finnish woman, rather shy. As to whether she is pretty, I am no expert in such things. I have a picture, if you would care to see it." He took a wallet out of his hip pocket and flipped it open to a plastic-covered picture that he held out to Laurian.

Looking closely at the photo, she felt the sudden prick of jealousy. The picture was a professional pose of a much younger Keska with his head bent close to an exquisite woman. She had very fair hair curling around a classically beautiful face and large, thickly lashed blue eyes.

Handing the wallet back to George, Laurian walked on

down the path by his side, kicking stones and leaves. "Did Keska love her very much?" she asked finally.

"I wouldn't be in a position to answer that, madam."

Lifting a shoulder in frustration and letting it drop, she asked, "How did the divorce come about? Did she leave him or did he leave her?"

"It isn't my place to speak of such things, please understand." George glanced at her apologetically. "You must wait for Mr. Lahti to tell you as much about it as he wishes."

"George," she groaned.

"Will it suffice to say that I am very happy you have come into Mr. Lahti's life?"

"I suppose it'll have to."

He smiled and touched her shoulder. "You must have patience."

"That's what Uncle Jules keeps saying."

"Ah, Uncle Jules! Could I meet that fine man?"

"He'd love it. You're two of a kind," she said, and led him back up the path to the school complex.

Much later, after George had left, Laurian went into Jules's office and dropped into a chair.

He was sitting behind his desk, a beatific smile on his face, as if he were hatching plans. "Well, my dear," he said. "Such a surprise that you visit me. I've seen so little of you lately."

"Busy, busy," she said blithely. "What did you and George Miller have to talk about?"

"Oh, about music, memories, the camp, you, the state of the world, and Keska Lahti."

"The concert?"

"The concert did come up in passing."

"Uncle Jules, don't badger Keska about playing at the concert. Please."

"It must be very difficult for a man of Keska's nature to give up the world of music that has been his life. He must miss the gratification of recognition, the joy of extending his gift to an audience, the roar of applause and bravos."

"I'm warning you, Uncle Jules. Don't interfere."

"Ah, so. Sometimes the old are impatient also. For us there is so little time left."

"What do you mean?"

"I've been thinking about my retirement. The pressures and the furor of this camp have begun to wear me down. This summer will be my last, I think, as director."

"Oh, Uncle Jules, you can't retire," Laurian cried. Pulling herself up in the chair, she leaned forward anxiously. "Nothing would be the same without you."

"I'll be available, of course, in a consulting capacity. But someone else must take over the burdens." He rested his elbows on the desk and raised his eyebrows. "Can I count on you to take over the camp when the time comes?"

Laurian had always known Jules meant her to take over the camp. She loved Camp Bryant almost as much as he did, and she owed a great deal to this loving man who had rescued her after Andrew. But now her shoulders slumped as she wondered how this development would fit into the life with Keska that seemed to be opening up for her.

"From your frown I assume you are not entirely thrilled by my offer," Jules said softly.

"I am," she began hesitantly. "But Camp Bryant simply won't be the same without you at the helm."

"I've trained you well, my dear. You can take command most capably."

"It's just that it's so sudden. I have to get used to the idea." Laurian got up and walked to the door. She looked back and smiled a worried little smile.

"It was just a thought, so don't let it trouble you," he said. Then he snapped his fingers as he remembered something. "By the way, the young flautist is arriving at the San Francisco Airport tomorrow afternoon. Would you have time to pick her up?"

"Of course," she said. "I'd love to. You can count on me."

But could Uncle Jules count on her? Laurian wondered as she left the office and climbed the stairs to her room. Camp Bryant took a great deal of time and effort to run. There were heavy obligations even in the winter season: organizational burdens, financial worries always, and upkeep.

Laurian stood before her window, looking down at the exuberant students running around the grounds, and wondered how she could fit Bryant Music Camp in with her blossoming love for Keska.

Nine

Laurian stood beside Keska in the waiting area of Gate 83 in the United Airlines concourse of the San Francisco Airport. The inbound 747 edged in so close to the second-floor window that they and the pilots were almost eye-to-eye. When the ramp swung into place against the side of the airplane, they moved to a spot where they could watch the stream of disembarking passengers.

"What is this flautist's name again?" Keska asked. "And how are we supposed to recognize her?"

"Her name is Patrice Hammond. She's thirteen, red-haired, and she'll be carrying a flute case. I don't imagine there'll be many people on the plane answering that description."

There weren't. Only one. Her red hair turned to fire under the lights and her complexion was flawless. Just clearing five feet in height, she had a body that was somewhere midpoint between coltish childhood and elegant womanhood. She was carrying a leather flute case.

Laurian stepped forward and said, "Patrice? I'm Laurian Bryant and I'm so happy you could come." They moved out of the pressing crowd to stand off to the side. "Did you have a nice trip?"

The girl gave Laurian a brilliant, nervous smile and said in a voice that came in little self-conscious, adolescent spurts, "Oh, I just can't *believe* I'm here! I've never *been* on an airplane before. So I just *loved* it. I mean, *totally*." She dragged out the *totally* for full emphasis.

Her jittery, skittish excitement was contagious and Laurian grinned in response. "I'm glad," she said, "and we're so pleased you're here. You don't know how badly we needed a flautist." She put her hand on Keska's arm. "Patrice, this is Keska Lahti. He came along to keep us company."

Keska put his hand out and Patrice put hers in it. "I'm delighted to meet you," he said in his mellow accent, and brushed her fingers with his lips.

Patrice jerked her hand away and stared up at him with her mouth propped open. Her body was tense and breathless in a yellow T-shirt and tight jeans. Suddenly a couple of stars blinked on in her wide hazel eyes. "Keska Lahti, the *violinist*?" she exclaimed.

"I'm afraid so," he admitted, his lips twitching.

The stars turned to adoration as she stared wide-eyed at him. Her knees seemed to go weak. "But I just *love* a violinist! I mean, I freak out over violinists. Really. I mean, *totally*."

"In that case," Keska said with a smile, "you ought to be very happy at Camp Bryant. Because I have a feeling we can scrape up a violinist for you. Our violinists come in every variety."

"Oh, *you*!" Patrice exclaimed, and gave an embarrassed, though interested, giggle.

Laurian glanced at Keska as she led the way down the concourse. His lips were compressed and she knew he was fighting not to laugh. She nudged his arm and leaned close. "Oh, you! Your nose is pinched again."

He turned his back just before the laugh broke loose. Then he hurried to catch up to Laurian as she stepped on the moving walkway behind Patrice. "Poor Roger," he murmured. "He hasn't got a chance . . . I mean, totally."

It was almost seven in the evening when they arrived at Camp Bryant. Laurian settled Patrice in one of the student residences, a chalet set close to the river with a few redwoods behind it. The building was deserted.

"Everyone is at a bonfire tonight, having a party," Laurian explained. "That's where your roommate, Sandy, is. I think you'll like her. She plays an oboe, so you'll go to classes together. I'll take you to the bonfire now, if you'd like."

"Neat," Patrice said, and they walked downstairs to rejoin Keska.

As they passed Laurian's building, they heard the sound of string music. "That's Roger," Keska said, stopping them. "Why isn't he at the party?"

"Roger?" Patrice questioned, turning toward the sound with alert interest.

"Yes, indeed—Roger," Keska said helpfully. "A violinist. Fourteen-years-old, reasonably good-looking, and very gifted."

"Keska!" Laurian poked him in the side with her elbow and whispered, "Poor Roger."

Stars blinked on in Patrice's eyes again as she stared toward the building and cocked her head to listen to the boy's impassioned music.

"Why don't we go see what our young violinist is doing in there all by himself?" Keska said, disregarding Laurian when she rolled her eyes up in futility.

When they walked into the huge practice room, Roger was standing near the front playing one of his own rebellious, agonized compositions. His brown hair was a mass of tumbled curls. He was wearing wrinkled shorts and a pair of disproportionately large running shoes. His T-shirt had been torn off at the stomach to show off a wiry young body. He lowered his violin at the interruption, a brooding, annoyed expression darkening his face.

The minute Patrice looked at the gangling boy, a subtle change came about in her body, a rounding out and softening. Walking slowly toward the front of the room, she gazed raptly into Roger's temperamental face, the stellar flashing of her eyes almost florescent.

A blank, astonished look washed away Roger's irritation when the red-headed girl stopped a few feet in front of him, her eyes bathing him in flaring sparkles.

Laurian stood behind the girl and said, "Roger, this is Patrice Hammond, our new flautist. She just got here."

"My *special* friends call me Patty," the girl said with a voice like satin, her lashes fluttering down and up again.

Roger threw a pleading, trapped look at Keska. His mouth opened, but no words came out.

"What were you playing?" Patrice-Patty asked. "I've never heard it before, but I just *loved* it. I mean, the *power*. It freaked me out." She reached out and touched his violin with one reverent fingertip. "I just *love* violinists."

Roger's eyes went completely vacant, and his Adam's apple bobbed when he swallowed convulsively. With considerable effort he managed to say, "It was . . . just something I wrote."

Patty gasped, the astral flash of her eyes blinking off and on again as her lashes lowered and rose. "You *wrote* it! But it was *marvelous*!"

Some sort of magic began to work within Roger. His eyes came back to life with a fatuous blue flame. His body seemed to stretch taller, so that he towered at least two inches over the girl who was gazing at him with enraptured eyes. "Oh, well," he said modestly in his changeable voice. "It was nothing—just something I threw down on paper."

"It was totally wonderful." Patty leaned forward and stared into his face. "Oh! You're growing a *mustache*! I adore mustaches."

The blue light in his eyes bathed Patty's face as he stretched his tongue up over his lip in a bemused exploration.

By squinting, Laurian could just make out a vague shadow over Roger's upper lip. But it was obvious he hadn't even noticed it before.

When she glanced at Keska, she could see his nostrils were pinched and white. He had his hand clapped over his mouth and every one of his laugh wrinkles had deepened. "*Sadist!*" she hissed at him.

Then she said aloud, "Roger, we were on our way to take Patty to the bonfire so she can meet everyone. Do you want to come?"

He nodded vigorously and put his violin in its case, giving it a pat of gratitude and affection as he glanced at Patty. Shrugging at Keska and Laurian, he said hopefully, "You guys don't have to come. We can find our way."

Then he walked across the room beside the adoring, red-haired girl. Opening the door with a sweeping flourish, he murmured as she passed through, "Roger Oliver will take care of you . . . Pretty Patty." Then he quickly closed the door between himself and the adults.

Laurian stood with her arms crossed over her chest, scowling fiercely at Keska when he collapsed onto a chair and burst into laughter. "That was a horrible thing to do to that poor shy boy!" she said when he appeared to be regaining some kind of control.

"Pretty Patty is just what Roger needed. You wait. Roger's temperament and personality will stabilize after she has blinked her lashes at him a few times," he said, then burst out in laughter again.

"That girl is going to twist him right around her little finger. You ought to be ashamed instead of sitting there laughing like an idiot. How could you have done something like that when Roger looks up to you as a kind of father figure? Did you hear what he said? He's even patterning himself after you." She snorted. " 'Roger Oliver will take care of Pretty Patty!' Good Lord!"

Keska took a long shuddering breath to put a brake on his amusement. He wiped his eyes on the backs of his hands. "Do I really sound that pompous and affected?"

Now Laurian laughed. "Totally pompous and affected," she answered, her dark eyes flashing. "I mean, it freaks me out. I adore it . . . totally."

"Like, *totally*?" he asked in his musical accent, grinning as he reached his hand out to her.

Laurian sat on Keska's knees and put her arms around his neck. His eyes turned to melted silver as he brushed her lips with his. "Do you want to go to the bonfire?" he asked softly. "Everyone must be there—I don't hear anyone in this building. I think it's possible we have it all to ourselves."

She cocked her head and listened. "I believe you're right. And I think I could miss the bonfire without a qualm. I've got a better idea. There's a bottle of blackberry wine up in my room. It has a fine bouquet, as you would so aptly put it. Would you like to come up and sample it with me?"

His hands were busy in her coils of hair. "Keska Lahti is always interested in fine blackberry wine," he whispered when her hair tumbled down over her shoulder in a thick, twisted rope. He unwound it and spread it into a black veil over her breasts. Picking up a strand in his fingers, he kissed it, then held it over his upper lip. "Would it freak you out if I grew a mustache?"

Laurian laughed and shook her head, twitching the tress of hair away. She ran her lips across his mouth from one side to the other, then kissed each of his closed eyes and blew in one of his ears. "It'd take you too long to grow a mustache. I'm already freaked out and I don't want to wait."

Keska buried his face in the silky, perfumed mass of hair. His lips were on her neck and his hands were caressing the firm, round shape of the breasts pressing against her blouse. Then with a delicious shiver, he stood up, holding her close against his body. "Let's go see about your blackberry wine, my lovely Laurian," he said in a husky, musical voice.

Kissing on each step, they made their slow way up the stairs, through the deserted building, into her room, and closed the door securely after them. Chintz-covered furniture surrounded them, and a dim light left on in the corner lit their intent faces. A large brass bed with a blue spread stood waiting.

Keska took Laurian into his arms and captured her lips, possessing them. He explored the now familiar territory of her mouth with the finesse of a lover who knows intimately and exactly how to please his woman.

Her body instantly exploded into sensual life as she pressed herself against the muscular tension of his slim aroused form. The faint lavender smell of her room receded, overwhelmed by Keska's delectable scent of lime and male musk.

Laurian's nipples sprang to rigid life at his caressing touch; her lips softened and throbbed. A desperate, eager ache began low in her pelvis; it was brought to a peak of urgency by his stroking hands. When she pushed off his sport jacket and ran her hands over the hard, sleek shape of his back and shoulders, her muscles and bones dissolved into swelling desire.

"Do you still want to have the wine?" Keska asked, breathing heavily. His fingers were working at her soft, lacy white blouse. When he had slipped the garment off her arms, he bent his head to touch his tongue to the valley between her breasts.

"What wine?" Laurian gasped as he unzipped and pushed her skirt down over the filmy silk of her panties.

The low light reflected a dim golden glow on his tanned skin after she had slipped off his shirt. Brown curling hair formed a Y on his chest, the arms extending from nipple to nipple, the tail disappearing into his trousers. Burying her face in that tantalizing mat, she reached down and undid his pants. When he pushed them down and kicked off his shoes, she eagerly fondled the prize at the bottom of the Y.

"Oh, my sweet Laurian," Keska moaned against her thick black hair when her hands held and cradled him. His lips moved over her eyelids, down her neck as his fingers ignited fire after he had slipped off her panties. Then his lips moved down over her breasts. He knelt before her and teased her to a fever pitch with the probing of his tongue.

He rose to his feet and lifted her into his arms to lay her on the bed. He lowered his body to cover hers and moved against her, using each muscle, every curve and plane of his body as a stimulating, tormenting caress. "Love me, my sweet, my Laurian," he gasped against her neck.

Laurian took him into her body and held him tightly with her arms. She brought him to a raging passion that matched hers as they moved together in perfect tempo. They reached a climax that was a tumultuous end to a soaring, ecstatic symphony.

When the delicious fury faded, Keska lifted himself away and took Laurian into his warm, moist arms. Burying his face in the mantle of hair that lay tumbled over the pillow, he held her as if she might fade away from him, as if she were a dream that he wouldn't be able to hold. His soft, tender Finnish words caressed her neck and shoulder.

She didn't need to ask the meaning of his words and echoed them in English. "I love you, too, my darling, my Keska. So very, very much."

He lay beside her silently for a moment, then she felt a

spasm of laughter jerk through his chest and stomach. "Totally?" he asked. "Do you love Keska Lahti totally?"

"I'm freaked out."

"Then we had better have your wine in celebration."

"It isn't blackberry," she said. "It's a good Napa Valley rosé."

His cheeks creased when he grinned. "I must admit I'm relieved. Perhaps this fall Keska Lahti will have better luck with the uncooperative blackberries."

Laurian laughed and got up. Her waist-length hair fell around her in lieu of a robe as she took the wine bottle out of her tiny snack-size refrigerator. She poured the mellow pink rosé into two stemmed glasses, then climbed back into bed and snuggled down next to Keska.

They sat braced against the headboard, naked and happy, cuddling together as they sipped wine and shared kisses.

Laurian watched Keska's face, forever fascinated by his mercurial expressions, by the artistic slant of his eyebrows. The color of his pewter eyes was set off dramatically by his black lashes. She touched the sensitive curve of his lips.

Then she glanced meditatively at the slim, tanned violinist's fingers around his glass and asked with curiosity and concern, "Are you still happy being just an apple farmer, Keska?"

His eyes darkened and the lines across his forehead deepened. He didn't answer for several seconds, and when he did, he hedged her question. "Just hold me, my sweet Laurian. Don't ask difficult questions at a warm time like this . . . just hold Keska Lahti."

Setting her glass down on the bedside table, Laurian wrapped both arms around him and pressed her face into his strong shoulder. They lay silently for a few moments, and then she whispered against his ear, "I haven't seen our apple for a few days, Keska. Is it doing well?" Is our love growing and maturing? was her true question.

"The apple is most beautiful. You must come see that it is developing color. Soon it will be ripe," he answered with a tender smile. His fingers threaded into her hair, spreading it smoothly across his chest.

Laurian stopped his hand, lacing her fingers through his. "If our love is maturing, then you can tell me if you miss performing on the violin, Keska. I love you and care about you. You don't need to hide your feelings from me."

He looked down into her intense dark eyes. "I miss playing the violin in concert very, very much, my Laurian," he said in an exhausted voice. "When I'm not performing, I feel I'm lost in an alien world. It is as if a part of me is dead."

Tightening her arms around him, she whispered, "If you feel that way, then why did you give it up, Keska? Help me understand."

"I told you before that I had to learn to know myself. I had become a very lonely man, isolated in my world of the violin and music and never-ending performances."

"Have you found happiness and fulfillment in your apple orchard?" she asked dubiously.

"I found you, my sweet, my lovely Laurian." He lifted her hand to his lips.

"Am I enough, Keska?"

"You are everything, my love."

His hand was gentle as it caressed her face and hair. But his sigh was deep and troubled.

On the next Thursday afternoon Keska and Laurian were sitting in the camp auditorium watching the student orchestra settle into their seats to rehearse. Uncle Jules stood behind the podium like a jolly gnome, rapping for order.

As the exuberant group began to settle down, Laurian leaned over and whispered to Keska, "I wonder if Pretty Patty can actually play the flute? It seems impossible that a talented musician might be lurking under that frivolous exterior."

He grinned. "I doubt it will make any difference whether she can play or not. She'll carry the orchestra by simply batting her eyelashes."

"Chauvinist!" Laurian snorted.

"Look at Roger," Keska said by way of explanation, and nodded toward the stage.

"Good Lord," she exclaimed, "his hair is combed. And his face almost looks pleasant."

"A miracle, no?"

"A miracle, yes!"

The large group of youngsters grudgingly came to attention and lifted their instruments. Jules's baton hung motionless in the air for a few seconds, then swept down in a signal to begin. The opening strains of Vivaldi's "Autumn—Allegro" from *The Four Seasons* ran through the large, empty room. Every student played at the proper pitch and in the correct tempo.

As the piece progressed Keska became increasingly restless. He crossed his legs, uncrossed them, then stretched them out. He folded his arms over his chest, then clasped his hands behind his head. He slumped in his seat, then leaned forward. Finally he folded his hands in his lap and stared moodily at his clasped fingers.

Laurian watched him defensively. He seemed pained by the performance of the orchestra, but to her ear the students seemed to be playing quite beautifully. With a notion of feeling him out for his opinion, she said, "Patty's flute sounds almost ethereal, doesn't it?"

But Keska's answering nod was distracted at best, so she leaned back in her seat to listen more closely, trying to hear what it was in the sound of the orchestra that bothered him.

The session ended, and they watched the youngsters crowd out of the auditorium. When they had all gone, Laurian turned to Keska. "What do you think of the orchestra now? Will they do all right?" The students had sounded almost perfect to her.

Keska pulled himself up straight in the auditorium seat. "They are excellent. Remarkably good. They could play the concert tomorrow, if needed."

Laurian opened her mouth to respond, then closed it thoughtfully. She glanced at him from the corners of her eyes. So it was the concert itself that was bothering him. Could it be possible he was coming to a crisis in his self-evaluation? she wondered sympathetically.

"Come to my farm," Keska invited after a few minutes of silence. There was a tense undertone in his voice. "Come see the marvelous color developing on our apple."

They walked through the orchard under boughs heavy with apples. Now that June had come to a close, the fruit had begun to take on a mellow golden color, the gold overlaid with scarlet striping in the distinctive pattern of the Gravenstein apple.

A few apples had fallen to the ground under the trees, jewels on the tilled brown soil. Bees and fruitflies danced around the decomposing fallen apples. The earth and the air smelled of hot, ripening summer.

The brook was almost dry, with only a trickle of water creeping between the rocks. Watching it made Laurian feel melancholy and restless.

She and Keska stood under their special tree. He pulled down the branch holding the apple, their apple, and touched it. "You see, it is much larger than the others. It hangs in a place of privilege and flourishes."

Laurian's melancholy faded away as she stood in the circle of his arm, admiring the apple, the symbol of their love. It had a much more glowing yellow base than the other fruit, and much brighter red stripes. It was, in fact, a thing of perfection.

"Look at those two stripes," she said, tracing them with her finger. "They've grown around each other as if they were hugging."

"Of course," Keska said, sounding pleased. "Who would have expected less? Our apple is unique."

"You are unique," Laurian said, laughing softly with affection. "What will you do with this wonderful apple when it's ripe? I hope it isn't going to market with the others. I'd hate to think of anyone making applesauce out of *our* apple." She smiled up at him, teasing.

"Don't talk sacrilege!" Keska exclaimed. "Of course not. I think I may have it bronzed and keep it forever in memory of this matchless summer, and of the love we have shared."

First he brushed the back of her neck with his lips. Then he stepped away from her and let the branch swing back into position.

Laurian stared up at the apple that hung trembling on its stem, just out of her reach. She tried not to dwell on the fact that Keska had spoken of their love in the past tense.

They walked slowly through the orchard with no particular destination in mind. After a time Laurian looked up at Keska. "Did you love your wife awfully much?" she asked. She needed to know what had happened so she could understand his motives for living this simple country life he had chosen.

"Helvi?" he said heavily, his eyes metallic and troubled. "Did I love her?" He walked on in silence for a few minutes, frowning at the ground. Then he looked up at Laurian. "I must have cared for her. She is a beautiful and warm woman. I see her when I visit Finland. She has married again, so now we are friends. But did I love her?" He shrugged in lieu of an answer.

Laurian stared at him. He seemed so troubled, it made her feel chilled and frightened inside. Perhaps he still wished for Helvi. "I'm sorry. It's none of my business and I shouldn't have asked."

Keska stopped and looked intensely at Laurian. "Of course, it is your business. You should know what kind of a man Keska Lahti is." His accent had intensified with emotion.

Taking her hand, he began walking slowly between the rows of fruit-laden trees again. "When I belonged to the world as a performing violinist, there was no time for such things as love and close, rewarding relationships. I traveled here, there, giving myself to the people who admired me and who wished to hear my music."

He paused and glanced at her with a slight frown to be sure she understood. "It may have been hectic, but it also was very exciting. I enjoyed my performing life very much."

Laurian nodded and pressed his hand. "I understand how it is. I've heard applause a time or two in my life also."

"My success was very thrilling and euphoric, but I found myself lonely even when the audience cried out for me and applauded."

"So you married Helvi?"

"I married Helvi. I met her when I was on holiday in Finland. She is a lovely person who could have made a good wife to any man." He shrugged again. "But she knew nothing of music or performing. It was difficult for her to understand my underlying drive to give my music to the world. Helvi wished to be a good wife, but I was so seldom there to tend."

"Were you her only interest?"

"I uprooted her from her home, her family, and her friends to bring her here to the United States. And then I left her alone while I traveled with my violin for company. Occasionally I would have a day, sometimes even a week, of freedom so I could go home to her."

Keska walked silently for a few moments, kicking at clods of dry earth. "We were very polite to each other, Helvi and I. We went through the motions of marriage. We even had the child—" His voice wavered, then he went on. "The baby girl—fitting in her conception between performances."

Laurian pulled him to a stop and put her arms around him.

Keska looked down into her eyes. "I wasn't present at the birth of our baby—I had a concert in Chicago. I wasn't present at her death—I was performing in New York City."

"I'm so sorry, Keska."

He didn't seem to hear. "After we lost the baby, I couldn't be with Helvi because I had commitments. So she divorced me and returned to Finland."

Laurian tightened her arms around him and he touched her cheek with the fingertips of one hand. "Why did I cease performing? I did it to find out what was lacking in me . . . why I should have allowed such a thing to happen."

"Believe me, Keska. There is absolutely nothing lacking in you," Laurian said intensely. "You are a wonderful, loving, sensitive man. I wonder if the lack of understanding wasn't on the other side of your marriage." She looked up into his troubled eyes and asked slowly, "Did you quit performing to punish yourself, Keska?"

"Perhaps," he said in a low voice. "But mostly to

search for some insight into my life. You asked, Did I love Helvi? God help me, I don't know. I didn't even know her . . . what she was like inside as a person . . . what her hopes and dreams were. I let all that slip past me in my preoccupation with the violin."

Laurian held him fiercely against her body, tears running down her cheeks. "Oh, my darling," she said, then her voice caught and she couldn't go on. There were so many things that needed to be said between them, but this wasn't the time. But at least they had reached a beginning of understanding.

With a low groan Keska wrapped his arms around her and held her so tightly, it took her breath away. He buried his face in her shoulder. "And that is why Keska Lahti is an apple farmer. So that I can be free to love you, my lovely Laurian. I would never, never subject you to being the wife of a performing violinist. If I should happen to take up the violin again, I would set you free."

"Oh, no, you wouldn't—"

"Shhh." He jerked his head up and stopped her with a finger pressed on her lips. "You don't know what you are saying."

Laurian held him and stared up into the trees, looking at the apples hanging in golden, rosy glory above their heads. She knew in her heart that this simple life was not enough to hold Keska Lahti forever. And when the time came, Keska would have to come to a much better understanding of what she expected from a marriage.

Ten

Next morning at seven Laurian joined Keska in the practice room as had become their habit. The thrill of listening to his violin enriched her life. They always began the practice period with a duet in a lover's pattern of nostalgia. His forcing her to respect and feel comfortable with her own talents had broadened her personality.

Playing her cello to accompany Keska's violin had become for Laurian a fulfilling emotional experience. She knew he felt the same. It was a daily interlude of sharing and accepting each other that welded them firmly together.

But on this particular morning the restlessness that had been growing in Keska was more evident than usual.

After he had played a sour note, he jumped up in disgust and clapped his violin and bow down on the table. His face was flushed and he seemed irritated. He kicked his chair and it toppled, crashing to the floor. Breathing heavily, his body stiff under his knit shirt, he gave the hapless chair another kick for good measure.

Startled by the outburst, Laurian stared at him. She pushed her cello forward and leaned on it. "Do you feel better now?" she asked.

"No, I don't feel better," he answered sheepishly, and picked up the chair, settling it on its legs. Then he sat down and took up his violin.

"What's wrong, Keska?" she asked. "What's bothering you?"

He sighed deeply, then smiled at her. "Nothing is

129

wrong." Lifting his bow, he began the music at the note he had misplayed.

Laurian positioned her cello and eased herself into the duet. After they had finished the composition, Keska practiced alone. His violin communicated an emotion that was close to intense desperation. The music swept around Laurian with a poignant longing that seemed to pull tears up from the very core of her being, from her soul. She studied his face, anxious over the inward torment she read in his features.

Later that afternoon, when the day's classes were over, Keska drove Laurian to his apple orchard. His restlessness had increased and he handled his car with abandon, speeding over the narrow, winding road from the camp.

Laurian breathed a sigh of relief when he parked in front of the big white house on the farm. "You're in a marvelous mood, Keska," she said. "What on earth is the matter with you?"

Lifting his shoulders in a high shrug, he helped her out of the car, then smiled apologetically. "I don't know what is the matter with me, my lovely Laurian. Autumn is coming. Perhaps the seasonal change has disturbed Keska Lahti's internal clocks."

"Internal clocks! Who do you think you're trying to fool," she scoffed, half trotting as he pulled her by the hand into the apple orchard. The subject was tabled because she could see it was difficult for him to discuss his frustrations.

The heavy, mature fruit swayed in the gentle breeze. Occasionally an apple would drop, rustling the leaves and plopping on the ground. The atmosphere smelled dusty and ripe from the weeds gone to seed in the dry California summer. The air hung sluggish and hot over the orchard. Laurian and Keska walked between the trees and down the wide rows, under a canopy of leaves that in the height of summer had turned to a tough bronzed green.

"Aren't the apples almost ready to harvest?" Laurian asked, studying the scattering of fallen fruit.

Keska stopped and looked up at the branches, his

brow wrinkled. "Yes, they are," he said irritably in something close to a challenge.

"Sorry I asked," she said, and smiled wryly at him.

Grimacing, he reached out to circle her neck with his arm, pulling her cheek against him. "You must forgive Keska Lahti. My disposition lately is unfit for so lovely a woman."

"I wish I knew how to help you with whatever is troubling you," she said softly, putting her arms around him.

"No one can help. Keska Lahti must come to terms with himself," he said, his lips against the smooth skin of her forehead.

"I'd like to try."

"You are the problem, my sweet Laurian."

"I don't want to be, my darling."

"And that is precisely *why* you are a dilemma. You are much too good for me." Keska laughed to end the discussion and took her hand to continue their walk through the trees.

"Do you miss Finland?" she asked softly, hoping to encourage him to discuss his worries. "Tell me what your home country is like."

He looked up at the patches of blue sky between the branches and shrugged fretfully. "Finland is a harsh, beautiful land and it holds many nostalgic memories for me. It is flat, covered with forests and lakes and rivers." He smiled. "Someday I would like very much to show Finland to you, Laurian."

"I'd like that."

"One must struggle very hard in Finland to wrest a living from the land, so perhaps that is what makes us Finns so very stubborn and individualistic." He glanced at Laurian and smiled slightly. "Sometimes I miss my parents and the old friends I left behind."

At the far side of the orchard, they stood under the last apple tree in the row, looking up toward the top of the sun-drenched hill and at blackberry brush that was heavy with glossy deep purple berries.

Laurian turned to Keska. "Do you ever think of moving back to Finland?"

"Of course not," he said, shuffling his feet restively,

kicking at a fallen apple. "This is my country now—the United States. I am a naturalized citizen," he said impatiently. "California is my state." He looked back at the orchard with a fidgety expression. "This is my apple farm. I am happy here." He said the last defiantly.

Meeting his flashing gray eyes, Laurian said, "Then if you're so happy, what *is* the matter with you? You're acting as if one of your internal clocks had its spring wound too tight."

Keska stood silently, scowling into the distance. She could see the explosion building long before the eruption. His nostrils became pinched and white. His brows were pulled down. His face turned pink, then flushed. His body was pulled up straight and tense, chest expanding, muscles contracting.

He suddenly gulped in a deep breath and shouted, "*But I am so bored!*" The *bored* echoed, rolling over the hills and back with a rippling, haunting, " *'ored . . . 'ored . . . 'ored.*" Then, with a theatrically dramatic gesture, Keska flung out his arms to demonstrate fully the broad scope of his boredom.

One of his wrists hit the tree, jarring it. Laurian hunched her shoulders and covered her head with her arms. The apples shaken loose by the jolt rained down around them, thudding and thumping on the ground.

When the shower was over, she cautiously looked out from under her arms, then cried in alarm, "Keska! You're hurt!"

His face was a mask of pain as he bent forward, holding his right hand and wrist—his bow hand. He had it pressed against his thigh, clutching it tightly with his left hand.

"Oh, God, Keska," Laurian said anxiously, running forward. "You haven't broken your wrist, have you?"

Gently lifting his left hand away, she looked at his injured right hand. The knuckles were skinned and bleeding. But more ominous was an angry patch of red swelling that had begun puffing up where his wrist joined his hand. "Is it awfully painful?" she asked rhetorically, considering the expression on his face.

"Not so bad," Keska said bravely, straightening up and lifting his arm up so he could look at the battered hand. "I don't think any bones are fractured." He wiggled his fingers cautiously.

"Don't move it!" she exclaimed. "For God's sake hold it still. Don't move a muscle in your hand until it's been X-rayed and a doctor checks it."

The same thought was written on Keska's face that Laurian had in her mind—of how vulnerable a musician was. Keska's entire professional life depended upon the supple pliancy of his hands and wrists. His eyes were veiled and darkened, hiding his apprehension as he stared at his swollen wrist.

Taking charge, Laurian bent his left arm to cradle the right wrist, pressing both of his arms tightly against his chest so the injured hand would be held as high as possible. "Keep it like that," she ordered. "Don't move it. Let's get back to the house."

As they set off across the orchard Keska gave a brittle, negligent laugh. "It's only a bruise, Laurian," he said in an attempt to play down the seriousness of the accident. "Such a fuss for a little bump." His color had gone pale under his tan, contradicting his unconcerned words. His accent was thicker than Laurian had ever heard it. She knew his wrist and hand were vitally important to him.

"Be quiet," Laurian said, tramping along beside him through the trees, over the lumpy earth. "This is no time to play macho. Little bump or not, we've got to get to the house immediately and call a doctor. And for heaven's sake don't trip and fall on your arm."

When they walked in the front door of the farmhouse, Laurian shouted into the silent, deserted hallway, "*George?* Where are you? Keska has hurt his arm."

George dashed out of a first-floor room instantly in his shirtsleeves and with his vest unbuttoned. For once his controlled demeanor was shaken. "Good Lord! This is terrible. What happened?" he demanded, grasping Keska's elbow, carefully supporting the wrist. He stared with horror at the blood and the swelling.

"He hit it on a tree," Laurian explained. "I'll put cold compresses on it. You call the doctor."

"All this commotion over a simple bruise," Keska said,

white-faced, his voice slightly tremulous. "Let's look at it first. If it isn't broken, I shouldn't need a doctor."

Anger pulled George's face up tight and his color rose. "Keska!" he said furiously. "Don't make me lose patience. I've put up with enough from you over this last year and a half. Now don't act like a nincompoop!" He glared for a second, then walked rapidly down the hall toward the telephone.

Keska stared after him with startled eyes, then turned to Laurian. "I think I had *better* worry," he said. "That is the first time George has ever called me Keska."

After almost three hours Laurian and Keska came out of the emergency room of the hospital in Santa Rosa. As she hovered over him, he climbed into the passenger seat of his car. "All this fuss over a simple bruise," he complained.

Laurian got into the driver's seat and glanced at Keska. His lips were twitching, and she guessed he wasn't so much impatient over all the attention as he was sheepishly enjoying it. His attitude annoyed her in an irrational way, and she began shaking with a postaccident reaction.

"I agree with George—don't act like a nincompoop," she snapped as she turned the key in the ignition and started the car with a roar.

Keska settled himself in his seat and examined the thick elastic bandage wrapped around his right wrist. A neat, white hospital dressing covered his skinned knuckles. "X rays, prodding, poking. I felt like some fascinating new biological specimen." He glanced at Laurian. "I told you it was only a bump and a scratch."

The aftershock of her fear and concern began rapidly accelerating into anger. Her lips were compressed and white-rimmed to keep from railing at him. How *could* Keska Lahti, of all people, have been so careless? Driving furiously out of the city, she turned the car onto the highway leading to his farm.

"You don't have to say what you are thinking," Keska said after a few minutes of silence.

"I wasn't going to say anything," she said angrily, her eyes glued to the road.

"I know what you are thinking."

She could feel his eyes searching her profile. "I wasn't thinking," she said grimly. "My mind is a blank."

"You're thinking Keska Lahti should know better than to throw his valuable hands around."

"You said it, not me. They're your hands, so you can treat them any way you want to." Laurian glanced at him, then back at the road.

He was as ripe for an argument as she was; they were both suffering shock reactions over the close brush with disaster. After a minute she added pointedly, "If you're bound to be an apple farmer, you have to expect these sort of accidents."

Keska poked at the thick elastic bandage with an annoyed finger. "I'm tired of being saddled with hands that are insured for millions of dollars."

"Then trade them in on a new pair," Laurian said angrily. After a moment she softened and apologized. "I'm sorry, Keska. I shouldn't have snapped at you. But it's just that you scared me so when I saw your hand all swollen and bleeding. I'm still shaking."

Reaching out, he touched her cheek. "I am the one who must apologize, my lovely Laurian. Keska Lahti was upset and worried also—I admit it." He grimaced with annoyance at himself. "I started the day feeling restless and irritable, and the accident hasn't caused my disposition to improve."

Laurian squeezed his hand and glanced at him, then returned her attention to her driving. After a few seconds she said softly, "I know why you're restless. We both know what your problem is, Keska. Why don't you face it? Unless you do, you really might fracture one of your arms out of sheer frustration."

"I don't know what you are talking about," he said stubbornly.

"Oh, yes, you do, Keska Lahti. You want to play again for an audience. You can't bear being away from what you were born to do—to perform on your violin."

The car motor sounded unnaturally loud in the brief hesitation that followed. "You don't know what you are asking, my sweet Laurian," he said finally in a taut voice.

"Why don't you stop torturing yourself?" she said, glancing at his troubled face. "Admit it. Your greatest desire is to be on stage again, sharing your talent and your violin with an audience."

His body seemed to tense in the bucket seat next to her, as if he had to fight to resist her words. "My greatest desire is to be with you, my love," he said miserably.

"You *are* with me, Keska," she exclaimed. "But you also want so very badly to play your violin at the students' concert next month. Don't you?"

There was no answer. Laurian turned the car into the driveway and drove up to the house. After she had parked and shut the motor off, she turned to Keska. "Why don't you just admit you want to play the benefit concert with the students? You want to be on the stage with them. You know you want it more than anything in the world."

"You are wrong." He put out both hands, pressing his left palm and the fingertips of his injured right hand against Laurian's cheeks. "My only wish is to make you happy. That is what I want more than anything else in the world, my sweet, lovely Laurian."

"Then make me happy," she pleaded. "Fulfill yourself."

The pewter color of his eyes darkened with indecision. "Would it make you happy if I played at the benefit concert?"

For a moment her breath stopped. Then she drew it in very softly and said, "It would make me happy, Keska, my darling. Because I know it would make you happy, and I'm happy when you're happy."

After a second Keska's body relaxed and loosened as if he had shaken free from a suffocating prison he had been caught in. "In the face of so many happy's—how can Keska Lahti refuse?" He smiled uncertainly. "I will play my violin at the Camp Bryant benefit concert."

"Oh, Keska," Laurian exclaimed, and put both her hands over his.

"*But,*" he interrupted. "But! I will play only the benefit concert. Just that one. Keska Lahti will do that one concert only. I am still an apple farmer, you must understand. And I will not give that up. I will not give you up, my sweet Laurian."

Laurian nodded. It was a beginning, and she was euphorically pleased.

George met them at the door and ushered them into the hallway. He had resumed his unflustered dignity, now that his vest was buttoned and his suit coat was on. "The verdict was?" he asked with concern.

"A bruise only," Keska said, waving the concern away with his left hand. "In a week I shall go back to have the bandages removed and to receive a clean bill of health." He stood poised in the hallway, looking restless and edgy.

"How fortunate." George sighed in relief.

"I wish I could stay and celebrate," Laurian said, "but I've got to go back to camp. There's a jam session tonight and I have to be there." She raised her eyebrows at Keska. "Will you be all right?"

"You mustn't worry," he said as he hugged her with his good arm and almost nudged her toward the door.

"Will you drive me home, George?" she asked.

"It will be my pleasure, madam."

"Sit down—or better yet, lie down and put your arm up on pillows. Don't let it hang down," she said to Keska. He stopped her words with his lips. "Ice packs, remember?" she said around his kiss.

"I remember," he agreed impatiently. "Go worry about your jam session before you make an invalid of Keska Lahti."

There was obviously something terribly important on his mind. Even before Laurian had reached the front door, Keska had disappeared into the sitting room.

George followed her out onto the porch, but they both stopped short just outside the door. Turning back toward the house, they listened to a scale being played on the violin in the music room. It swept up high into a thin, piercingly clear sound, then undulated down to a low, deep moan. The sound died away and was not repeated.

"Keska was a lot more worried than he wanted to let on, wasn't he?" Laurian said.

"Yes," George answered. "His gift is very precious to him."

"I think he was so concerned about the injury that it shocked him back into his senses," she said quietly. "He's agreed to do the benefit concert."

A flash of relief lit George's face. "I'm so very pleased," he said with consummate gratitude.

Suddenly it became a real and tangible fact to Laurian. Keska was taking up his violin again. She felt an overwhelming excitement building inside her. "No matter how he fights against the idea," she said, "music and the violin are the largest and most thrilling parts of Keska's personality. They make him the exceptional, emotional, and vividly alive man he is."

"The fact that you accept him for what he is, madam," George said with one of his warmer smiles, "will cause him to accept himself."

"He hasn't agreed to go any further than the benefit concert," she said, "but I think he will in time. How can he not?"

As Laurian walked toward the car a feather of anxiety as chilly as an arctic breeze ran over her skin. "I hope things don't change too drastically for Keska and me," she said slowly, then laughed away the worry. "But why should anything change for us if—when he decides to go back to performing?"

George merely nodded encouragingly, though his eyes were pinched with private, unspoken worries of his own.

Camp Bryant exploded into enthusiasm upon learning of Keska's decision to play his violin at the concert. The students were thrilled over the drama of the great man—one who had reached heights they could only dream of—making a comeback.

They considered it an honor and a privilege to perform as an orchestra on the same stage with a violinist of Keska's status. Consequently they stepped up their practice, both in groups and in private. The teachers were delighted and took full advantage of the phenomenon.

Keska practiced slavishly, his violin held at a rakish

angle to accommodate his injured right wrist. After a week the bandages were removed, and fortunately he had suffered no permanent damage.

Publicity for the concert and for Keska Lahti's appearance had gone out to all the major newspapers, causing a flurry of excitement to ripple around the world. The concert was immediately a standing-room-only sellout.

The weeks before the concert passed hectically. The problems and the joys were as predictable at Camp Bryant as they were anywhere a large group of exuberant and active youngsters were involved. This group was different from other adolescents only in that they possessed superior musical talent and a dedication to classical music. Other than that they behaved normally, and the usual incidents occurred.

Laurian was kept busy solving a variety of problems. The timpanist in the orchestra, a sixteen-year-old boy, fell off a horse. Luckily he broke his ankle, not his arm, and was able to clump around the stage in a cast. Two of the female cellists got into a fight over a boy, a trumpeter, and they couldn't bear the sight of each other. Their positions in the cello grouping of the orchestra had to be changed to put as much distance as possible between them. Unfortunately the fickle boy almost immediately lost interest in both girls and began romancing a lovely young clarinetist. Then both cellists were heartbroken and wanted their positions changed back so they could commiserate with each other.

As summer accelerated into August and the concert came closer, Keska began to spend all his waking hours at the music camp and became involved in the internal workings of the school.

It pleased him to offer suggestions concerning the orchestral selections and to listen to the young musicians play. Occasionally he personally directed the orchestra quite ably. He spent many extra hours of time encouraging the eager string students, advising them in methodology and technique.

For the concert Keska had chosen a couple of fairly short, complicated violin compositions to play at his cameo appearance. They would demonstrate his abilities, but since they were brief, they wouldn't overwhelm the efforts of the orchestra.

In the evenings, after their work was done, Keska made love to Laurian. An ardent and devoted mate, he touched her with more tenderness and passion than she could have ever dreamed of experiencing.

As the end of the summer season approached, the world seemed a very secure and happy place to Laurian.

On Thursday morning of the third week in August, Laurian smiled at Jules as she sat in his office. "Keska is so excited," she said. "It will have been a year and seven months since he last played on stage for an audience. The prospect of doing the concert on Sunday has him acting like a child at Christmas."

Jules smiled and nodded. "We can feel quite pleased and smug with ourselves for having brought this about, can't we?"

"It's only a beginning," Laurian said. "He still hasn't agreed to go beyond the Camp Bryant concert with his musical return. But I'm confident he will." Frowning slightly, she added, "I don't think anyone can fully appreciate the torture it has been for him to deny himself the life he loves."

"Each of us who is connected in any way with music can sympathize," Jules murmured. "You went through your own brand of insecurity over your abilities, questioning your focus in life. I know you understand him."

"Keska forced me to face my fears. I've become twice the woman I was before I met him. He's quite persuasive." She laughed affectionately. "I'll bet he has a marvelous stage presence. He's a natural actor, besides being a brilliant violinist. A ham, to be exact."

"That he is . . . that he is."

Laurian nodded. "A ham like you."

"A ham! Me? How can you say such a thing about your uncle Jules?" He laughed. "Keska isn't at camp today?"

"No. His precious apples are ripe, and he has someone coming to harvest and send them to market. He'd been putting the harvest off until the orchestra and the concert were under control. Now all that's left to do is keep the students from flying off into nervous flights of fear."

She laughed wryly. "We can handle that, so he decided to take care of his apples."

Jules smiled.

"Keska acts like a doting father with that orchard of his. He'll probably go through empty-nest syndrome when his apples are gone." Her dark eyes softened. "They'll all be gone but one."

Jules raised his eyebrows. "One?"

"You wouldn't understand," she said, grinning as she got up and walked to the door. "It has to do with the birds and the bees, and that sort of thing."

"And Uncle Jules wouldn't understand that sort of thing?" he scoffed. "You think I've been an old man all my life?"

"I'll bet you used to be a corker in the birds-and-bees department," she said, and nodded sagely. "You probably still are. At any rate this is Keska's first harvest, so he's terribly excited about it. Maybe after all the dust settles, he'll have gotten apples out of his system." She opened the door and went out, then popped her head back. "Except one apple."

Eleven

There was a telephone call for Laurian the next afternoon. She took it in Jules's office, fully expecting to hear Keska's exciting, accented voice saying he missed her.

Instead to her surprise, she heard "Good afternoon, madam. This is George Miller."

"George," she said, her fingers tightening on the receiver. Why would George be calling her? He never had before. "Hello. What a surprise to hear your voice."

"I trust I'm not disturbing you? Perhaps you are busy."

"I'm not busy. Is something wrong, George?" Her lips felt numb. "Has something happened to Keska?"

"Oh, no . . . not exactly."

"What do you mean, not exactly? George, has Keska been hurt?"

"Calm yourself, madam. I assure you, he hasn't been injured."

"Well, *what* then?" she demanded.

"It isn't my place to meddle, still . . ." he said tentatively before his voice died away.

"*George!*" she cried. "Will you tell me what's wrong!"

"Could you find a few moments to visit the farm, madam? I suspect Mr. Lahti needs you."

It was pointless to waste time prying an explanation out of him, so she said, "I'll be right there."

"Very good. Good-bye, madam."

Laurian didn't stop to change out of the white shorts and the blue T-shirt she was wearing. She grabbed her purse, tossed back her long thick braid, and ran to her car.

The winding, narrow road between Camp Bryant and Keska's farm had never seemed so long as when Laurian drove the ten miles that afternoon.

George had been watching and met her in the yard. Stiff with worry, Laurian jumped out of her car and demanded instantly, "What's wrong with Keska, George?"

"I'm not sure, madam," he answered, his face wrinkled with lines of concern. "Mr. Lahti hasn't spoken to me since yesterday afternoon, and he gives every appearance of being extremely unhappy. He has been wandering in the orchard most of the time. I don't believe he has eaten any of his meals, and I have no idea when he came in to retire last night. I thought it might be helpful if you could speak to him and perhaps offer comfort?"

"Of course I will. Where is he?" Laurian asked urgently.

"He's still wandering in the orchard. I can't say for certain which direction you should try. You'll have to search for him, I'm afraid."

Laurian turned and ran through the thick, tough hay toward the orchard. The apple trees closed in around her, and she hurried across the rows to first check their special place. When she stood under their tree, her heart dropped heavily in her chest. Keska wasn't there.

The hidden haven that had been so achingly beautiful in the dewiness of spring now looked harsh in late summer. The brook had dried up, and the rocks lay dusty and abandoned in the cracked streambed. The grass and weeds were brown and broken from the summer drought.

Laurian looked up. The apple was hanging on its branch, large and rosy and ripe; their love, she thought, must surely be safe and well. Seeing the apple gave her an irrational feeling of comfort, but it didn't help find Keska.

She began to walk randomly through the rows of trees, across the orchard. Occasionally she would stop to call his name and listen. When there was no answer, her apprehension grew.

A sudden breeze wafted in from the west, cooling the

perspiration on her face. It disturbed the branches on the trees. Several apples shook loose, thudding to the ground.

Laurian stopped, unsure in which direction to walk. Anxiety sat heavily in her stomach. She looked around, peering through the gnarled gray tree trunks.

A carpet of apples lay under each tree—circles of rotting fruit with clouds of fruitflies hovering hungrily in the heat. A pungent, ciderlike smell arose from the fermenting apples.

When she looked closer, Laurian noticed that alongside of the rotten windfalls were several fresh apples that had been sliced in half and thrown down in the aisle between the rows of trees. The open surfaces of white meat were turning brown in the air. She could scarcely believe Keska would have cut up his precious apples in this way. It was a foreboding sign.

As she stared down at them her forehead knitted with uncertainty, Laurian noticed there was something like a trail of bisected apples leading across the orchard. She followed it curiously.

The slashed apples became fresher as she made her way diagonally through the trees. The meat was white and beaded with juice now, so she speeded up her pace. When she had crossed over three more rows between the tall, heavily branched trees, she found Keska.

The picture of total desolation, he was sitting on the ground, his back propped against the trunk of a tree near the far side of the grove. His jeans were dusty, his blue work shirt wrinkled, smeared, and sweaty. With his legs cocked up, he had his elbows resting on his knees and one hand clasped the other wrist. A pocketknife dangled from the free hand. Sunlight dappled through the leaves, gilding his wavy light brown hair and flashing on the steel of the open blade of the knife.

A scattering of dropped fruit lay brown and pungent and rotting all around him. The cider smell rose in waves as Keska looked up at Laurian with eyes that were tragic and disconsolate.

Laurian ran across the aisle separating her row of trees from his. Falling to her bare knees between his heavy work boots, she put her hands comfortingly on his upper arms. "What is it, darling?" she asked softly. "Tell me what's wrong, Keska."

He sighed deeply, dismally. "Codling moths," he answered.

Laurian mulled that over in her mind for a moment or two before she repeated, "Codling moths?"

"Codling moths," he echoed, his eyes dark and sorrowful.

She frowned as she tried to understand. She shifted one bare knee off a sharp clod of dry soil. "What *about* codling moths?"

"Eggs."

Laurian began to seriously suspect Keska had drifted over the far edge. He didn't seem to be playing from a full score. "Eggs?" she inquired dubiously.

He nodded and sighed again.

A fairly long silence elapsed, and then she said, "If this is another bug fable, you'll have to tell me the rest of the tale. I'm not following you."

"No fable, this," Keska said. His accent had thickened with melancholy. "Unfortunately this is a true story. The codling moths lay eggs on apples."

"They lay eggs," she said placatingly, and patted his shoulder.

Keska picked up an apple that had fallen on the ground nearby. Cutting it neatly in half, precisely through the middle with his pocket knife, he held the two juicy surfaces up, only inches in front of Laurian's face.

She stared at them for a second. Then she gasped and pulled back in repugnance. The core of the apple had been eaten away into brown crumbles. The worm who had done the deed waved its head convulsively at her, bewildered by its sudden exposure to fresh air and light.

"*Worms!*" Laurian exclaimed, and grimaced with disgust.

"Worms. Lahti's apple has worms," Keska said with a dejected nod. Throwing the two halves of worthless, infected fruit down on the ground, he propped his elbows on his knees again and braced his chin on one fist. The knife dangled limply from the fingers of his other hand.

The fruit hung so beautifully, red on gold, on the branches above her head. But even as she stared up into the tree, one apple dislodged and plopped to the ground only a few feet from her. A brown spot on the side indicated that a worm had made its exit.

It had never occurred to her that the fallen apples were a symptom of disease. "Surely not *all* the apples," she said in disbelief.

"The experts with whom I meant to arrange harvesting claim a large enough percentage of the apples are infested with worms to render all of them unsalable," Keska answered. "My apples are useless garbage." He closed his knife and slipped it into the pocket of his jeans.

"But, Keska, how could that be? The apples developed so perfectly." Laurian moved closer to him, between his knees, and put her arms around his shoulders. "We've watched them grow."

A deep, deep sigh lifted his chest and dropped it. He lay his head despondently on her shoulder. "Obviously Keska Lahti did not watch them closely enough as they grew. Some chemical or spray was needed that I didn't know about."

Laurian tightened her arms around him, running her hand up his back to smooth the tumbled wave of his light brown hair. "Honey," she said softly, "it isn't the end of the world. There'll be another season for apples. Don't feel so bad, my darling."

Lifting his head, Keska looked into her face. "There will be no other seasons. Keska Lahti knows nothing of apples. It was an absurd notion that I could make a life as a farmer."

"Apples aren't everything, darling," she said soothingly, massaging the tense muscles in his lean back.

Keska's gaze moved very slowly, with aching love, over the heart shape of her face. He looked sadly into her dark eyes. "No," he said in a heavy Finnish accent. "Apples are not all for Keska Lahti. But I had so many hopes. . . ."

They sat silently for a few minutes while Laurian comforted him with her hands and lips. Finally she gave him a gentle little shake. "Why don't you come up to the house with me and sit in your sauna for a while? That'll make you feel better, won't it?"

"Nothing will ever make me feel better again," he said melodramatically, but he allowed her to hold his hands and pull him to his feet.

"You're being silly," she said, lacing her fingers through his as she walked beside him toward the farmhouse. "Next year Keska Lahti's apples will be perfect."

"There will be no apples for Keska Lahti next year, or ever again," he said firmly. "It was stupid of me to think I could change my life."

They walked past the flawed fruit, rotting on the ground. Laurian squeezed Keska's hand and said, "You might not have apples, but you have other things, darling. George, and the camp, and all the people who love you." A slight anxious frown ran across her face. "You have your violin." She glanced up at him. "You have me."

Keska's hand closed tightly, almost painfully around hers, but he didn't answer. His face was a map of conflicting emotions as they walked across the field toward the back of the house.

The small building housing the sauna was heated even through the summer sun was at its hottest. A tendril of smoke curled out of the chimney, drifting down across the bright blue swimming pool to spread the smell of fragrant burning wood over the yard.

In the tiny anteroom of the sauna Laurian pulled off her shorts and T-shirt. She watched Keska strip off his work shirt and jeans, then modestly cover his hips with a towel. Over the summer they had become free and uninhibited with each other, so now the towel puzzled her. It seemed an ominous clue that serious problems were brewing.

Feeling oddly naked and vulnerable after Keska had covered himself, Laurian wrapped a large white towel around herself and preceded him into the fiercely heated inner chamber.

The two benches in the sauna were tiered like a couple

of wide, oversize wooden stairs. Keska sat down on the lower bench and dashed several dippers of water over the hot stones. Steam boiled up furiously, clouding the small room.

Laurian climbed onto the upper bench to lie on her stomach on the hot boards. Steam settled down on her, pressing on her body like a leaden blanket. Bracing an elbow on the bench, she propped her chin on her fist and looked down at Keska. He had stretched his lithe body out on the bench below her. His arm was cocked over his face, positioned in such a way that it hid most of his expression. All she could see was the unhappy twist of his sensitive mouth.

It wasn't difficult to guess why the loss of his apple crop had affected him so acutely. It wasn't the financial loss; he had plenty of money. His frustration stemmed from the fact that Keska Lahti had never experienced failure before—ever. Since he had quit performing all his creative energies and his entire interest had been directed toward managing the apple orchard, and now his well-developed ego couldn't be expected to accept defeat gracefully.

Reaching down, Laurian touched the tanned forearm that was thrown across his face. She caressed him comfortingly, moving her hand slowly down his arm, pressing his slender fingers. "They were just apples, Keska," she said softly. "Don't feel so bad."

His chest lifted in a sigh and she watched the hair-sprinkled muscles rise and fall. "But they were Keska Lahti's apples," he said.

"I know. The nerve of those codling moths and worms to lay one buggy little foot on Lahti's apples. Don't they know who they're dealing with? Whatever happened to respect?" she teased, hoping to raise a smile from him.

His hand closed around hers, and he moved his arm away from his face to look up into her eyes. There wasn't a hint of a smile on his features. "The codling moths and their worms were a sign."

"A sign of what?"

"A sign that the things you said to me after I had

injured my arm were so very true, my sweet Laurian. I'm a violinist. The orchard is not enough."

"Everyone knew that except you, darling," she said.

His eyes were dark and brooding as he looked through the steam swirling about them. "I was born to perform on the violin. I can't be a complete man unless I resume my career, but I wanted so badly to build a different life for us. I pitted all my hopes for happiness with you on the apples I might have grown on this farm. It was an unrealistic wish."

Apprehension sprouted, full-fledged, at his words. "Keska," she said quickly, "we'll find happiness when you take up your violin again. Everything will be different this time."

Bringing the backs of her fingers to his lips, he kissed them lingeringly. "Do you know that Keska Lahti loves you more than life itself? My sweet, my lovely Laurian."

Her muscles tensed, pressing her into the hot boards of the bench. Suddenly the steam seemed oppressively heavy around her body. It formed a thick white barrier between Keska and her. Apprehension escalated into anxiety. "I know you love me, Keska," she said, speaking through the heavy steam that seemed to be pushing them apart. "I love you, too, my darling. You're everything to me."

"If only I could be," he said sadly, and kissed her palm, his lips soft and hot on the slippery film of sauna moisture on her skin. "I wanted us to be together so badly, to be husband and wife. But this catastrophe has wiped away all those wonderful plans."

Placing her hand on the hot boards, Keska lifted himself off the lower bench in one sinewy motion and walked out of the steam chamber.

"Keska!" Laurian cried out in shocked protest, her heart contracting in a jolting, frightened surge. Leaping off the upper bench, she ran out of the sauna after him.

His towel lay in a heap on the colorful tiles, and Keska stood poised at the edge of the Olympic-sized pool. Each muscle was tensed and his slim masculine body was achingly sensual. When he launched himself out over the water, he was a lean, tanned arrow shooting away from Laurian. Water splashed high into the hot summer air, a glittering explosion that sent birds squawking out of the trees at the end of the yard.

Laurian threw her towel down on the tiled apron at the edge of the pool and waded into the shallow end. Her breath caught in shocked gasps as the cool water crept up her body, feeling icy when it touched her steam-boiled skin. The coolness crept up her body until it lapped at the heat and perspiration coating her rib cage.

She hooked her elbow over the tiles at the edge of the pool and watched Keska worriedly. The laps he was swimming were a punishing marathon of frenetic speed as he tried to cope with his crisis and work off his frustration. She bit her lip in alarm. There had to be some way they could work out a life together.

Presently he stopped swimming and paddled over to the edge of the pool. Pulling himself up to sit on the tiles near Laurian, he picked up the towel he had dropped and draped it in front of his glistening nude body. After he had wiped his face, he rubbed his sun-streaked hair into a bright halo.

Laying her hand on his knee, she asked in a choked voice, "Your decision to take up the violin again doesn't necessarily have to affect our relationship, does it? Why do things have to change?"

His hands dropped and he clutched the towel in his lap. "Since it became known that I will play at the Camp Bryant concert, a deluge of requests for performances have come in from all over the world. I have received invitations from the White House, from London, from Vienna, and from all points in between. Since I can't be an apple farmer, I will accept the invitations."

"It doesn't surprise me, Keska," Laurian said. "But you didn't answer my question."

"Keska Lahti and the violin are one. One can't live without the other. I cannot force myself to be what I am not." He looked at her intensely.

"I realize that, Keska. You'd soon become a bitter, frustrated man if you didn't fulfill yourself," she said miserably, leaning toward him in the water. "I understand. A return to performing is what I want for you."

"In your last marriage you were caused great suffering by a husband who was egocentric and engrossed in his performing career. In much the same way I brought misery and unhappiness to my wife." He looked at her with tormented, wistful eyes. "A marriage to me would be dismally lacking for you."

"Keska," she whispered, "maybe it would be different this time—for us?"

"Would you be happy having me absent from your life most of the time?"

Laurian hesitated for a moment, gazing at him yearningly as she imagined what it would be like—the loneliness. From the first his violin had been her reason for knowing him. She had wanted Keska to play the Camp Bryant concert and to return to his performing career. In her stupidity it had never occurred to her that this wish would threaten their happiness.

"I'd hate having you gone," she admitted in a low choked voice, then cried out, "But what about our apple? It grew so beautifully?" Our love?

Keska looked toward the orchard, then back at Laurian. His eyes were as dark and sad as a winter raincloud, filmed with tears. "Our apple is full of worms, my sweet Laurian. I had no right to allow this to happen, to open my heart to your love. I have brought you to this unhappiness."

When the image of an ugly worm eating away the core of their apple rose in her mind, a pain like a vise clamped her chest. "I love you, Keska," she whispered desperately.

He nodded slowly. "And I love you much too much to subject you to the performing life I must follow. I cannot bear to offer you a life of loneliness and unhappiness. It would destroy Keska Lahti to watch you begin to hate me for the life I must lead and for my violin."

Laurian forced her body against the water of the pool. She climbed the steps up to the tiled apron, picked up her towel, and wrapped her petite body from chest to knees. Then she stood over Keska, gazing hopelessly down at him. "I'd never hate you, Keska Lahti. Never."

"Laurian, my sweet, don't," he said, and pulled himself to his feet. Positioning the white towel around his slim hips, he knotted it at the side. "If I could amputate my need to create music and to perform, I would."

She blinked back the tears welling up in her eyes. "If I had been perceptive enough to look ahead, I would have chained you to your miserable apple trees instead of encouraging you to face the truth. Isn't there some way we can make a life, Keska?"

"We have lived a beautiful dream life this summer on my apple farm. The love we shared has been so very important and dear to me," he said, searching her face. "And I will not— I refuse to allow the dream to turn into a nightmare for you."

Taking her hand, he pulled her close to him. He covered her mouth with his, drawing the essense of her into him. Throwing her arms around him, she clutched him to her, hands molding around solid muscles. He pressed his face feverishly into the curve of her neck.

Finally he lifted his head and looked down at her. "My memories of this summer will be a bright treasure to hoard for the rest of my life, lovely Laurian. A treasure to warm me and torment me forever."

Dropping his arms, he gently put her embrace aside and turned away with an effort that took all his strength. His shoulders were bowed and his steps heavy as he walked away from Laurian.

When he had disappeared into the house, she stumbled to the sauna, her eyes blinded with tears. She picked up her scattered clothing and slipped numbly into shorts, T-shirt, and sandals.

When she walked into the house and down the silent hallway, George came to the door of his room. "What is it, madam?" he asked when he saw her ravaged face.

"Where's Keska?" she asked miserably.

"Why, he went to the music room, I believe."

"Oh, George," she whispered. "How am I going to live without him?"

Before she could go on, the sound of Keska's violin filled the house with an anguished wailing. No composer had written his theme. The grief in his music came straight from the depths of his heart.

The throbbing, despairing strains tore at Laurian, shattering her. Very slowly she walked through the sitting room and stopped just outside the tightly closed French doors. The painfully sweet sobbing of the violin enveloped her, tearing her apart.

Laurian listened to the celestial perfection of his music and knew she had been right in pushing him into returning to his performing career. That was where Keska belonged. But she was lost and drowning in the chasm that had opened between them because of it. "Oh, Keska," she whispered against the French doors that closed her away from him. Tears flooded down her face.

The agonized music seemed to become more intense. The plaintive, despairing beauty of the violin strains surrounded Laurian, filled her with aching, pulled her. The love for her that rode on each note inundated her.

But even as it drew her, Keska's violin shoved her away with the strength of a battering ram. Laurian hugged herself and cried in quiet hopelessness as she listened to the grief in his heartbroken outpouring.

After a few minutes George took her arm and drew her away from the French doors, pulling her out into the hallway. He offered a sparkling white handkerchief and awkward, fumbling sympathy. "What has that foolish, infuriating man done now?" he asked.

"Keska isn't foolish, George. He might be driven by a compelling talent, but he's also tender, sensitive, caring, and very, very unahppy," Laurian said in a disconsolate voice. "He's unselfishly doing what he feels best for me."

Turning abruptly, Laurian ran out of the house and climbed into her car. As she drove slowly away the anguished, weeping sound of Keska's violin followed her down the driveway toward the road. The emotion in the music said farewell in a thousand clear, exquisitely agonized notes.

After she had driven a little way down the road, she could no longer hear the violin through her open window. Then her loss became real, and the reality crushed her.

* * *

When Laurian got back to the music camp, she walked into her building on stumbling and grieving feet. Numb and shocked, she closed herself into a room that suddenly seemed a lonely prison cell. Her bond with Keska was broken. That knowledge hung about her shoulders like a crushing yoke.

Music drifted through her open window. The sounds of trumpets and oboes and drums came from separate buildings all around the camp. String music seeped up through the building from below. The students were practicing for the concert.

Laurian wished she had never heard of the concert, that it could be struck from her life. Because of the concert, Keska was going to rocket right out of her life.

Covering her ears to shut out the enthusiastic music, she threw herself down on the bed where she and Keska had once made joyous, passionate love. Burying her head under the pillow, she pressed the muffling feathers over her ears and pinched her eyes tightly shut, trying to shut out the pain.

But a memory popped up to torture her. A picture rose in her mind of the beautiful apple, the product of tender love between a honeybee and a flower. The rosy, golden apple, the symbol of Keska's love, danced elusively in front of her closed eyes. With X-ray vision she could see a sickening, voracious worm eating the center of the apple, destroying the sweet perfect flesh, separating Keska from her.

Laurian wept, spiraling down into despair.

Laurian awoke the next morning, the day before the concert, to sit straight up in bed with her heart leaping like a crazy jumping bean. She listened analytically to the violin music coming up from the room below, then glanced at her watch. The music was quite professional and it was only seven forty-five, so surely it must be Keska practicing.

The sound surprised her because Laurian hadn't expected him to come for his routine practice period after yesterday. Perhaps he had changed his mind; perhaps there was some way they could be together, she thought. Then she shook her head because she knew it was a hopeless wish.

The memory of their impending separation pierced through her heart as keenly as Keska's knife had sliced through the wormy apples. But, despite the pain, the prospect of seeing him sent futile excitement leaping through her breast.

Jumping out of bed, she dashed through her morning preparations and yanked on a pair of yellow cotton pants and a white T-shirt with lace around its low round neck. She brushed her hair and tied it back with a yellow ribbon, then flew down the stairs and threw open the door to the practice room.

But after she had rushed into the room, Laurian stopped abruptly. Disappointment sent dark spots dancing behind her eyes. Sinking into a chair just inside the door, she said in a choked, let-down voice, "Oh, Roger, it's you. Patty. . . ."

Roger had stopped playing his violin the instant Laurian had opened the door. In his usual shorts and T-shirt, he sat near the front of the room, staring at her uneasily. He seemed bewildered by the facial expression of suffering she was trying to hide.

Patty sat near him, fresh and young in a halter top and pale green shorts. Her coppery hair was fluffed around her face and her flute was in her hand. "You don't look so, like, great, Mrs. Bryant," she said with concern. "I mean, really."

Laurian forced a smile and nodded. "I'm fine. You surprised me, that's all. I didn't expect to see you and Roger here at this hour in the morning."

Roger shuffled his worn running shoes. "I'm waiting for Mr. Lahti," he said. "I wanted to ask him something about a composition I'm working on. He's usually here by now. I've only got today to talk to him, because I'm going home right after the concert tomorrow. He's coming today, isn't he?" His blue eyes were pleading, and he was beginning to look betrayed.

Laurian felt as if a knife were twisting in her chest, and she clasped her hands in her lap, staring at the white knuckles. "No, I don't think he'll be coming. I'm sorry, Roger."

Patty jumped up and grabbed Roger's wrist, dragging him after her across the room. She threw herself into a chair near Laurian and cried, "Oh, my gosh. You guys didn't break up, did you? I'd die if you have. I mean, I'll *die*."

"It's a long story," Laurian said, fighting a tinge of hysteria that wanted to creep into her voice.

Clutching his violin in one chapped hand and his bow in the other, Roger perched himself awkwardly on the edge of a chair. "He'll be back next summer, won't he?" he asked.

"Mr. Lahti has decided to take up his performing career again, so he'll be awfully busy." Laurian tried to smile. "You know how it is, Roger. Practice, practice, practice."

"You *have* broken up, haven't you?" Patty said with a worldly-wise, womanly look in her eyes. Her overdone speech patterns disappeared in her commiseration. "Oh, Mrs. Bryant, I'm so sorry."

Laurian got up. She couldn't handle much more of this without crying. "It's all right, honey. I'll be all right. Some loves just don't work out, that's all."

Patty reached out and clutched Roger's hand again. Her lashes fluttered anxiously at him as she asked, "Ours will—won't it? We'll still like each other when we both come back to Camp Bryant next summer, won't we?"

Roger's head jerked up and down in a nod. Then he peered at Laurian, lost in a situation that was far beyond his understanding. "Why isn't Mr. Lahti coming back?" he asked helplessly. "Doesn't he care about us anymore?" There was a suspicious dampness in his eyes. "Can't you talk him into coming back to the camp next year?"

Laurian put her fingers over her lips until she had the trembling under control. "Of course, he cares about us, Roger. It's just that he has his own life to lead too. You've progressed so beautifully with your violin this summer that you don't really need Mr. Lahti any longer. In fact, you're doing so well that I mistook your playing for his before I came in the room this morning."

"But why did you break up?" Patty demanded, getting

back to the more important basics. "Don't you love him anymore?"

"No, no, it isn't anything like that," Laurian said, pressing a hand against the side of her head, feeling as if she were on trial. Suddenly it seemed so important that she find the right words to say to an impressionable girl and a vulnerable boy who were just beginning to feel their way into the mystical, precarious world of romance and love.

She sat down again with her back held ramrod-straight and explained carefully. "I still love Mr. Lahti and he still loves me. It's just that he's a star, and his performances are so demanding, they don't leave time for anything else. He'll be traveling most of the time. Can you imagine how it will be?"

Laurian glanced at each of them. They nodded. She went on. "Marriage is a commitment that requires lots and lots of understanding and effort, even when two people are in love. Happiness doesn't just magically happen. So, since we would have so little time together, Mr. Lahti and I chose to separate, rather than take a chance on future unhappiness." Brow puckered, she realized her explanation sounded weak, that something was missing.

"You mean—if Mr. Lahti can't be home, then neither of you can work on knowing each other?" Patty asked, clarifying everything.

Laurian took a relieved breath and said, "That's right. That's what I meant."

Patty looked at Roger for a long time, studying him and the violin held in his hand. He looked back at her with a fatuous, sick-puppy expression on his face.

Then she turned back to Laurian and said inflexibly, "If I loved someone, I'd never let him go away from me. I'd go with him."

There were several minutes of silence in which Patty peered wide-eyed at Laurian, watching her hopefully while Roger gazed out the windows, bewildered by all these unfamiliar quandaries.

And during which time Laurian stared off into space with new and speculative thoughts popping up in her mind like mushrooms. "Well, speak of missing pieces," she muttered finally, and got up and walked to the door. "I'd better let you get back to your practicing."

After she had left the room, Laurian stood motionless in the hallway for quite some time, nodding, shaking her head, and frowning as she organized her thoughts. Then she walked into Uncle Jules's office. Closing the door, she plopped herself into a chair, crossed her legs, and sighed deeply.

Jules sat behind his desk in his shirtsleeves, leaning back in his chair drinking a cup of morning coffee. Laurian knew he must have at least a hundred last-minute details to take care of because the camp would close down as soon as the concert was over. "Do you have a few minutes?" she asked.

"I always have minutes for you, my dear." His eyes gleamed as if there were secrets and speculations running through his mind. "Though I have a very fascinating and curious appointment to go to in a little while. Did your deep sigh indicate you have the weight of the world on your shoulders?"

"I have." Laurian stared at him for a moment, then tried out her new idea verbally. "I'm going to travel around the world with Keska."

"Around the world!" Jules's eyebrows lifted in surprise.

"Maybe he won't want me with him," she added hesitantly.

"It's much too early in the morning for riddles," Jules complained.

"Keska is going to pick up his career again. He's been receiving invitations to perform all over the world."

"But that's wonderful!" Jules exclaimed. He peered at Laurian. "Isn't it?"

"Yes-s-s, I suppose. . . ."

"But?"

Laurian gave him a very brief rundown on what had happened. Then she blinked several times and rubbed the tears that escaped with the backs of her hands. "I can't bear to think of being parted from him," she finished in a wobbling voice.

Jules leaned forward and put his coffee cup down. He clicked his tongue several times, his face echoing his sympathy, and said softly, "Such unhappiness the young must face." He hesitated as if he wanted to tell her something, then seemed to change his mind. "Can nothing be done?"

Wrinkling her forehead, she picked at the crease in her yellow slacks and said slowly, "This morning I heard wisdom from the mouths of babes. They wondered why I'm letting Keska go off on tour by himself."

"Ah, so. . . ?"

After several minutes of silence and thought, Laurian looked up and said, "Which led me to think that I ought to be with Keska every minute to stop him from becoming too enthusiastic and leaping into things—like his apple orchard, or taking on too many commitments. He needs someone to arrange his itinerary, someone who isn't afraid to shout at him when he goes off on tangents."

Jules raised his eyebrows. "And Keska has agreed to allow you to organize his schedule for him?"

Laurian frowned, hunching her shoulders in worry. "I haven't talked to him about it yet. The idea only just occurred to me this minute. I'm thinking all this up as I go along." Her hunched shoulders slumped. "He probably won't accept the plan because he has some pretty definite ideas about what a marriage should be like."

"That wouldn't surprise me. The European attitude."

Laurian glanced up at Jules and nodded. "If I want him to accept the idea of me traveling with him, then I have to have my arguments down pat." She twisted her fingers together anxiously. "So I've got a lot of thinking to do. The reason I came to visit this morning was so I could practice on you first to see how the idea sounded."

He gazed at her for a few moments. "And, just incidentally, to gently suggest that I must find someone else to take over after I retire? Is that so?" Smiling ruefully, he ran his fingers through his soft hair, raising a white halo around his head.

"Oh, Uncle Jules," Laurian cried out, jumping up to sit on the edge of his desk and take his hand. "I feel so guilty. You've done so much for me, and now I'm deserting you when you need me most. I know how much you wanted me to take over the music camp."

He smiled. "Don't worry, my dear. I have several other solutions in mind. In fact, just this morning something . . ." He let the sentence die.

Laurian suspected he was fabricating to comfort her. Guilt cramped her stomach because he was so kindly downplaying her obligation to him. "I adore Camp Bryant and our students, you know I do," she said miserably. "But I love Keska so much. He's everything to me, Uncle Jules."

Jules pressed her hand gently. "Not to worry, my dear." He gave a little laugh. "Things have a peculiar way of working out."

"What do you mean?" she asked cautiously.

"Nothing to concern you, my dear," he said, and rose from his chair.

Laurian studied him for a moment, then shrugged. "Can I use your telephone? I want to call Keska to warn him that I'm coming to the farm for a talk." She picked up the receiver.

Jules put his finger on the button. "Let Keska stew in his juices until after the concert. If he feels as unhappy as you look, he'll be even more receptive to suggestions given another day. One must make use of every advantage in this case, mustn't one?"

Laurian paused thoughtfully, staring at the phone, and then she gave him a suspicious look. "Do you know something I don't?"

"What would I know?" he asked. "It's just that while I'm gone to my appointment, I need you here at camp. Someone has to comfort our terrified young musicians as they anticipate their big day at the concert tomorrow. If all works out, you'll give Keska the rest of your life. So you can afford to give Uncle Jules this one day, eh?"

The fact that she meant to give up Camp Bryant without a thought to Uncle Jules made Laurian feel sufficiently guilty to agree to stay. Though everything about her—her mind, her heart, and her body—wanted to fly to Keska.

As the day passed, Laurian thought from every angle

about her plan to travel with him. Her eventual conclusion was that Jules was probably right. If she talked to Keska tomorrow after the concert, he would be riding on such a euphoric high after his violin performance that he'd be open to almost anything. She hoped.

Twelve

The next day, Sunday, dawned clear, sunny, and very warm, even on the river. The concert was scheduled for two o'clock that afternoon.

Laurian got up early to spend time with the student musicians, who were milling around the camp in a state of agitated stage fright. They kept all the teachers and personnel busy applying comforting hands and words of encouragement. Their emotions rose and fell like roller coasters.

Laurian's emotions were no better. One minute she was breathlessly eager to see Keska play, the next minute found her in desolation, picturing him leaving her forever.

Shortly before noon she slipped away to dress for the event, taking great pains with her appearance. She showered, then dressed in her prettiest lingerie. Coiling her hair into a sleek, gleaming ebony crown above the deep inverted V on her forehead, she pushed glittering, jeweled combs into the sides. Her hands were trembling so badly, she could barely handle her makeup.

Spraying a flowery perfume on her wrists, her neck, and between her breasts, Laurian hoped the scent would befuddle Keska into agreeing to her career-sharing plan. After all, the scent of the apple blossom had successfully seduced the honeybee to do its bidding. Then she dismally reminded herself that the apple conceived in the union between honeybee and bloom now lay flawed and rotting by a lifeless, dry brook.

The rest of her life would stretch before her like an endless desert full of rotten apples if her plan didn't work, if she and Keska couldn't find a way to be together, Laurian told herself.

The dress she had chosen to wear was a soft, glowing blue in draped, clinging crepe. He liked her in blue. She fastened a gold chain in a neckline that ended at the valley between her firm breasts.

Slipping into a pair of matching shoes, she picked up her clutch bag, ready to face Keska with dignity and beauty. She refused to listen to the inner whispers of anxiety tormenting her.

Taking a deep breath, Laurian walked downstairs to inspect the dark-suited, scrubbed, and combed boys. The sophisticated girls were wearing long black skirts and white blouses. Now that the hour was upon them, the students had sunk into silent terror. She knew how they felt because her own stomach had shrunk into a knot the size of an acorn.

After the young musicians and their instruments had been loaded into buses, Laurian climbed into the passenger seat of Uncle Jules's car and they followed the last lurching vehicle out of camp.

The Luther Burbank Center for the Arts, situated north of Santa Rosa, was done in the Spanish style with stuccoed walls and pink-tiled roofs. It had a tall curving sculpture in front of the main building, the concert hall.

After the buses had unloaded the jittery student orchestra and their instruments in the rear of the concert theater, Laurian and the other teachers shepherded them into a large room where they would wait until it was time to file on stage.

George Miller came to the doorway to watch the agitated activity with interest. He caught Laurian's attention and smiled.

"Is he here?" she asked softly when she stood by his side.

"He's upstairs in one of the dressing rooms, going through much the same torment as these youngsters. Nausea, cramped fingers, and hysteria." George smiled wryly. "I'd better go back and comfort our prima donna."

Laurian herself would have liked to comfort that particular prima donna, but there wasn't time. Instead, she marshaled the young musicians into an orderly, if restless, line to march through the narrow passageway to the stage.

When the last student had entered the stage door, Laurian and the other teachers breathed a sigh of relief and went out to take their seats in the front row.

The theater was large and tranquilly exquisite, done in glowing light wood and soft upholstered pews. It had a capacity of fifteen hundred people and all the seats were filled. There were also a good number of standees. The crowd of excited classical-music lovers buzzed with impatience, chatting, rustling their programs, and coughing.

The sudent musicians were sitting on a stage that was elevated by about three feet and exposed on all sides but the back. They were filling the huge room with the sound of tuning instruments, a melodious cacophony.

A couple of television cameras were set up in front of the stage, anticipating Keska Lahti's long-awaited return engagement.

Laurian sat in the audience to the left of the podium, which was centered before the open space on the stage where Keska Lahti would stand to perform magic on his violin. She would be no more than twenty feet away from him, and her entire body was trembling with anticipation. It seemed like years, not just two days since she had seen him last.

The house lights dimmed. The students ceased their tuning. The lighting became brighter above the stage. The audience became hushed. For several long moments the theater hung motionless and deathly silently.

Then Jules Bryant walked with quiet dignity from a door at the right rear of the stage to the podium, commanding in his black formal suit, carrying his baton in his hand.

Laurian took a sharp breath and her muscles tensed as she watched Keska follow Jules along the path between the orchestra members. The second he appeared, the packed audience exploded into a roar of applause and shouts. The noise was tumultuous and deafening. Laurian didn't hear it. Her eyes, her ears, all her senses were attuned only to that one man, Keska, who walked across the stage with his graceful, loose-hipped stride.

He looked so unutterably handsome in the black exquisitely fitted tails that were his professional trademark. The cropped jacket lay smoothly at his slim waist and swept away behind to frame his hips. The black satin stripe down the outside of each leg bent and straightened with every step he took. She adored each pearl stud that held his stark white shirt closed over his chest. A crisp white tie was tied into a bow over the pulse in his neck. She gazed lovingly at the slender hands carrying his violin, his bow, and a small white box.

Agonized longing ran through her as she studied his face. His sloping eyebrows, his angular jaw, and his aristocratic nose were lighted by the spotlights. The lights made blazing gold of the hair waving around his collar and over his ears.

A broad, delighted smile had spread over his lips for the roaring, welcoming, elated audience. His eyes, his marvelous pewter eyes, were lit with exhilaration. When he looked out over the sea of faces, it was as if his eyes were touching each person individually.

For this hour or two Keska would belong to the wild, adoring crowd. Laurian could see instantly that they were his sustenance. She didn't mind sharing him if only she could carve out her own niche in his life. Would he accept her plan to be his traveling companion? As she looked at the magnificent, formidable man on the stage, it seemed less and less likely.

The applause was still roaring when he took his seat at the left of the podium, just in front of the student violinists. But now Keska's eyes sought out Laurian. They rested on her with a haunted, wistful look that seemed almost a palpable touch. His eyes fingered her face, connecting them as if by a wave of energy passing over the distance separating them.

He dropped his gaze and leaned over to place the small white box under his chair. Then Keska settled back, lay his violin and bow over his knees, and smiled at Jules, who stood waiting on the podium.

At Keska's nod Jules turned to the audience and raised his baton for quiet. The thunderous applause died gradually away, replaced by expectation.

"Greetings, my friends—old friends, new friends, parents of our fine musicians," Jules said, the microphone amplifying his voice. "You seem unusually happy to see our humble company this afternoon." His pink face beamed. "And of course, I understand your joy over the appearance of the illustrious Mr. Lahti. We, too, are thrilled. It has been a privilege to have him share his expertise with our young musicians this summer at Camp Bryant."

Laurian let her eyes and her mind wander to Keska as Jules drifted off into a description of the music camp, explaining its principles and functions.

But her attention leaped back to Jules when he said, "Since this is my last summer as director of Camp Bryant, I have doubly enjoyed working with these most delightful and exceptionally talented young people." His face became sober, almost sad, as he gazed around at the young orchestra, and then looked back at the audience. "I have made the difficult decision to retire."

When a hubbub of groaning protests arose from the audience, Jules pointed toward Laurian with his baton. "My lovely niece, Laurian Bryant, will take command of the camp. She is a talented cellist, and she will be a very capable camp director."

As the applause billowed again, Laurian cringed in her seat and stared at Jules with impotent worry and reproach. She could see complications twisting her plans awry. Why hadn't he taken her seriously when she had told him she wanted to be with Keska?

Jules held up his hands. "And Laurian will have a most able-bodied partner to help her in this enterprise, not that she particularly needs assistance."

Laurian groaned inwardly. What had he done now?

"After this summer we will change the name of our facility to the Bryant-Lahti Music Camp. Mr. Keska Lahti will take on his shoulders an equal share in the joys and the woes as a full partner." Jules beamed under his silvery halo of hair. "We couldn't be more pleased."

The applause exploded, roaring through the theater.

It vibrated around Laurian as she stared at Jules, her mouth hanging open. Keska was going to be her partner? Why hadn't he told her?

Then she glanced penetratingly at Keska. He was giving his violin a keen inspection, pegs, gut, vents, and shape, from one end to the other, his lower lip pushed out. Just one flicker of a glance lifted to Laurian, then he instantly looked back down. His expression was unreadable.

Suddenly she stiffened, and her palms broke out in icy sweat. Uncle Jules had surprised Keska with this announcement! Laurian contemplated the thought with sheer horror. In his way Jules had meant to help her. But surely he knew better than to try to manipulate a man like Keska Lahti! It simply wasn't done.

Her heart thumped a depressed knell as she tried to imagine what was going on behind Keska's stage face. He'd never listen to her again if he thought she was responsible for this trick. She figuratively kissed her hope to travel with him and their life together good-bye.

Now that Jules had dropped his bombshell, he turned his back and raised his baton. The young musicians positioned their instruments and he led them into the sweeping, whirling strains of their first selection, an "Artists' Life" by Strauss. The orchestra was in perfect harmony and pitch. They had never sounded so professional and exciting as they did at this moment.

Laurian took a deep breath and studied Keska hopelessly, delegating every inch of his body to her memory. She studied him closely, squinting for signs of anger. At least his nose wasn't pinched.

Just before the selection ended, Keska turned slightly to look back at Roger to nod approvingly. A momentary bond of affection passed between the two before he turned away again. Laurian would have given anything to know what was going on in Keska's mind.

Applause roared enthusiastically when the orchestra came to a rousing finish. The noise died away and a breathless, anticipatory hush fell over the theater when Jules turned to face the audience.

"I give you Keska Lahti and his magnificent violin, playing 'Romanza Andaluza,' " he announced simply. "I think everyone will agree that it is very wonderful to have him back on stage after his long absence."

A tumult of applause thundered forth. Keska rose from his chair and stepped forward, almost to the edge of the stage. Standing motionless, he let the sound flow over him, around him and through him. He soaked in the love directed toward him from the throng of people.

Suddenly his face exploded into a smile that dimmed the stage lighting. Lifting his arms, violin in one hand, bow in the other, he threw them out wide to embrace the audience who adored him. With his gesture he made the crowd a part of himself. Once again his eyes swept the theater, seeming to touch each face.

Then he dropped his arms. After positioning his violin under his chin, Keska raised his bow. Silence fell instantaneously as the audience settled back to hear the first note. A student accompanist played a brief introduction on the piano.

Then the clear, sure, full-bodied sound of Keska Lahti's violin swept across the enormous room in a gentle, romantic beginning. The sound swept to heights, teasing and playful. Then it grew wilder and faster in tempo. The music tumbled and washed over the upturned faces, taking them into its spell, Keska Lahti's spell.

Every leaping, dancing phrase reflected itself upon his intense, inward-directed expression. His mouth moved in tiny smiles, or pursed with the depth of a low note.

His eyes moved sightlessly over the audience, involving them in his trance, in the joy of his music. Perspiration drawn up by his intensity and concentration gleamed on his tanned face.

Then Keska's eyes touched Laurian as she sat in a dream, gazing up at this impossibly attractive, charismatic man. His attention didn't leave her again, and he seemed to be sharing his lilting music with her alone. A subtle change crept into the sound, a sensuality that sent shivers over her skin and caught her breath. *Come dance with me,* the violin enticed. *Come love me.*

Keska's sensuality folded Laurian tightly into a spell so strong his arms might have been around her. The clear seductive notes pulled her close and touched her in secret places. Only the two of them were there, together in the link of their eyes and in the bond of the music.

When the melody came to an end, Laurian felt bereft and alone, empty of will.

Lowering his violin, Keska turned away to give himself to the cheering audience who were beating their hands together and roaring their bravos. They stood on their feet and claimed him as their own. His smile was brilliant. Pressing his hand to his lips, he threw a kiss to his worshipers, spreading it with a wide, expansive sweep of his arm. He bowed deeply from the waist, again and again. And still they clamored for more.

Finally Keska brought the crowd under control by shaking his head and gesturing toward Jules Bryant and the young orchestra. Only then did they allow the concert to go on.

Laurian remained imprisoned in Keska's dancing, inviting, loving music. It rang through her mind and sent sensual tremors quivering over her body. Their eyes met and melded, and neither one of them heard the rest of the first half of the concert.

Intermission was riotous. The young musicians all talked at once and consumed gallons of fruit juice. They were thrilled and excited, pleased with their own performances and fascinated with Keska's magic.

Laurian listened to them in an agony of wanting to be upstairs in Keska's dressing room, sharing his excitement and happiness. Uncle Jules's shocking announcement held her back, because she had no clue as to how Keska would react.

After the orchestra had filed back on stage, they began the second half of the concert with Vivaldi's *Four Seasons*, playing with tact and mature emotion.

Laurian sat fidgeting through their performance waiting with a thundering heart until, for the second time, Jules announced Keska.

He again approached the brink of the stage, but this time he had left his violin on his chair. He had the small white box in his hand.

A wave brought silence. "Perhaps I have a responsibility to explain why I deserted you for so long," he said confidentially in his soft Finnish accent to the crowd of people. "Certainly it was not because I didn't love you or my music. I simply felt I needed time to come to know the heart as well as the soul of Keska Lahti. To accomplish this I have made many blunders and I have wandered onto several mistaken paths."

His gaze rested on Laurian for a moment, then drifted over the audience. "Keska Lahti has come close to the soil and to nature. My success as an apple farmer has been far from spectacular, but—" he held the small white box up so everyone in the audience could see, then turned to Laurian—"I have grown one perfect and precious thing of matchless beauty."

He opened the box and lifted high by its stem a flawless apple. "Behold, Keska Lahti's apple."

He was smiling a puckish, wry smile but the eyes he turned to Laurian were filled with love and loneliness and pleading. "It has become clear to me just in the last day that one must value an apple of perfection above all other things. Everything else is meaningless."

The silence in the theater was complete. The audience wasn't certain whether he was making a joke or revealing a great truth.

Keska held Laurian's eyes for only a moment. Then he said to the audience, "Because of this apple"—he lowered it to rub the glowing skin with his thumb—"because of this apple Keska Lahti will make only a limited comeback." There was a spatter of puzzled applause and a few objecting groans.

Keska grinned. "And now I will play for you." That was something the crowd could understand, and they responded with exuberant approval.

Keska slipped the apple back into its box, put it under his chair, and took up his bow and violin.

Laurian couldn't figure out anything that was going on, so she simply allowed herself the joy of becoming imprisoned in Keska's ethereal music. The rest of the concert passed in a haze for her.

The final orchestral selection had been played, and the audience would have kept Keska on stage indefinitely for encores if he hadn't finally gone backstage and ceased to respond to their continued applause.

With his withdrawal the Bryant Music Camp concert and the summer term were over for another year.

The next few hours were so hectic, Laurian had no chance to talk to Keska. The young students and the visiting parents had to be returned to the camp. A post-concert farewell party was held. Then the final good-byes of the summer were said, and the community began to disperse.

Roger and Patty held hands until the red-headed flutist was taken away to catch a plane to New Jersey. Then Roger left with his parents to return to Southern California.

Laurian stood beside Keska and swallowed convulsively around the lump in her throat. "I can't believe I'm going to miss Roger so much," she said. "He and Patty were so cute together. I'm not sure, but I suspect those two have sworn in blood to meet again next year at Camp Bryant."

Keska laughed and waved after the last car. Since he had shed his jacket, he was dubiously casual in satin striped black trousers, with his white tie open and hanging around his neck and his hair completely tousled. He glanced around the grounds. "The camp looks lonesome and abandoned."

Laurian sighed. "I know. There's no one left but the service people, who will close everything down. Every time a summer ends, it gives me such a sad feeling, I want to cry."

"I understand. Perhaps Keska Lahti has a bit of that feeling too." He put his arm around her. "But I have an idea. I have some excellent blackberry wine at the farm. It should be a perfect remedy for this sort of nostalgic reaction."

Laurian glanced up and grimaced. "I think I'll pass on the wine, but I'll go to the farm. We need to have a little talk, don't we?"

"It certainly seems we should," he said emphatically. "We'll leave George here to thrash out this partnership business with Jules. Then we can go to the farm and thrash out our own problems in privacy."

His determined expression made Laurian's heart sink

as they got into his car. As they drove the winding miles in silence and she held his tailed jacket in her lap, she realized her plan to build a life with this man was nothing but a silly pipe dream. She had seen him become one with the audience today. He belonged to the world.

Thirteen

It was early evening by the time Keska parked his car in front of the farmhouse. A hot orange sky silhouetted the rolling black hills on the horizon. A couple of shredded clouds had turned purple. In the orchard a catbird mimicked a warbler, repeating the notes over and over. The hard cider smell of Keska's fermenting apples drifted in from the surrounding orchard, intoxicating the air.

They walked through the house to the sitting room and Keska threw his jacket on a chair, took his violin out of the case, and laid it on the table in the music room, then handed the small white box to Laurian. "There," he said, walking with his graceful stride to the liquor cabinet. "Now for the blackberry wine."

Laurian sat down on the silver and blue brocaded love seat, arranging her full blue crepe skirt around her thighs. She watched Keska get out a bottle and two glasses, then asked hopefully, "Have you ever thought of getting rid of that horrible blackberry wine?"

Glancing back, he laughed. "As a matter of fact, I have already poured it down the sink. That wine was one of Keska Lahti's most notable failures."

He walked back to the love seat with a labeled bottle and two Brandy glasses. A grin pushed creases into his cheeks as he handed her a glass and sat down beside her, stretching his long legs out and crossing them at the ankles. "This is blackberry brandy put out by a quite reputable distillery. It will do as well as my wine, don't you think?"

Laurian sipped and laughed as she glanced at Keska.

"It'll do nicely. And I'm eternally grateful to the distillery." She looked down and picked at a loose seam on the white box in her lap, hesitant about mentioning Jules's fiasco concerning the partnership.

Keska sipped his brandy, his brows raised contemplatively as he studied her face.

"I hope—" They both started together, then laughed nervously.

"You first," Laurian said.

Keska took a deep breath. "I hope you aren't angry because I went behind your back to buy into Camp Bryant. It only occurred to me afterward that my partnership will cut your inheritance in half. Keska Lahti has bypassed logical thinking and has done the impulsive thing again." His eyes were worried as he studied her. "Maybe after I caused you so much distress and pain, you don't even want me for a partner."

"Not want you!" Laurian's eyes were wide and stunned as she looked at him. She swallowed two or three times before she could exclaim. "*You* went behind my back! You mean it wasn't Uncle Jules who went behind *your* back?"

"It was I."

"But I don't understand. How did this come about?"

Keska shrugged and sipped some more brandy before explaining. "The plan came quite suddenly to me in the middle of the night. After the apples went bad, I thought there was no way for us to marry and make a life. But when I imagined leaving you, I had no wish to live, much less play my violin for anyone. So I lay awake, desperate to find a solution so that we could build a life together. And then I thought that it would be a logical step if I should become connected to Bryant Music Camp."

"A logical step? I doubt that you've ever taken one in your life, Keska," she said, and gave a little laugh of anticipation.

"There's always a first time, isn't there?" His eyes were silvery gray with intensity. "Then after I had formed this wonderful plan to buy into Camp Bryant, it didn't seem likely that Jules would agree. He was quite hesitant when I called him yesterday morning to put out a feeler about a partnership, though he agreed to come to the farm to talk about it. When he arrived, something seemed to have changed his outlook and he had become quite amenable to a full partnership. He and George acted like boys with a new toy."

Laurian stared at him, astonished. "That must have been after I had gone to his office for a talk. I thought he had a secret burning his tongue." She laughed, and then frowned. "But you do realize the music camp is going to tie you down horribly, don't you?"

Keska nodded slowly. "I realize, but I won't mind. I have found over this summer that I enjoy very much working with these young musicians. I imagine I understand them, and I have felt quite useful and fulfilled. When the idea of a partnership came into my mind, I discovered that I wanted to be a permanent part of the camp quite badly—as badly as I wished to play my violin."

He lifted his glass and sniffed appreciatively, then sipped the dark liquid. "I was wrong the other day when I told you we could have no marriage. I can't live with the decision. This once I will admit I acted like a fool."

She smiled. "I should never have listened to you and let you tell me it wouldn't work. We're both fools. I wonder if two fools can have a successful marriage?"

"At least we have something in common," he said, and shifted position, turning to face her. "After you had left, it was clear that there was nothing important in my life except my lovely Laurian." He touched her cheek with the tip of a finger. "I couldn't bear to think of an empty, lonely life stretching endlessly in front of me."

"I know," Laurian whispered. "I couldn't bear it either."

He studied her for a moment, then said, "I'm not such a bad music teacher, am I?"

"You're a marvelous teacher." She moved closer to him.

Keska stretched one arm out along the back of the love seat, just short of touching her shoulders. "Lahti-Bryant Music Camp will be a tie that holds me down for three months out of the year."

"Bryant-Lahti Music Camp." She poked one of his pearl studs with a forefinger.

"I can see there may be a few bugs to be ironed out," he murmured.

"But you're so good with bugs," she murmured back. "I'm sure you can handle it."

"We'll see. . . . At any rate the camp will be an obligation that will ground me every summer. Then we can spend all our time together." He frowned thoughtfully. "I can't imagine why I didn't think of it long ago."

Laurian laughed softly. "Falling in love doesn't do much for mental acuity, does it? I haven't been thinking clearly either."

"George can hardly wait to get his hands on the functions and finances of the camp. Both he and Jules were very eager to take care of all the details of the partnership for me."

"I'll just bet they were," Laurian said. She watched the dark brandy swirl as she twirled her snifter. Then she set it down on the coffee table and put her hand on Keska's knee. "It'll be nice to have you available all summer."

He inched closer to her, the black satin stripe on his thigh touching the soft blue crepe that clung to her leg. "I will be nothing but available all summer. Here. With you, my love." One finger touched her shoulder, grazing the bare skin at the curve of her neck. "Are summers enough to build a marriage upon, lovely Laurian?"

She rested her head against his shoulder. "Oh, yes, they certainly are. Especially since I've been making plans of my own while you've been busy with your little surprises."

"Plans, have you?" he murmured, his lips against her forehead.

"I've decided you need a keeper, Keska Lahti," she said firmly. "I intend to travel around with you to your performances and concerts to keep you out of trouble. I'm going to supervise your itinerary for you, so you don't get bogged down with too many engagements."

She lifted her head and gave him a fierce look. "After sneaking that partnership in on me, you wouldn't *dare* tell me I can't go on tour with you." Behind the determination, she was watching him apprehensively for his reaction.

For a long time Keska didn't answer. His expression was very serious as he studied her face. "What about a home? Perhaps children? Your career? All these things are important. How can you have these if you follow me in a nomadic life?"

"First I want to be close to Keska Lahti, then the other things will work themselves out."

"And what of your own life, Laurian?" he asked, searching deep in her eyes for her inner feelings. "The symphonic orchestra you play with, and your music? How will you be fulfilled if you give that up?"

"I can carry my cello and my music anywhere you go, Keska. You've bolstered my confidence and you've reinforced my abilities. If I build upon that, I'll be happy."

He hesitated for a moment, then took her hand in his. "You have seen tonight the response to my performing life. Can you be happy following in another's shadow?"

Laurian paused and thought for a moment, and then she said slowly, "Music is my business, but not necessarily just the playing of it. So if I applied my training to assisting you in patterning your career, I wouldn't be in your shadow, Keska. I would be standing shoulder to shoulder beside you. We'd have an equal partnership in this as well as in the music camp."

Freeing her hand, she took the two ends of his loosened tie to give his neck a couple of determined yanks. "I won't listen to any vetoes."

"In that case," Keska said, rising to his feet, "I had better show you something." He went out of the sitting room for a few moments. When he came back, he had a peck-size wicker basket in his hands and a couple of folders clenched between his teeth.

When he upended the basket on the coffee table, letters and telegrams showered out, piling up, bouncing and spilling over onto the floor. "If you intend to be Keska Lahti's keeper, there you are," he said through the clenched teeth holding the folders. "Your work is cut out for you, my Laurian. You can organize with all Keska Lahti's blessings. To me the planning is nothing more than a burden. You can choose anywhere in the world you want me to travel."

Taking the folders out of his mouth, he held them out

to her, his grin pushing humor into his face. "But I have the first choice of where we go. I have already made arrangements for both of us to go to Vienna to discuss a performance, so there is no changing that."

Laurian stared up at him, then at the airline tickets. "Keska," she said with annoyed patience, "don't tell me that after all my worrying you had already thought of taking me with you on tour."

"Perhaps it had crossed my mind, but I would never have imagined putting you to work. That was your own flash of genius," he said, his laugh lines deepening.

"Genius!" Laurian gave an irritated sniff.

Keska grinned, and then he held up the other airline folder. "After Vienna we'll go to Helsinki so you can meet my parents. Perhaps we could call both trips a honeymoon?"

Bewilderment, excitement, and warmth began building as Laurian stared at the tickets in his hand. "You were busy, busy, busy yesterday, weren't you? Why didn't you tell me what you had in mind?"

"Constant traveling is a harrowing existence. I wasn't sure you would care to come with me," he said softly, and sat down on the love seat again, placing the plane tickets on top of the letters piled on the coffee table. "I bought the tickets and hoped." Reaching out, he curved his warm hand and teasing fingers around the back of her slender neck.

"And I was so worried that you wouldn't want me with you," she said, and laughed softly. "This is like a fairy tale come true." Her fingers worked at the top pearl stud on his shirt, then the next, and the next.

"The apple made the fairy tale come true," he said, his breathing speeding as her fingers worked over his chest.

"The apple!" she exclaimed, and picked up the small box that had gotten pushed aside. "I almost forgot it." Removing the top, she lifted the apple by the stem. "It's really the same one, isn't it? See the two stripes hugging each other?"

"The very one," Keska said, smiling. "The apple of our love. No disease . . . strong . . . healthy . . . no worms."

Twirling it by the stem, she looked at it dubiously

from all sides. "How can you be sure there aren't any worms?"

His eyes gleamed as he grinned and captured her in the circle of his arms. "No worm would dare touch Keska Lahti's love apple. Take a bite of it and you will see, my sweet lovely Laurian. There is a risk that one bite might put you under my spell, but there is no worm."

"Under your spell, is it?" Laurian licked her lips and stared at the apple, then shuddered and shook her head. "As tempting as it sounds, I don't think I'm brave enough to take a chance." She glanced up and laughed. "You bite it, Keska, then you'll be under my spell."

"I already am," he said, and took the fruit out of her hand. "But I have faith in our apple—in our love." Opening his mouth, he positioned the apple between his teeth and hesitated for a moment, looking at Laurian out of the corners of his eyes.

Her entire face puckered in a grimace, anticipating disgust as she listened to the crisp, juicy crunch when he bit down. A shudder ran through her body when she pictured half a maggoty worm left behind. She could barely bring herself to look when he held the apple out.

The meat was white and virginal. "Thank God!" she breathed. Then she glanced at Keska. "How did you know there wasn't a worm?"

He chewed and swallowed, then answered, "I had it X-rayed and scanned at the hospital in Santa Rosa."

"X-rayed and scanned!" she exclaimed, and shook her head. "I don't believe it."

"I couldn't bring myself to cut it, but I had to know if our apple was strong. Because I love you so very, very much, sweet Laurian. I had to know the apple was pure, so we could become one in the eating of it." He pulled her close and laughed happily. "Taste Keska Lahti's apple, my sweet." He held it out to her.

Laurian gazed at him for a moment, her eyes dark and deep with emotion. Then she took the apple out of his hand and whispered, "I love you so much, my darling. You're everything to me." Lifting the apple to her lips, she bit deeply into its luscious, very sweet flesh.

When she had swallowed, Keska lifted her chin and lowered his head. He kissed the sweet taste of love off her lips. Touching his tongue to the inside of her mouth, he shared the sensual, fruity juice. They ate the apple, sharing bites, becoming one in a love they had watched grow to maturity.

Then Keska pulled the jeweled combs and the pins out of her coils of hair. The thick, long mantle tumbled down around her face and over her breasts. Taking the silken mass in his hands, he looked at her with eyes that were hot with seductive invitation and whispered, "Do you know what Eve did after she bit into the apple in the Garden of Eden?"

Laurian moaned softly as his talented fingers traced the low, wide neckline of her dress. He brought the skin of her breasts flaring into a fire of eager anticipation that spread instantly through her body. Giving a tiny, delighted laugh, she gasped, "Does the question about Eve have to do with one of your bug fables?"

"Don't make fun. Keska Lahti is very serious," he murmured, his lips tickling the side of her neck as he reached around to unzip her dress.

"I'm gullible," she said, her voice low and breathless. "What did Eve do after she bit into the apple?" Slipping off his white vest and undoing the last studs in his shirt, she spread her own brand of fire over his heaving chest.

Keska spoke with a thick and mellow accent in broken gasps. "Eve immediately"—he smoothed his hands up the silk of her hose under the blue skirt—"learned to . . . play a—"

Laurian got up to facilitate the dispatch of her panty hose. Her dress made a pool of blue beside the brocaded love seat. "Learned to play what?" She asked breathlessly when his hands made a slow, all-inclusive journey down over her satin slip. Slipping his stiff white shirt off, she counted his sleek muscles.

Taking her hand, Keska led her into the music room. "Eve learned to play the cello," he murmured softly into her ear, holding her against his body as he closed the French doors firmly. On the table behind them his violin was glowing with a golden sheen in the faint light.

"The cello!" Laurian repeated against his soft seeking lips. After she had unzipped his black trousers, he slipped out of pants, briefs, socks, and shoes in a few efficient, fluid movements.

Then with languorous, talented hands caressing her body, he eased her slip up and off over her head, and her lacy panties off over her feet. He looked at her body in the dim evening light coming in through the windows and sighed deeply.

Laurian ran her palms over the crisp hair on his chest and teased his nipples. "Why did Eve learn to play a cello after she had bit into the apple in the Garden of Eden?" she whispered.

Taking her into his arms, his eyes glowing with desire, he said softly in his musical accent, "Because then when Adam's violin cried out for love, Eve would answer with her cello in a husky, sexual voice." He nipped gently at her lower lip. "And ever after, they would fiddle around and make beautiful music together."

Laurian groaned in protest and pulled him down on the soft thick rug. "I love you, Keska Lahti—even after *that*. Oh, darling, I love you so much. Forever."

"Forever, my sweet, my lovely Laurian. . . ."

THE EDITOR'S CORNER

Readers who are new to our LOVESWEPT romances have been writing to ask how they can get copies of books we published during our first year on sale. So I thought it might be helpful for me to point out that a list of our books, accompanied by an order form, can be found in the backs of many of our LOVESWEPT romances. (Once in a while there isn't enough space for the whole list—due to my Editor's Corner being too long!) If you send the form along with your check to the address indicated on the blank, our folks in Des Plaines will get your order back to you within four to six weeks. In future LOVESWEPT books, you'll be seeing all or a part of a listing that we put together. It gives just a few lines of description about each of our first fifty titles; if you've missed any of them, do be sure to order.

Speaking of being missed . . . doesn't two months seem too long to wait for another of Helen Mittermeyer's powerful love stories? Next month you'll be treated to **VORTEX,** LOVESWEPT #67, by Helen, and it's just the sort of dramatic romance you've come to expect from this talented storyteller. Heroine Reesa Hawke is beautiful, spirited . . . and troubled; Dake Masters is as magnetic and forceful and attractive as a hero can be. Reesa and Dake have been separated for seven long months, months in which Reesa remembered nothing about her life before a fisherman pulled her out of the storm-tossed waters of the Caribbean Sea. When Dake suddenly appears, bringing back the torrid memories of their life together, Reesa finds herself just as wildly attracted as in the past, but with a wealth of new and enriching insights into the values that had

(continued)

been missing in their relationship. Yet Dake is a changed person, too. How they reconcile their troubled past and their optimism for the future makes for a provocative and tender love story that you won't want to miss.

Another very talented Helen—Helen Conrad—provides a delightful romp in **UNDERCOVER AFFAIR,** LOVESWEPT #68. Helen's heroine Shelley Pride and hero Michael Harper certainly meet in a unique way: Shelley captures him ... literally ... in a citizen's arrest! But soon Michael turns the tables, hotly pursuing the woman he's discovered he can't live without. A merry chase follows and reserved Shelley is forced to unbend—even, at one point, to become a daring impostor! There's danger, too, though, because of Michael's work, and the lovers are almost parted by it. I'll bet that you're going to relish the way Michael "shadows" Shelley ... as well as all the other heart-warming episodes in **UNDERCOVER AFFAIR.**

It's always exciting for us to bring you new talent—and never more so than next month when Marianne Shock debuts as a published author with **QUEEN'S DEFENSE,** LOVESWEPT #69. Witty, warm, and just plain wonderful, this romance gets off to a marvelous start when heroine China Payne's mother—she's just a little batty—threatens to hire a "hit man" to go after her fifth husband. That gentleman happens to be hero Reeve Laughlin's father. What follows between China and Reeve is a love affair to remember ... coupled with a chess game that predicts the bold moves of a well-matched man and woman. I believe you'll be delighted to join us in giving a warm welcome to Marianne as a LOVESWEPT author!

Touching and funny by turns, **THE MIDNIGHT SPECIAL,** LOVESWEPT #70, is another grand romance by Sara Orwig. As you know from her biographical sketch, Sara is a mother. But the four monster children who look like angels and behave like devils in her November LOVESWEPT romance come purely from the author's imagination. I've met Sara's lovely family and I can assure you that her own children do not bear the slightest resemblance to her hero's, Nick Bannon's, nephews! Those boys have sent more than a dozen teachers packing . . . but they—and their uncle—have never met the likes of Maggie Linden! A determined beauty, Maggie prevails over mice in her suitcase and snakes in her bed. But her heart won't let her prevail over Nick. His pursuit is determined . . . and delicious! **THE MIDNIGHT SPECIAL** is *very* special indeed . . . another winner of a love story from Sara Orwig.

Do be sure to look in the back of this book for the excerpt from **HEARTS OF FIRE**, the latest historical from Christina Savage. I trust you'll find the teaser intriguing and that you'll be sure to ask your bookseller for the novel, coming to you from Bantam next month. Have a glorious November!

Warm wishes,

Carolyn Nichols

Carolyn Nichols
  Editor
LOVESWEPT
Bantam Books, Inc.
666 Fifth Avenue
New York, NY 10103

A special preview of

HEARTS OF FIRE

by Christina Savage
author of LOVE'S WILDEST FIRES

On sale November 1, 1984 wherever
Bantam paperbacks are sold

She was a Tryon and a lady, a proud, raven-tressed beauty from a great Philadelphia family divided by war—a family now driven to open conflict by notorious rebel Lucas Jericho, who challenged Cassie Tryon to love as never before. Dynamic, passionate opponents, soon they were swept away on a feverish tide . . . until family tragedy trapped Cassie between her Rebel lover and her loyalty to her Tory brother. As a patriot heiress in a Tory-occupied city, Cassie achingly surrendered her dreams of Lucas and his maddening touch. She would live dangerously, love recklessly, and command her father's mighty empire until she could reclaim the pirate prince torn from her arms by a brother's betrayal and the cruelties of war.

Turn the page for a dramatic excerpt from
HEARTS OF FIRE.

HEARTS OF FIRE

By Christina Savage

Cassie escaped into the tiny rear foyer and onto the porch. The garden, she saw instantly, was empty. Which was curious, she thought, descending the steps and looking around the corner of the house. She was certain Robal had said the rear garden, but there wasn't a soul in sight.

A joke? Not likely. Robal was noted for a total lack of humor. Unheeding of the shade and slight, cooling breeze, she hurried down the path of chipped rock and peered through the wrought-iron oak foliage of the rear gate. The drive, too, was empty. "Hello?" she called. "Louis?"

Silence was her only answer. Concerned, she stepped into the drive in time to hear a jangle of harness and see a horse and carriage emerge from the stable, the driver hidden in shadows. "What in heaven's name . . . ? Louis? Robal said—"

"My compliments." Lucas reined the mare to an abrupt halt in front of her. He leaned out of the carriage and offered her his hand. "C'mon up."

"But I . . . I can't," Cassie stammered, thrilled to see him and yet reluctant to obey. "I have guests. Robal said you were in the garden."

"I was, at the time. C'mon."

Common sense and social obligations would prevail if she hesitated. Before she could change her mind, she caught his hand and allowed herself to be pulled into the carriage.

"See here!" Louis shouted, running from the stable.

"Take care of my horse," Lucas called back over his shoulder. "She's had a long run. I expect her watered and fed by the time we get back. And rubbed down, too, Miss Tryon says."

Louis jerked off his cap and stared up at Cassie. "Sorry, miss," he gulped. "I didn't know . . . That is, I thought . . ."

"It's all right, Louis." Somehow, she managed to appear as if the whole episode had been planned. "Do as he says, please."

"But be careful," Lucas warned, sending the mare forward with a burst of speed that left Louis dodging a shower of gravel. "She bites."

"This is insane," Cassie said as they turned into the alley. "There must be fifty people back there who'll . . . Whatever will I tell them?"

"That you were kidnapped," Lucas said matter-of-factly.

"Oh, God, Lucas."

"Very well, then." He grinned, took her hand and tucked it in his arm. "Will rescued do?"

He was mad. But then, Cassie thought, so was she. And quite content to be so, under the circumstances.

The carriage rumbled down the alley, slowed for the turn onto Fourth Street, and left Jedediah's wake behind in the settling dust. They turned west on Walnut and drove the two and a half blocks to the entrance of South East Square. Seemingly misnamed—it lay to the southwest of the packed and bustling center of town—the park consisted of twenty carefully tended acres that served as a symbol of beauty and serenity in the midst of otherwise untrammeled growth. The land rose and fell in emerald swells whose sweep was broken by widely separated shade trees. In its center, protected by a ring of weeping willows, wild ducks and white swans glided tranquilly across a broad, deep blue pond that was adorned, at one end, with soft green lily pads and creamy white blossoms. Lucas steered the mare off the path and to a halt beneath a giant elm. "Walk?" he asked.

Cassie nodded her assent. "How did you hear . . . the news?"

Lucas jumped down and rounded the carriage. "My first mate returned from town this morning. I rode out immediately when I heard." He took Cassie's hands to help her down. "It's a hell of a thing."

"I hadn't thought of it in those terms," Cassie said with wry sarcasm, and then stopped short as her dress snagged in the bench seat's leaf spring. "Damn!" she cursed, falling against Lucas.

"Hang on. Let me see . . ." He held her with his left hand, reached around her with his right, and caught a provocative glimpse of ankle and calf. Almost suspended, she would fall if he let her go to free her skirt without damage, so he shrugged and gave a sharp jerk. The hem tore free, leaving a small piece behind. "Sorry," he said, still holding her though the need had passed.

Cassie caught up her skirt, inspected it, and let it drop. "It can be mended," she said with a sigh of resignation.

"But how about you?" Lucas asked. "Can you be mended?"

"I thought we were going to walk."

After four solid days of talk, the silence was blissful. No carriages arriving or leaving. No women chattering, no men deep in serious discussion. No questions, no solicitous comments to be acknowledged. Only the soft soughing of the wind in the trees, the occasional cry of a bird or chatter of a squirrel. Lucas walked at her side. The breeze ruffled his sunbleached, golden hair. His shirt was open to midchest, revealing a soft blanket of tight curls, starkly white against deeply tanned, bronze-colored skin. A broad black belt with a steel buckle shaped like a helmsman's wheel circled his waist. His nankeen breeches were cut tightly, almost too revealingly, and tucked into high-topped, soft black boots that were molded to his calves by a year's hard wear. More dashingly handsome than any of the dozens of other men she had seen in the past four days, he seemed not more piratical, but rather more natural and less ill at ease than he had in the scrivener's garb in which he'd arrived at Tryon Manor. "Is it that obvious, then?" she asked, almost painfully aware of his scrutiny.

"Your eyes betray you. You haven't been eating, I daresay. Haven't slept . . . and you've yet to have a good cry."

"Oh?" Cassie bridled. "And what makes a pirate—privateer, I beg your pardon—like yourself such an authority on tears?"

"I watched my mother being raped and wanted her to die and to be dead myself. I blamed myself, then and years later again when she walked into the sea. I have cared for Barnaby, and held his head in my arms so he wouldn't have to watch them hang our father, as I did." His voice was soft, as if lost somewhere in dreams or time. "I know about tears, Cassie. I'm an expert on tears. I am . . . an authority."

Cassie swallowed a knot in her throat. Her eyes burning, she fought her grief, tried desperately to push it back into the privacy of her heart. But so delicate a vessel was no match for her overwhelming sadness. "The Tryons . . . the Tryons are not given to tears," she gulped, and, as a great sob wracked her body, stopped and stood rigid and trembling.

"Come," Lucas said simply, leading her to the

willows. And there, hidden from the world by the soft green canopy of leaves, took her into his arms, dropped to his knees and to the ground, and held her like a babe.

The grass was cool, his arms around her and his body against her warm, a promise of safety. Society forbade her to be with a man like Lucas, but she no longer cared. In him was comfort; in him was safety. With him she needn't fear revealing her weakness. Slowly, the tension subsided and she relaxed and wept openly and unashamedly. She wept for her loss, for her loneliness. She wept for her fear and her uncertainty, for her father whom she had loved so deeply, and as all those who have known sorrow know so well, wept for herself.

Tears of anguish, tears of desolation. Hot and bitter tears that as they spilled, cleansed the soul of the poisons of excess grief. Lucas's hold was firm yet tender. His voice soothed her, and his arms gave her strength. One hand soothed her hair as her tears wet his chest. One emotion denied stifles all other emotions. The control over heart and head, the injunction not to feel, spreads. All is dulled until the door is opened and, so long pent up, a flood of emotion is released. Sometimes comes anger, sometimes fear, sometimes gratitude. Sometimes, too, comes a ravenous hunger for a contradiction of death and an affirmation of life, and even more a desire beyond all bounds to love and be loved. Blindly seeking him, Cassie found his lips, crushed her body to his, and breathed his name over and over again in her need to envelop his soul, to drink in his very being.

Lucas was at first taken aback, then swept along by the tide of her emotion. Pleasure overcoming surprise, he pressed her against the grass as his tongue slid along hers. His hands, roughly and then tenderly, caressed her sides, paused beneath the mounds of her breasts, moved gently to cup them for one brief, sweet second before continuing to the pale white of her throat and the string holding her bodice closed.

The kiss ended abruptly with the sound of laughter. Their eyes snapped open and their heads turned as one. "Oh, dear!" Cassie gasped, her voice lost under Lucas's heartfelt curse.

Two children, a boy and a girl of no more than ten years, stood peering between the draping branches of the willow. "Get out of here, you!" Lucas ordered.

The girl giggled.

Shoeless and dressed in homespun, the boy grabbed her hand and tugged at her. "C'mon, Beth."

Lucas jumped to his feet and feinted in their direction. "Go on. Git!" He added as the girl squealed in terror and the pair darted away.

Cassie rose shakily and smoothed her skirts.

"Damn kids," Lucas muttered. "Get underfoot when you least expect them—or want them."

"I think providence must've taken a hand," Cassie said, fiddling with her hair to hide her embarrassment. "What must you think of me?"

Lucas took her hands and kissed one and then the other. "None the worse, believe me. I think you're a remarkably brave young woman."

"Brazen, perhaps. Hardly brave." Her face and eyes felt puffy, but she counted that a small price to pay for the relief her tears had brought her. "We were going to walk, remember?" she asked, more kindly than before.

"All too well," Lucas admitted. He held out his arm for her to take, parted the screening branches so they could pass. "Mademoiselle?"

The land sloped gently toward the water's edge. As they approached, a mallard guided her half-grown brood to the safety of the far side of the pond. "I prayed you'd come, you know," Cassie said. "I was so lonely and frightened. Richard's been so distant, and Abigail and I don't get along at all. Jim is marvelous, as always, but I wanted to talk to you."

She smiled shyly up at him. "Do you think that terribly forward of me?"

"No." He turned, followed the water's edge. "I was thinking, when you were crying, how much I wished you'd been there to hold me when I cried."

Cassie squeezed his arm to her side. "I wish I had been too."

"I've learned something from this," he said softly. "If you find someone you trust . . . and love . . . enough to cry in front of, I've found the woman . . . that is, you've found the person you've been looking for, and you'd better not let her, or him, go."

Cassie stopped and turned to him. "Do you know what?" she asked, her fingers light on his cheek.

Lucas smiled. "What?"

"I think you're right. But—" she stretched up on tiptoe to kiss him fleetingly "—this is the wrong time and place, and since I don't trust myself, let's keep walking."

They rounded the end of the pond, startling a sleeping turtle into splashing flight. "You should have sent for me the moment it happened. Espey and Ullman knew where I was. An accident, wasn't it?"

Able at last to talk about her father's death with some degree of equanimity, Cassie recounted the events of the previous Saturday morning. "It's strange," she went on, "but I can't walk past his study without looking in and expecting him to be there and to tell me this has all been some macabre misunderstanding. A joke we'll laugh about as we sit around a winter fire."

It wasn't a joke. It was a calamity. The news of Jedediah's death had struck Lucas like a bombshell. Their agreement had been verbal, and it was a foregone conclusion that Richard, Jedediah's natural heir, wouldn't honor it, which meant he'd have to find a new investor before the end of the next week or face losing *The Sword of Guilford*. His one cause for hope had been an additional piece of information that could more properly be classified as a rumor. Billings, his first mate, had heard that the son had been cut off in favor of either the wife or the daughter. Grasping at this as a man overboard would have grasped a lifeline, Lucas saddled his mare and rode immediately and openly to Philadelphia.

He had been tempted to ask the moment he'd seen her, but had known that to do so would have been impolite. But as much as he loved her, as much as he sympathized with her grief and honestly tried to give her solace, the question had never been far from the tip of his tongue. An hour after his arrival, he was still burning with curiosity. "I won't be able to stay in town long," he said in an oblique approach to the all-important question. "I, ah, suppose you'll be living in town until Richard gets things sorted out?"

"Until Richard . . . ?" Cassie looked up at him quizzically and then understood. "Oh. No," she said, evidently troubled. "I'm afraid Richard won't be doing any sorting out."

Lucas's heart leaped, but he disguised his joy. "He won't? I don't understand."

"I mean Father cut Richard off. He left everything to me."

"It's true, then!" Lucas blurted without thinking. "Thank God!"

"I beg your pardon?" Cassie asked, unwilling to believe what she'd just heard. She stopped abruptly and stared up at him. "What did you just say?"

Lucas cursed mentally.

"You knew," Cassie went on accusingly.

"No," Lucas said, trying, too late, to explain. "Heard. A rumor. But it seemed like the wrong time to talk about . . ." He paused, threw up his hands. "The truth is, your father and I had an agreement, and I was afraid that if Richard had inherited everything, I'd be in danger of losing my ship."

"And just what did father promise you?" Cassie asked coldly.

There was nothing to be done but to continue and hope for the best. Haltingly at first, embarrassed by having been caught out, Lucas explained the terms of the agreement and the importance of receiving the money by the end of the next week.

"You couldn't have cared less," Cassie said sadly. "You didn't care about Father, didn't care about me—"

"That's not true," Lucas protested. "Asking a perfectly sensible question, under the circumstances, doesn't preclude caring."

"Caring for what?" Cassie snapped. "My money? So you can build your damned boat and sail around killing Englishmen? That's the reason you came rushing here so fast. The *only* reason. You were worried that your agreement with my father was buried with him."

"Cass—"

"And I played the fool, didn't I? The grieving daughter. Throw your strong arms around her. Tell her about your own tears. What was it? An expert on tears? An authority?" Her voice crackled with sarcasm and her eyes blazed with fury. "Tell me how brave I am? How bold? Well, what about how easily manipulated? What about gullible and trusting and . . . and . . ." Near tears again, she whirled and fled toward the carriage.

"Wait!" Lucas said, catching up with her and grabbing her arm. "I meant nothing of the sort and you know it. You're not being fair, damn it."

"Not being fair?" Cassie asked with exaggerated sweetness that only emphasized her anger. "Why, of course I'll be fair, Lucas. You needn't worry about that. I'll see my father's bargain through. You'll get your money, sir, and your cursed boat." She stared at his hand until he loosed her arm, then into his eyes. "And now"—the sweetness became acid strong enough to etch glass—"I should like to be taken home, if you don't mind. I trust you are gentleman enough not to refuse."

Lucas sighed. "All right, Cassie," he said, stepping out of her way. "Whatever you say."

"Exactly," Cassie hissed, and with a contemptuous toss of her head, she stalked past him.

A dozen expletives flashed through his mind, but none of them seemed appropriate. Lucas stared down at his reflection on the surface of the pond. A water- wind-rippled privateer stared back. He stooped down, picked up a stone, and threw it into his likeness, then wheeled around in disgust and started after Cassie.

A TRIUMPHANT NOVEL
BY THE AUTHOR OF
THE PROUD BREED

WILD SWAN

Celeste De Blasis

Spanning decades and sweeping from England's West Country in the years of the Napoleonic Wars to the beauty of Maryland's horse country—a golden land shadowed by slavery and soon to be ravaged by war—here is a novel richly spun of authentically detailed history and sumptuous romance, a rewarding woman's story in the grand tradition of A WOMAN OF SUBSTANCE. WILD SWAN is the story of Alexandria Thaine, youngest and unwanted child of a bitter mother and distant father—suddenly summoned home to care for her dead sister's children. Alexandria—for whom the brief joys of childhood are swiftly forgotten . . . and the bright fire of passion nearly extinguished.

Buy WILD SWAN, on sale in hardcover August 15, 1984, wherever Bantam Books are sold, or use the handy coupon below for ordering:

Bantam Books, Inc., Dept. Loveswept-1, 414 East Golf Road, Des Plaines, Ill. 60016

Please send me _____ copies of WILD SWAN (Hardcover • 05059-1 • $16.95 • $18.95 in Canada). I am enclosing $_____ (please add $1.25 to cover postage and handling. Send check or money order—no cash or C.O.D.'s please).

Mr/Ms _____

Address_____

City/State _____ Zip _____

Loveswept-1—7/84

Please allow four to six weeks for delivery. This offer expires 1/85. Price and availability subject to change without notice.

AN UNFORGETTABLE FAMILY SAGA

THE MOONFLOWER VINE

BY JETTA CARLETON

Beginning in the timeless era of turn-of-the-century America, this is the story of four women bound by love, blood and family secrets . . . four very different sisters attempting to come to terms with the past and themselves. As spirited and eternal as *Little Women, To Kill a Mockingbird* and . . . *And the Ladies of the Club,* here is a warm, moving and powerful saga you will never forget.

Buy THE MOONFLOWER VINE, on sale October 15, 1984, wherever Bantam paperbacks are sold, or use the handy coupon below for ordering:

Bantam Books, Inc., Dept. Loveswept-1, 414 East Golf Road, Des Plaines, Ill. 60016

Please send me _____ copies of THE MOONFLOWER VINE (24422-1 • $3.95). I am enclosing $_____ (please add $1.25 to cover postage and handling. Send check or money order—no cash or C.O.D.'s please).

Mr/Ms _____

Address_____

City/State _____ Zip _____

Loveswept-1—10/84

Please allow four to six weeks for delivery. This offer expires 4/85. Price and availability subject to change without notice.

LOVESWEPT

Love Stories you'll never forget by authors you'll always remember

☐	21603	**Heaven's Price #1** Sandra Brown	$1.95
☐	21604	**Surrender #2** Helen Mittermeyer	$1.95
☐	21600	**The Joining Stone #3** Noelle Berry McCue	$1.95
☐	21601	**Silver Miracles #4** Fayrene Preston	$1.95
☐	21605	**Matching Wits #5** Carla Neggers	$1.95
☐	21606	**A Love for All Time #6** Dorothy Garlock	$1.95
☐	21607	**A Tryst With Mr. Lincoln? #7** Billie Green	$1.95
☐	21602	**Temptation's Sting #8** Helen Conrad	$1.95
☐	21608	**December 32nd . . . And Always #9** Marie Michael	$1.95
☐	21609	**Hard Drivin' Man #10** Nancy Carlson	$1.95
☐	21610	**Beloved Intruder #11** Noelle Berry McCue	$1.95
☐	21611	**Hunter's Payne #12** Joan J. Domning	$1.95
☐	21618	**Tiger Lady #13** Joan Domning	$1.95
☐	21613	**Stormy Vows #14** Iris Johansen	$1.95
☐	21614	**Brief Delight #15** Helen Mittermeyer	$1.95
☐	21616	**A Very Reluctant Knight #16** Billie Green	$1.95
☐	21617	**Tempest at Sea #17** Iris Johansen	$1.95
☐	21619	**Autumn Flames #18** Sara Orwig	$1.95
☐	21620	**Pfarr Lake Affair #19** Joan Domning	$1.95
☐	21621	**Heart on a String #20** Carla Neggars	$1.95
☐	21622	**The Seduction of Jason #21** Fayrene Preston	$1.95
☐	21623	**Breakfast In Bed #22** Sandra Brown	$1.95
☐	21624	**Taking Savannah #23** Becky Combs	$1.95
☐	21625	**The Reluctant Lark #24** Iris Johansen	$1.95

Prices and availability subject to change without notice.

Buy them at your local bookstore or use this handy coupon for ordering:

Bantam Books, Inc., Dept. SW, 414 East Golf Road, Des Plaines, Ill. 60016

Please send me the books I have checked above. I am enclosing $_____ (please add $1.25 to cover postage and handling). Send check or money order—no cash or C.O.D.'s please.

Mr/Ms_____

Address_____

City/State_____ Zip_____

SW—9/84

Please allow four to six weeks for delivery. This offer expires 3/85.

LOVESWEPT

Love Stories you'll never forget by authors you'll always remember

☐	21630	Lightning That Lingers #25 Sharon & Tom Curtis	$1.95
☐	21631	Once In a Blue Moon #26 Billie J. Green	$1.95
☐	21632	The Bronzed Hawk #27 Iris Johansen	$1.95
☐	21637	Love, Catch a Wild Bird #28 Anne Reisser	$1.95
☐	21626	The Lady and the Unicorn #29 Iris Johansen	$1.95
☐	21628	Winner Take All #30 Nancy Holder	$1.95
☐	21635	The Golden Valkyrie #31 Iris Johansen	$1.95
☐	21638	C.J.'s Fate #32 Kay Hooper	$1.95
☐	21639	The Planting Season #33 Dorothy Garlock	$1.95
☐	21629	For Love of Sami #34 Fayrene Preston	$1.95
☐	21627	The Trustworthy Redhead #35 Iris Johansen	$1.95
☐	21636	A Touch of Magic #36 Carla Neggers	$1.95
☐	21641	Irresistible Forces #37 Marie Michael	$1.95
☐	21642	Temporary Forces #38 Billie Green	$1.95
☐	21646	Kirsten's Inheritance #39 Joan Domnnig	$2.25
☐	21645	Return to Santa Flores #40 Iris Johansen	$2.25
☐	21656	The Sophisticated Mountain Gal #41 Joan Bramsch	$2.25
☐	21655	Heat Wave #42 Sara Orwig	$2.25
☐	21649	To See the Daisies . . . First #43 Billie Green	$2.25
☐	21648	No Red Roses #44 Iris Johansen	$2.25
☐	21644	That Old Feeling #45 Fayrene Preston	$2.25
☐	21650	Something Different #46 Kay Hooper	$2.25

Prices and availability subject to change without notice.

Buy them at your local bookstore or use this handy coupon for ordering:

Bantam Books, Inc., Dept. SW2, 414 East Golf Road, Des Plaines, Ill. 60016

Please send me the books I have checked above. I am enclosing $_____
(please add $1.25 to cover postage and handling). Send check or money order
—no cash or C.O.D.'s please.

Mr/Mrs/Miss _____

Address_____

City_____ State/Zip_____

SW2—9/84

Please allow four to six weeks for delivery. This offer expires 3/85.

LOVESWEPT

*Love Stories you'll never forget
by authors you'll always remember*

☐	21657	The Greatest Show On Earth #47 Nancy Holder	$2.25
☐	21658	Beware the Wizard #48 Sara Orwig	$2.25
☐	21660	The Man Next Door #49 Kathleen Downes	$2.25
☐	21633	In Search of Joy #50 Noelle Berry McCue	$2.25
☐	21659	Send No Flowers #51 Sandra Brown	$2.25
☐	21652	Casey's Cavalier #52 Olivia & Ken Harper	$2.25
☐	21654	Little Consequences #53 Barbara Boswell	$2.25
☐	21653	The Gypsy & The Yachtsman #54 Joan J. Domning	$2.25
☐	21664	Capture the Rainbow #55 Iris Johansen	$2.25
☐	21662	Encore #56 Kimberly Wagner	$2.25
☐	21640	Unexpected Sunrise #57 Helen Mittermeyer	$2.25
☐	21663	Oregon Brown #58 Sara Orwig	$2.25
☐	21665	Touch the Horizon #59 Iris Johansen	$2.25
☐	21666	When You Speak Love #60 B. J. James	$2.25
☐	21667	Breaking All the Rules #61 Joan Elliott Pickart	$2.25
☐	21668	Pepper's Way #62 Kay Hooper	$2.25

Prices and availability subject to change without notice.

Buy them at your local bookstore or use this handy coupon for ordering:

Bantam Books, Inc., Dept. SW3, 414 East Golf Road, Des Plaines, Ill. 60016

Please send me the books I have checked above. I am enclosing $_____
(please add $1.25 to cover postage and handling). Send check or money order
—no cash or C.O.D.'s please.

Mr/Mrs/Miss _____

Address _____

City _____ State/Zip _____

SW3—9/84

Please allow four to six weeks for delivery. This offer expires 3/85.